Everyone Dies in Youngstown

A Gripping Suspense Thriller

James Dain

Brown & King

Cover art by Anna Mitchell

Contents

A Note on the Style

I strive to capture the authentic rhythms of certain kinds of American speech as-it-is-actually spoken.

That might mean long meandering sentences, pronouns considered incorrect, odd spellings and contractions and numerous other errors that make English teachers wince.

Readers: I hope you enjoy it.

Teachers: I share your pain.

Civilization will not attain to its perfection until the last stone from the last church falls on the last priest.

– Emile Zola

Chapter One

The Product

The supplier in Newark was late with the coke and MJ Shea had been awake over 30 hours by the time he got to northeastern Pennsylvania. He didn't like to stop when carrying product and seldom used coke himself, but when he started falling asleep at the wheel in mid-afternoon, he pulled over at a Super 8 in Bloomsburg for a few hours of rest.

He paid cash for the room using the same fake I.D. he had used to rent the car, a 1986 Chevrolet Celebrity with no flash and little power. He parked the car outside the motel window and dropped his overnight bag, with its three keys of coke and a 9 mm Browning, on the mattress. Then he flopped on the bed himself and clicked on the boob tube.

On the TV, President Reagan was meeting Gorbachev and Jimmy Cagney had died. MJ cared nothing for politics but liked Cagney's cool toughness, which reminded him of his old man.

Soon sleepy, he put the overnight bag under the covers with him and the gun under his pillow while he slept. Having covered all the angles, he slept soundly and woke at 7 p.m., feeling groggy but better. After loading his stuff in the small Chevy, he headed for the Interstate entrance.

Bloomsburg was an old farm town injected with a bit of life by the construction of Interstate 80. The sun was setting, lighting orange fire under the clouds to the west. On this Monday night at the end of March, there was little traffic along the motel-and-restaurant strip leading to the nearby Interstate.

250 more miles to Youngstown. He should have the coke to Waylay by 1 a.m. His take for the run would be the usual three grand.

As he passed a flood-lit Howard Johnson's, a local cop car pulled out from the parking lot and followed along behind him. MJ felt a moment of anxiety, but then relaxed. He always checked his vehicles carefully for little stuff that might attract a cop's attention--shit like broken tail lights--and he always drove the speed limit. The overnight bag with the coke was in the trunk and his gun in his waistband, hidden under his untucked shirt.

He rode along nonchalantly with both hands on the wheel, observing the cop in his rear view. The officer, in a grey hat, appeared to be sipping coffee and didn't seem too interested in MJ.

A green sign indicated the entrance to I-80 a block ahead, and MJ pulled into the right lane in anticipation of turning.

Even as he did so, he realized that he had failed to signal his turn. The cop car's flashers and siren came alive as it swerved into MJ's lane and came right up on his tail.

Fucking shit, thought MJ, jolting upright. *How could I do that?* The Interstate entrance was just ahead and MJ had a split second to decide whether to make a run for it or play innocent. But what were the chances of outrunning the police in this piece-of-shit car? Besides, he knew from past experiences that if he just played polite and stupid, he could easily talk his way out of a simple moving violation.

He pulled over, but left the engine running.

"Good evening, officer," MJ said as the cop came up to the window, wielding a huge black flashlight which he shone in MJ's face. MJ wanted to rip the light out of the guy's hands and shove it up his stupid ass, but merely said, "Did I do something wrong?"

"Don't you know you're supposed to signal before changing lanes?" the cop said, finally shining the light away. He was a meaty, balding guy with a big brown hickey someone had planted above his collar on the left side of his neck.

"Oh, I'm real sorry officer, I thought I signaled," said MJ.

"You could have caused an accident," the officer said.

Accident my ass, thought MJ, who figured this was the cop's scam for writing up tickets on out-of-towners.

The patrolman continued: "Let me see your license and registration."

Reluctantly, hoping the cop was as dumb as he looked, MJ passed the documents over. The Avis registration was legit, but his driver's license was a fake in the name of "Melvyn Purdue" that his brother-in-law Lee had ordered up from some mob friends. While the cop examined it, MJ tried to distract him by saying, "I'm real sorry to disturb your nice town. I know you police have a hard time, what with catching all the criminals and stuff."

The cop, who had apparently been expecting an argument, looked up from the license. "We keep busy," he said.

MJ kept talking: "My uncle was a police officer and I know he sure worked hard. He taught me always to respect the law."

"Where was that?" said the cop, glancing at the city on the license. "Cleveland?"

"Yeah, Cleveland. My Uncle Jack. He was on the vice squad. Say, officer, do you think you could let me off with a warning?"

"I don't know," the cop said. "Changing lanes without signaling, that could have been dangerous."

Yeah, right. "Please, sir. I've got a wife and three kids and can't afford no ticket."

"Three kids, huh?" said the cop. He looked at MJ and grinned. "Boy, you must have started early, and kept on going."

MJ forced himself to laugh. "Yeah, three kids is a lot for 25. You a dad?"

"Yeah, I've got two. But they live with my ex."

"So what do you say?" pressed MJ. "A warning?"

The cop thought a moment, then handed back the license and registration. "All right, I guess we can let this one go. But drive careful, Mr. Purdue."

"Melvyn. You can call me Melvyn," MJ said with a little wave, thinking what a sucker the cop was.

It was this smart-ass gesture that got MJ into trouble, for when he gave the wave, he accidentally dropped the paperwork in his lap.

The cop leaned in (friendly now, the not-from-his-ex-wife hickey huge on his neck) to shine his flashlight into MJ's lap to help find the papers--and jumped back, startled, when he caught sight of the Browning poking out of MJ's pants where the shirt had pulled back.

"Whoa!" the cop yelled, drawing his weapon. "Put your hands on the steering wheel where I can see them! Now!"

Shit, thought MJ, his mind racing, thinking that the three bricks in the trunk meant 40 years in prison if he were caught.

He was going to have to make a run for it.

He made a big show of raising his hands to the wheel, then quickly dropped the car in gear and floored the accelerator.

The underpowered Chevy didn't exactly peel out, but it did lurch forward fast enough to startle the officer, whose cop hat flipped to the ground as his head snapped back.

MJ kept his foot mashed on the pedal as he sped toward the turn-off for the Interstate.

A ragged hole magically appeared in the windshield to MJ's right and a glance in his rear view confirmed that the cop was in a wide-legged stance--actually shooting at him. What a yokel, shooting at him for nothing, wasn't that illegal?

MJ barreled through the red light and swerved in front of a slow-moving dump truck onto the Interstate ramp, continuing to accelerate up the ramp. In the mirror, he saw the cop frantically running to his cruiser and grabbing the hand mike through the open window--probably to call in even more cops.

The Celebrity was doing 80 now, but that seemed to be its top speed on the long highway upgrade MJ found himself on. The cop, in his more powerful vehicle, would be on him in a minute.

MJ knew he would never make it to the next exit. He wove in and out of the night time traffic, looking for an escape route. A sign flashed past, something about low-clearance, and then he found himself approaching an overpass spanning the road ahead---big steel beams solidly set on angled buttresses of concrete.

As he neared the pass, MJ realized the buttresses would make a perfect screen to hide behind.

He flashed under the bridge and swerved onto the shoulder beyond, jamming on the brakes. The little car fishtailed as MJ struggled to keep it out of the ditch.

Then he threw the car into reverse and backed up as fast as he had ever backed up before, banging the Chevy's bumper hard into the stone-and-concrete buttress of the overpass.

He turned off the car lights and slid down into his seat. It was the kind of setup the police liked to use for speed traps. He was sure that the bridge abutment would hide his car and the pursuing cop would blow on by--assuming the guy was not checking his rear view mirror.

Just then, a huge tanker trunk went rumbling past--and beyond it, in the far lane, a patrol car zoomed ahead with lights flashing and siren sounding--the hickey-necked cop from Bloomsburg.

MJ watched the car speed up the grade until it disappeared around a curve, then MJ re-joined the highway and followed along cautiously, taking care to blend with the traffic.

Here the highway was split with a grassy median down the center, and MJ moved into the left-most lane. When he found a place where the grass strip leveled out, he slowed and pulled onto the left shoulder, then crossed the strip and joined traffic in the other direction.

Wedging himself between two slow-moving trucks, he passed the exit for Bloomsburg, then traveled several miles further to get off at the next exit, U.S. 11, heading south.

When he was absolutely sure no one was following him, he pulled over next to a farm field and lit a cigarette, pissed to find his hands were shaking. To calm down, he turned on the radio and tuned through the dial searching for some music until he found a static-y Harrisburg station playing Karen Carpenter, "Close to You."

He sat listening for a minute, keeping an eye on the rear-view mirror, then snubbed his cigarette and turned the radio off.

"Close to You." That was Cassie's favorite song. She had put it on a mix tape she made for him, right before they had broken up.

He checked the map, looking for routes to Youngstown that would keep him off major highways.

Chapter Two

Lonely Pennsylvania Night

A ll the way across Pennsylvania, MJ couldn't stop thinking about Cassie, even though she wasn't talking to him and he hadn't seen her for a year.

She was smart, beautiful and ambitious--studying to be a nurse with the nuns at the Sacred Heart School of Nursing--and totally unlike any girl MJ had ever dated or even known. They had only slept together once, and only gone together for six short weeks. But it was the best six weeks of MJ's life, until Cassie found out that his "business" was not selling construction equipment, but running cocaine.

After that she wouldn't have anything to do with him, cutting him off and leaving a hole in his heart like a wound that wouldn't heal. MJ had always gotten over chicks before, easy, but every time he thought of Cassie his mind started churning with I-should-have-done-this and I-should-have-said-that. He didn't understand her. Even though she had grown up on the streets of Manila and had only made it to the U.S. by the skin of her teeth, she talked about returning to the Philippines to work in some government do-good program. And she had already hooked up with some lame-ass project that was feeding sandwiches to the homeless in downtown Youngstown.

Most girls he could figure out, but not Cassie. All he knew was, she didn't want *him*--"a no-account drug dealer" she called him, even though he didn't really deal and was saving up like he told her, to escape Youngstown.

His heart ached.

Shit.

He had told himself a thousand times that there were other girls, that the longing he felt when he thought of Cassie would eventually fade.

But now, in the lonely Pennsylvania night, with "Close to You" ringing in his ears, there was no use denying it.

He was in love with her.

Stupid and crazy, maybe, but he couldn't help it.

"Damn," he shouted to the empty car. He had to get her back.

He would have to swallow his pride and crawl to her, somehow try to patch things up.

But first there was the delivery, which was giving MJ a major headache. Waylay was already pissed at the delay in New Jersey, and now, taking the back roads, MJ was really going to be late. Bad things could happen if Waylay thought MJ was dicking him around, so he decided to call Promo and explain the situation. "Promo" Reule was MJ's main point of contact with Waylay's operation-- one of the inner circle that managed the actual distribution of the coke Waylay was bringing in.

He found a phone booth outside a closed gas station in Elderton and dropped in the five quarters the recording demanded.

"Hello?"

MJ recognized the voice as Promo's, but had to be careful in case the line was tapped. "It's me," he said.

"What's up?"

"I had a problem with a cop. I had to get off the Interstate."

"Is the pizza okay?"

"Yeah, but I'm going to be even later than I said. Maybe 3, 4 in the morning."

After a pause, Promo said, "He ain't going to like that. We got a guy here."

The "guy" would be a distributor, anxious for his cut. "I'll be there as fast as I can," MJ said. "But I have to be careful."

"I'll tell him," said Promo, and hung up.

MJ still had some quarters left from his roll, so he decided to call his sister, who worried herself sick about him when he was on a run.

"Hello, Peg," he said, when she picked up.

"There you are, you bastard, I've been paging you for hours."

"Oh. Sorry sis. I had the damn thing turned off. Is everything okay?"

"No it's not okay. When is anything ever okay around this crappy joint? I've been so busy."

"Yeah? Doing what?" said MJ. Regardless of when he talked to her, Peggy always complained about feeling frazzled and overwhelmed. And maybe she had cause, since she was caring for their mother Anne, who had Alzheimer's, as well as her two kids from her marriage with Lee. She and Lee were still married but had separated the previous summer. Since then, Peggy and MJ's younger brother Danny lived with her off-and-on, but that was another story in itself.

"What do you mean, doing what? I've been shopping, fixing dinner, scrubbing dishes--by hand since the dishwasher is still broke. The kids have been screaming all night and Queen Anne peed the bed again. So now I'm still doing laundry at, what?, midnight."

"Well get some rest, sis, go to bed."

"Yeah, go to bed, that's exactly what I'm going to do, as soon as I finish this load. Oh, and it's been raining for hours and there's a wet spot on my kitchen ceiling."

Peggy lived in the house they had grown up in, and there were always problems she wanted help with. "I'm still on the road," MJ said. "I won't be back 'til morning."

"Well what am I supposed to do? Every time I look the spot's bigger. That's why I wanted you to come over."

"How bad is it?"

"What do you mean, how bad is it? How am I supposed to know that?"

"How big? One inch? Three feet?"

"Oh, maybe a foot."

"That doesn't sound serious. I'll come by in the morning," MJ said. "If it starts to drip, have Danny take a look."

"Right, like what the hell would Danny do? He's not even here."

"What do you mean?"

"He left in a huff three days ago and I haven't seen him since."

Danny was a problem. He had started doing crack a few years earlier and had been going downhill ever since.

"Did you look for him?"

"Ha. Like I have time to go chasing Danny. He could be anywhere."

"Damn," MJ said. "I'm supposed to take him to rehab tomorrow, remember?" A bed had finally opened up at St. Elizabeth's Hospital and Danny had promised to go in if MJ took him.

"Well all I know is, he's not here," Peggy said.

MJ was thinking that after he delivered the shipment, he would have to go hunt down his brother and bundle him off to rehab before some other crackhead got the open bed.

"You still there?" Peggy asked.

"Yeah, I'm here."

"I'm going to sleep. I'll page you if the ceiling gets worse."

"Yeah, sure," he said. His sister's ceiling was the least of his worries right now. "And definitely page me if Danny shows up."

Just then a recorded operator demanded that he deposit another $1.00 for the next three minutes, so he hung up.

Chapter Three

Crack in the Smile

Wearily, he climbed back into the car and headed west, feeling overwhelmed. The last time Danny had disappeared he turned up at Central State Hospital in Anchorage, Kentucky--suicidal and psychotic from coke withdrawal. MJ would have to find him, fast. On top of that, he'd have to go see Cassie in person, since she'd just hang up on him if he tried calling. His sister's ceiling was small potatoes and could wait, but nonetheless he'd also have to show up at the house, if only to keep Peggy from flying off the handle. And he still had three hours driving on the back roads of Pennsylvania before he could get the coke off his hands. It was a lot of things to be worrying about, but for now, the coke had to be his priority, unless he wanted Waylay on his ass as well.

And he sure as hell didn't want that. Waylay killed guys that fucked around with him.

***

Big Man Donuts was a 30s adobe-style storefront located between a motel and a bird feed store just south of Youngstown, in the suburban sprawl of Boardman, Ohio. Boardman was the home of the first Arby's, now closed, and the first strip mall, also now closed, but it still had plenty of residents left over in the surrounding cheap tract houses and enough hungry shift workers to allay any suspicions about a 24-hour donut shop. In fact, MJ had heard that after Waylay had fixed up the place to make it look respectable, he was pissed with the shop's success, since he had bought it strictly as a front for his drug business and didn't like all the people around.

On this rainy Tuesday night at 3 a.m. there were still two cars out front and a pickup truck in the side lot, but MJ pulled past the customers to the back of the building and parked in the shadows of the alley by a dumpster. Relieved to have arrived with no more problems, he sat in the car a minute, smoking a cigarette and scoping out the surroundings. Waylay's operations were the target of multiple state and local investigations and MJ wanted to make sure there were no cops around to screw up his delivery. At this point, he wanted nothing more than to hand over the bricks to Promo and get what he was owed.

The office for the shop was in the back corner, and MJ could already feel eyes on him as he opened the trunk and took out his duffel bag, the cold drizzle running down his neck. The back door opened before he even finished reaching for the knob.

"Yo, MJ," said the guy inside, who MJ recognized as Wonder, a stash house guard.

"What's up?" MJ said, a little surprised to see him since Wonder and Promo didn't get along. They called him "Wonder" after Stevie Wonder, because he was black and wore sunglasses day and night--even now, in the dim hallway.

Wonder stepped back to let MJ inside. He was a huge man, looking extra menacing tonight with what looked like a Walther semi-auto dangling from a shoulder holster. "Up against the wall," he said. "I've got to frisk you."

That was also unusual, but MJ's weapon was in the car. He put the bag at his feet and leaned against the wall. "What gives?" he said.

"Just business," said Wonder, finishing his pat down and reaching for the bag.

MJ stomped on it with his foot. "That goes to Promo."

"I got to check it."

"Check it my ass. How long have you known me?"

"Open it," said Wonder, in a tone that let MJ know he wasn't screwing around.

Reluctantly, MJ unzipped the bag, holding it as Wonder rummaged through it with his big hands, finding the bricks but pushing them aside, looking for weapons.

"Okay?" said MJ when he had had enough.

"Okay," said Wonder. "Go on in."

MJ walked the few feet to the office door and pushed it open, intent on complaining to Promo about the treatment Wonder had given him.

But sitting at the little desk was not Promo, but Waylay May himself, with a beefy-looking bald guy MJ didn't recognize leaning against a file cabinet. Wonder came in behind and closed the door.

"It's about time," Waylay said, looking up from his Chinese food. He was in his mid-30s, his black hair slicked back with pomade, and a form-fitting purple shirt over his thin frame.

"I ran into a little problem," said MJ.

Waylay grunted and nodded at the overnight bag. "Let's see what you got."

MJ was suddenly nervous. He had never actually met Waylay before, only seen him at the Pig Iron, and he wondered where Promo was. He also didn't like the setup--the tiny locked room, the bald-but-brawny stranger and Wonder with his sunglasses and gun.

Something was wrong, and MJ felt like he was on trial for some unidentified screwup. He hadn't done anything, but then again he knew of guys who'd been whacked because someone *thought* they screwed up. He'd have to be very careful to make sure Waylay realized that--whatever had happened--it wasn't from MJ's side.

Suppressing his nervousness, MJ put the overnight bag on the desk, unzipped it, and put the three kilos on the tabletop. The bricks were white and wrapped in clear plastic and duct tape. "Like I told Promo, I ran into some trouble," he said. "This jerkwater cop was tailing me, and I had to ditch him. That's why I'm late."

Waylay ignored him and turned to the bald guy, who MJ now saw wasn't really bald, but had shaved his head like Mr. Clean. "Check it, Angel," Waylay told him.

The bald guy ambled forward, flicked open a switchblade, and punched a hole in one of the bricks, pulling out some coke on the knife tip and dumping it on the table. "It's been cut alright," he said. "Just look at the shit. It's fucking grey."

Angel took a pinch with his fingers and tasted it, then used his blade to lay out a line, which he hoovered up with a rolled bill.

He stood up sharply and threw his bald head back, staring at the ceiling, then looked at Waylay with a goofy expression on his face. "Not bad, but cut," he said, loudly and sloppily. "Just like I told you."

He laid out another line, then snorted it, closing his right nostril with his forefinger. After the hit, he sucked air twice, then started gesticulating wildly. "It's good but not what we agreed. I paid for primo, and this ain't primo."

"Okay, we get the message. You can wait outside."

"I told you. Didn't I tell you?"

Angel bent one more time toward the table, but at a signal from Waylay, Wonder grabbed his upper arm and escorted him out.

The door closed with a bang when Wonder re-entered, and Waylay leaned back and scrutinized MJ through steepled hands.

"You don't think I had anything to do with that, do you?" said MJ. "Because I never touched that dope. Those bricks are exactly what the Fahey brothers gave me."

"Tell me again why you were so late."

"The Faheys, they dicked me around for an entire afternoon, said there was a delay at the airport, so it was rush hour by the time I got out of Newark, and then there was an accident on the parkway. Then like I told Promo, I got pulled over by a cop and had to take back roads."

"Did you make any stops?"

"Just a couple hours at a motel near Bloomsburg. I was falling asleep at the wheel and had to get some rest. That's where the cop stopped me. He put a bullet through my windshield if you don't believe me."

"Go look," Waylay told Wonder.

When Wonder was gone, Waylay said. "No other stops? Like maybe in Pittsburgh?"

"Pittsburgh? Why would I stop in Pittsburgh?"

"Just answer the question."

"Hell no I didn't stop in Pittsburgh. I drove around Pittsburgh, not through it."

"Did you sample any of the product along the way?" asked Waylay.

"I'm not into that shit," said MJ. It was true. He seldom used coke anymore. The high wasn't worth the let-down, and he didn't like what it did to his brother.

As if reading his mind, Waylay said, "What about Danny? When was the last time you saw him?"

"What's he got to do with it?" said MJ, annoyed. Then, remembering who he was talking to, he said, "I don't know where Danny is. I ain't seen him for like a week, maybe last Sunday at my sister's house."

"So the bricks are exactly like you got them? You haven't touched them?"

"No," said MJ, emphatically.

Waylay leaned back into his chair, sizing MJ up.

"Come on, Waylay, you know I've always played straight with you. If that coke's been cut, it was cut when the Faheys gave it to me."

Just then, Wonder returned. "There's a bullet hole in the front and rear windshield, and another in the rear quarter-panel."

Waylay looked at MJ through narrowed eyes, then sighed and opened the desk drawer. *Holy shit, he's going for a gun,* thought MJ, feeling every muscle in his body tighten as he prepared to run.

Waylay picked up on that. "Relax," he said, pulling from the drawer a brown envelope stuffed with bills. "Here you go, MJ," said Waylay. "Good work."

MJ forced himself to breath normally, trying to calm his heart and look cool. "Thanks," he said. He couldn't read Waylay's face, but it was clear to MJ that he had passed some important test. He picked up the envelope, glanced at the stack of 100s and slipped it into his pocket, knowing better than to count it in front of Waylay.

"Take a week or two off," Waylay said. "I won't need you for a while."

"Okay," said MJ.

"Everything will be all right," Waylay said. "Just chill with your family and keep your nose clean."

"Always," MJ said, wondering what the hell he was talking about.

"Send Angel back in," he told Wonder. "And get this man some donuts on the way out."

***

An hour and three sprinkle donuts later, MJ drove away from the Youngstown-Warren Regional Airport. The Avis guy got seriously worked up about the bullet holes, but in the end there was nothing he could do: Melvyn Purdue had taken full comprehensive to cover just such problems. So, after a fist full of paperwork, MJ picked up his van and headed downtown in search of his brother Danny.

Normally after a successful job, MJ felt relieved and happy, but tonight, despite the $3,000 now in his pants pocket, he was just depressed. The deserted road, the yellow streetlights, the rain drizzling down--the city had never looked uglier.

MJ had grown up in Youngstown but hated it. The whole place had been going downhill on a fast shit slide ever since "Black Monday" nearly a decade before, when Youngstown Steel & Tube laid off 5,000 men in a single afternoon. The company--a hundred-year fixture of "Steeltown USA"--was a bankrupt, abandoned hulk within two years, followed quickly down the drain by U.S. Steel, Republic Steel and Youngstown Cement, along with all the little companies that had supplied the thousand odd products, from chemical solvents to paperclips, that kept the big industries going. Ultimately, 50,000 people lost their jobs and the mass exodus began.

Overnight, Youngstown went from a busy, prosperous city to a toilet bowl of unemployment, foreclosure and bankruptcy. MJ's dad was in the first wave of workers that got canned. As a 16 year old, MJ remembered that time well: his

Dad sitting around the living room for months on unemployment while his Mom berated him bitterly for not doing more to find work.

Then one night his father complained of chest pains and was dead before the ambulance could get him to the hospital.

The Shea family didn't do too good after that. His mother, always a clean freak, redoubled her efforts with Lemon Pledge. The house became spotless, but within a year of the funeral, her grip on reality began to slip, as she first began repeating stories and then started forgetting where--and finally who--she was. Peggy got married and predictably separated, having popped out two kids and successfully signed-up for public assistance. Danny boosted his first car (a two-door Eldorado that belonged to Dr. Sherman), sold pot, then coke and finally became a crackhead, tweaking around Youngstown for his next hit, his guitar slung over his shoulder like some Mexican mariachi man from an old tv Western.

And MJ after high school had a pill gig going, then started running dope from the East Coast--a "no-account drug dealer."

Screw Cassie, calling him that. What she didn't understand was that there was nothing left for a man to do in Youngstown. The factories were gone, school was for smart people, and the only jobs, if you could find one, were chump jobs paying chump change. It was like God had smiled on Youngstown for so long, his face had cracked and he shriveled up and died, leaving the residents to fend for themselves. That was why you had to be a hard ass to survive in this town.

In any case, his family was in Youngstown, and like Mom always said, family is all you got. MJ was the only one making good money, so he had to help his sister and brother out--pay the taxes on the family house and the bills for Danny's treatment.

Oh shit, MJ thought, Danny's treatment. Who knew how much that was going to cost this time? And screw Danny, too, for messing up his life and the lives of everyone around him. Danny was the reason why Waylay still didn't entirely trust him.

A few years earlier MJ, trying to help his brother out, had gotten him a gig with Promo--cutting and packaging coke and waiting on customers at the stash house on Chaney. But that was around the time Danny's partying was getting out-of-hand, and he apparently helped himself to some of Waylay's product.

The next time Danny showed up at the stash house, a couple of Waylay's enforcers dragged him out to a parking lot behind Schwebel's Bakery and beat the crap out of him, breaking a few of his ribs and detaching one of his retinas. It was MJ who Promo had called to haul Danny's busted-up ass to the hospital--both as a favor to MJ and a warning. But Danny's bad behavior had somehow worn off on MJ, and it was months before Promo threw him any more jobs.

Danny. The last time Danny had been to rehab he had been kicked out after three days for smoking pot, and MJ wasn't optimistic that he would do any better this time. Still, his brother had promised to try it again and MJ had to get him there. This morning, April Fool's Day, MJ had a pretty good idea where to find him. He'd be with the rest of the fools in the crack house on Walnut that used to be Christ the King.

MJ headed there.

Chapter Four

Steeltown USA

MJ Shea moved silently through the nave of the church, searching for Danny among the unconscious bodies sprawled in and around the remains of the pews.

There were a pair of passed-out black girls under a plastic tarp, a white guy MJ's age wrapped in newspapers, two dudes who looked like brothers lying end-to-end on a broken pew and a dark form curled in a fetal position in the shadows of the smashed remains of the organ.

With dawn, rain was again pouring down outside and the room was cold and damp. The windows had been boarded when the church closed, but wind and crack-addict-ingenuity had loosened the plywood and busted the windows, letting in a hint of wan light, and just enough rain to leave cold puddles on the floor.

MJ stepped over an inert body and climbed over a pile of fallen plaster, heading for the organ in case the form was Danny. It wasn't. The church had only been closed three years, but already it looked like every other abandoned building in Youngstown--falling walls, dangling plumbing, ripped-wiring--with added drug-den touches like scattered crack vials, McDonald's wrappers, plastic lighters, piss jars, cigarette butts, foil, candles, beer cans and a package of cornstarch for burn.

"Hey, MJ," came a voice from behind. Startled, MJ whirled, but it was only Carnival Jane, an emaciated runt of a girl, maybe 17, the youngest sister of Cherise Longman from the Rayen School.

"Carnival," MJ said. "Don't sneak up on me like that."

"I wasn't sneaking," she said. "I was trying to sleep over there and I saw you come in." She pointed to a makeshift bed made of crushed cardboard and torn fragments of carpets. "Got anything for me?"

"Better ask Danny," MJ said sourly.

She looked at MJ, irritated, then her first idea of the day hit her and she looked around, her eyes suddenly brighter. "Where is he?"

"That's what I was gonna ask you."

"He's not with you?"

"Does it look like he's with me? When's the last time you saw him?"

She furrowed her brow and stared at him, but her crack-addled brain was already losing the thread of the conversation.

"Danny?" he reminded her. "Have you seen Danny?"

"Oh, yeah, Danny. I seen him."

"You did? Where?"

A sly look crossed her face. "Got any gravel?"

"You're too young for gravel. Does Cherise know you're here?"

"Cherise don't care," she said in disgust. "She's the one kicked me out."

That didn't surprise MJ since Peggy had kicked Danny out a half-dozen times.

MJ sighed. "I might have something for you," he said. "If you can tell me where my brother is."

"We was together over at Harrison. He was playing his guitar."

"When was this? Last night?"

"What is today? Sunday?"

"Tuesday."

She looked confused. "Are you sure?"

"Yeah, I'm sure. When were you with Danny at the field?"

"That was last night," she said. "No, wait, that was... Sunday, I think. Under the bleachers where he played that song."

Worthless. It was a shame too because if she wasn't so messed up she would have been a good looking chick. She had nice tight little titties but her hair was in knots and her teeth already starting to turn crack-addict yellow.

"Whatcha got for me, MJ?" she asked. "Gravel?"

"Go away," MJ said, surveying the room to see if there were any bodies he missed.

She grabbed him by his arm. "You said you'd give me something."

"If you knew where Danny was."

"But I told you, he was here."

"Here?"

"Well, there, in that there room," she said, pointing to a door off the altar.

"When was this?"

"Last night. We came in when the storm started."

MJ climbed a few steps to the level of the altar and made his way for the door. Inside was a smaller room, black as night, with no window.

"Right there," said Carnival, pointing into the shadows. "We did a pipe together."

MJs eyes adjusted as he slowly stepped into the room. More vials, more foil, more cigarette butts but no Danny or anyone else.

He could have been here. Or maybe not. MJ didn't know whether Carnival had actually seen him or if she was just handing him a line of crackhead bullshit. "You sure he was here?"

"I told you, yeah, last night. We was together."

"What time?"

"Um, uh, I don't know. Midnight? One?"

"Where did he go?"

"Some stupid place. I can't remember."

"Come on, Carnival. Try to think."

"I can't remember. I went out for a crap and when I came back, he was gone."

She sounded real but how the hell did he know? "You're not kidding me?" MJ said.

"No, I swear, he was here. Last night. I swear on a stack of bibles."

MJ snorted, but decided she was probably telling the truth. Wherever Danny was, he wasn't here.

"Come on, MJ, you promised," whined the girl.

Her whining set him on edge but he was done here. He had some pot and a few tweeners of coke under the floormat, left over from Rhonda's party. Maybe he'd do a joint with Carnival. She'd be pretty if she cleaned up.

"Come on," he said. "My van's in the alley. Let's see what I got."

Her eyes lit up in excitement. "Danny," she said. "He always says good things about you, MJ."

Still worried about his brother, MJ led Carnival back over the bodies and through the side door of the church toward his van. With crack rolling over the city like some monster flood of the Mahoning River, beds were limited at St. Elizabeth's, and six more weeks would be wasted if he didn't get Danny into rehab today.

The alley was deserted. Carnival followed him like an eager puppy to the van, which was parked next to a mound of garbage and broken furniture.

MJ paused with the key in the lock. "Was Danny dealing? Did he have a lot of shit on him last night?"

"No. What we smoked, that was the last of his stuff." Her eyes flicked back and forth between MJ's face and the van door, waiting for the surprise inside.

He reached under the floor mat for one of the tweeners, but held it in his hand instead of giving it to her.

"You sure you can't remember where he was going?"

"He went to meet somebody."

"Who?"

"I don't know!" said the girl, wanting her reward.

The rain made her matted hair stick together into greasy strands. In the morning light, her eyes looked hollow and MJ suddenly wanted to be rid of her.

"Here," he said. "Don't snort it all at once." He was joking her because he knew she would go back into the church to turn the coke into smokable crack.

The bag disappeared into her pocket in a quick fluid motion. "Thanks," she said. "Can I get another for later?"

"No," said MJ, climbing into the van.

She grabbed the door. "Come on, MJ. I can pay you tonight."

He should have known better than to give samples to a crackhead. "I said no. Now let go my door handle unless you want to lose your arm."

MJ put the van into gear and started off down the alley, Run-D.M.C. blaring from a tape in the cassette player. In his rear view mirror, Carnival receded, looking wet and alone. It made him wonder if Danny was standing somewhere in the rain with the same forlorn look.

He stopped the van and honked the horn. Carnival came running up, her fine tits showing against her wet shirt.

"You have some place to go, get cleaned up and out of the rain?"

She looked disappointed. "Yeah, I got a place."

It sounded like she was lying. "Do you need a ride?"

"I don't mind the rain," she said. "Can I get another bag?"

He should have known. "Go the fuck home," MJ said. "Cherise will be wanting you."

Exhausted by all the drama, MJ rolled up the window and pulled away. Carnival's head was totally screwed up but she had given him an idea. Danny got his product from a guy named Skeevy Jones, over on the South Side. If Danny was out of crack like Carnival said, he was probably heading to Skeevy's right now.

MJ turned the van onto Rayen. He'd hang out until Skeevy opened for business, then trick Danny into the van and whisk him to St. Elizabeth's.

At the old library, he turned south on Wick and headed toward the Market Street bridge, which would take him across the river towards the South Side. The rain kept falling from the grey sky, and the trees along the route--full-grown maples that were planted 50 years back, when Youngstown had a future--shed sodden green leaves onto the black pavement.

MJ cursed as he approached the bridge. Traffic was snarled at the foot of the ramp, and beyond, blurry in the falling rain, tow trucks and ambulances were scattered across the bridge deck. A cop in a yellow safety vest waved traffic along a waning string of flares into a single lane.

On the bridge, a big Pepsi truck had skidded across the divider and smacked a little Pontiac head on, crumpling the car's front end and shoving it against the far railing almost into the river.

The truck driver, uninjured, was standing with some cops, but the occupant of the Sunbird wasn't so lucky. Firemen were still blasting water on the flames which engulfed the vehicle. As he drove by, MJ caught a glimpse of the dead driver's blackened face. It looked like a potato charred in a campfire.

MJ mentally shrugged and turned his attention back to the traffic. There were all kinds of fucked up ways to die in Youngstown, so what difference did it make? Everyone was going to die. That's why life didn't mean crap. Grab what you can, while you can--that was his philosophy.

The only thing, thought MJ, if I was the guy in the Pontiac, I'd damn well want to take the bastard in the truck out with me. MJ tried to imagine how the car driver could have made that happen--maybe speeding up and smashing the truck even harder, or shooting the trucker at the last second before the vehicles collided. It just wasn't fair that the truck driver was hanging around with a cigarette in his mouth while the car driver--probably some old schmo left over from the last round of layoffs--was burnt-up dead.

Then MJ caught himself and laughed. *Just wasn't fair*--what a fucking joke. That was something Cassie would say. Of course it wasn't fair, only an idiot would think that life should be fair. That was another thing about Cassie that he didn't understand. She hated the nuns and thought Catholics were full of shit, but still believed in God. How stupid was that? When MJ told her the only God he believed in was himself, she just shook her head.

Finally off the bridge, MJ took a side street to get out of the traffic and headed toward Skeevy's corner. He was tired of screwing around. Danny and his stupid guitar were going into St. Elizabeth's as soon as he saw him.

But MJ only got another block before his beeper went off. He looked at the number on the display: Peggy. Danny must have showed up. He'd have to find a phone and call her, find out what was going on.

MJ pulled into a gas station lot and found the pay phone by the air machine. It was an outdoor phone in a box on a post and MJ didn't have an umbrella.

Peggy picked up on the first ring. "MJ," she said as soon as she heard his voice. "You've got to get over here right away."

He knew it. Danny pulled crap like this all the time--going off on his own and then coming back, high and causing trouble.

"What's he doing now?"

"Who?"

"Danny. Isn't that why you paged me?"

"Hell no," she said. "I paged you because the kitchen ceiling's caving in and I've got water everywhere."

MJ couldn't believe it. Peggy was always getting hysterical over nothing, and he had other things to do. "Where's it dripping?" he asked.

"Dripping?" Peggy screamed. "I didn't say it was dripping. You never listen to me. A *pipe* burst. Water's coming out the ceiling like a fire hose and it's ruining the table, the floor, *every fucking thing.*"

"Peggy, I've got to find Danny. Just turn the valve off in the basement."

"It don't *work. Nothing works in this house!*" she screamed. "It's falling *apart!* I swear, if you don't get over here right away, I'm walking out and letting the whole damned kitchen float out the door!"

"Okay, okay," he said. When his sister started with the screams and the threats, he knew she'd make him miserable for weeks if he didn't help. It was early yet. He could run by and turn the valve off, and still catch Danny at Skeevy's. "I'm on my way now."

"Hurry," his sister said. And hung up.

MJ had to laugh. Peggy was a pain in the ass but that's what made her Peggy. If it wasn't for her, their mom would be in a nursing home and Danny permanently on the streets.

                                    ***

Twenty minutes later MJ was back at the house on Carlton, the familiar two-story wood frame rectangle where he grew up. Since the mill closings, Smoky Hollow wasn't what it used to be. When MJ was little, it had been a dowdy-but-respectable neighborhood of white clapboard homes on narrow lots, where men walked to the mill to work while the kids played on the brick street. Now, half the houses had for-sale signs leaning out front, and the other half were either owned by the bank outright or burnt to the foundations by Italian lightning, the local nickname for insurance arson.

Peggy talked frequently about doing some Italian lightning of her own, but everyone knew she was bullshitting since the house was her life. The home on Carlton had been bought by their parents in 1944 and was fully paid for, if showing its age. The white paint was gray and peeling and the roof shingles were mottled with makeshift patches. The block retaining wall out front had missing cinder blocks where roots from an old maple tree had pushed them out. Tall weeds choked the lawn, and the sidewalk was a soup of muddy puddles from the rain.

Still, it was a house, free to live in except for property taxes and insurance. MJ dutifully paid property taxes at the assessor's office twice a year since Peggy was taking care of their senile mother. Peggy herself took care of the insurance, unwilling to trust anyone else with what she saw as an indispensable safeguard.

He pulled into the drive behind Peggy's dented '78 Mercury Zephyr and climbed the stairs to the entry, steeling himself to deal with his sister, who tended towards hysteria whenever it came to problems affecting the house.

The front door was open and the hallway was sopping wet--literally awash with water. The house stank, as usual, of cats. His mother, sitting in the recliner in the living room, looked up from *Captain Penny* and then back at the tv screen, sunken in her Alzheimer's daydream.

"Hi Mom," said MJ, out of habit since there was seldom any sign of recognition in his mother's face.

But Shannon and Lee Jr., lying together on the sofa, perked up as he entered. They were five and six now, getting big. "Uncle Mike," they cried, running over and grabbing his legs.

"Hey, kids, not today, okay?"

"There's water," said Lee Jr., pointing to the wet towels and a rag throw-rug crumbled in the hall at the kitchen entrance.

"I can see there's water," said MJ, plopping the kids back on the sofa. Their clothes were dirty and damp, and Shannon had a scratch across her fore-head--mercurochromed but not bandaged in Peggy's usual half-ass way.

MJ made his way through the hallway puddles to the kitchen and saw imme-diately that his sister hadn't been exaggerating the damage. A four-foot section of the ceiling above the breakfast bar had come down where the pipe in the upstairs bathroom had burst, and water sprayed in multiple streams through the broken lathe down over the blue Formica of the breakfast bar. Plaster and chunks of horsehair insulation littered the countertop, and two of the wood cabinet doors were for some reason torn off their hinges.

Peggy was dumping a bucket of water into the sink, a cigarette dangling from the corner of her mouth. Her reddish-brown hair was soaked and her glasses were sliding down her wet face. "Could you have got here any slower?" she said as MJ appeared in the doorway.

"For Christ's sake, Peggy, I told you to turn off the valve."

"And I told you it's stuck. You think I'm an idiot?"

MJ shook his head in annoyance and headed for the basement, tripping over a bucket along the way. He tugged the pull cord on the overhead light bulb. The shut-off valve was in the far corner of the basement, behind the furnace, where the water main came in from the street.

He tried to turn the rusted wheel handle but it was locked in place.

"See? I told you," said Peggy, who had followed him down; the two kids, attracted by the excitement, took places on the stairs. "It don't turn."

"It's just corroded," said MJ.

"Everything's corroded," said Peggy, wrapping her arms around her chest. "The whole house is corroded. We got pipes bursting, no pressure in the shower, and I got to reach into the toilet tank to make it flush."

MJ ignored her bitching and went to his old man's workbench, basically untouched since his Dad's death almost a decade earlier. The tools were organized and neat, lined up like in a store (unlike MJ's tools, which were thrown together in a metal box). The yellow, dented can of Liquid Wrench was still on the shelf with the old cans of paint and jars of odd nails, and the red pipe wrench hung by its handle in the slot above the anvil.

At the shut-off valve, he squirted some penetrating oil onto the stem, banged it a few times with the wrench, then adjusted the teeth around the valve handle and turned. The valve resisted momentarily, then freed. He twisted it, *righty-tighty* like his Dad had taught him, to shut off the flow of water.

"There," he said. "It will stop now."

"Oh, like I'm the water meter man? I'm supposed to know how to fix a valve?"

"Peggy, I didn't say that."

She turned in a huff and marched up the steps, the kids following. MJ was irritated. While he couldn't blame Peggy for feeling frustrated, she had no cause to criticize him after he dropped everything to come to solve her plumbing problem. Next time she could call a plumber.

He put the tools back where he had found them and checked his watch. It was almost 9:30, but he might still be able to catch Danny at Skeevy's if he hurried.

Chapter Five

What Happened to Danny

U pstairs in the kitchen, the leak had stopped, though water still dripped from the sodden ceiling. The floor was a mess of ruined pantry items, broken crockery and soggy *Vindicator* newspapers. Peggy was mopping the floor with a ragged mop head, stabbing it into puddles, sobbing and carrying on a conversation with the mop end:

"You guys never listen to me. You treat me like your maid and your cook. You act like this house just takes care of itself--you and Lee and, and Danny. And it doesn't!"

"Peggy..."

"And then there's Queen Anne sitting in there, waiting for her meals and her medicines and her enemas! And Lee, when we separated he promised he'd lend a hand, at least with the kids, but how often do I see him? If I don't get some help around here I swear I'm going to go insane!"

"Peggy, I have to go find Danny."

"Danny, don't talk about Danny, he's another one, burning down my microwave with his crack fire. I should have kicked him out a long time ago, everyone would have been a lot happier."

"We have to get him admitted to St. Elizabeth's today, remember? Otherwise we're going to have to wait another six weeks."

"And what am I supposed to do in the meantime, with no water in the house? I can't use the toilet, or wash dishes, or even get the kids a glass of water."

"You're going to have to call a plumber, Peg." He peeled two $100 bills from the wad he got from Waylay. "Here. If it's more than this, let me know."

Just then, the doorbell rang. Peggy, already stressed from the dripping ceiling, anxiously peered out the kitchen window.

"Who is it?" MJ asked.

"I don't know," she said. "Just a black car."

Since the mill shutdowns, the neighborhood was plagued with out-of-work geezers trying to sell brushes, awnings, encyclopedias and siding.

The doorbell rang again, but Peggy didn't move.

"Aren't you going to get it?" asked MJ.

She pulled herself away from the window and smoothed her dress. "Stay here, okay?"

"I've got to go."

"No. I might need you. Can't you wait one more fucking minute?"

The salesmen must really be giving her shit. He followed her into the hallway and hung back while she cracked the door. The guy outside wore thick black glasses but otherwise was your typical salesman type--wrinkled suit, white shirt, red tie. Over the blare of the tv, MJ couldn't hear what the man was saying, but Peggy was holding her own and he didn't seem to be any threat. MJ headed for the back door to make his escape.

"MJ!" came his sister's voice sharply, and he turned to find the door wide open and Peggy sinking to her knees on the hardwood floor, one hand on the wall to support herself.

The guy with the glasses bent down to help her but MJ screamed, "Don't touch her!" and shoved him out of the way.

His sister was kneeling on all fours on the floor now, her head hanging down. She was breathing in great heaves, like an exhausted runner.

MJ knelt beside her. "What's wrong, sis?" MJ said, kneeling down beside her, thinking she was having a heart attack. The kids, on the couch, were frozen in fear.

When she finally raised her head, he saw that she was crying. "Danny," she gasped. "Danny's dead."

"What?" MJ said, believing he had mis-heard.

"He's dead, he's dead!" she moaned.

MJ looked up sharply at the man in the door, realizing with a shock that he wasn't a salesman in a rumpled suit but some sort of cop.

"Is it true?" he asked.

The cop with the glasses nodded--just the slightest gesture--but MJ felt like he had been punched in the gut. His head swam and, if he hadn't been holding up his sister, he might have passed out himself.

Peggy felt him wobbling. "Oh, Mike," she said, looking at him in anguish before burying her head on his shoulder to sob.

He held her, wanting to say it would be okay but knowing in his heart it wouldn't. Danny dead. Nothing would fix that.

The kids came over and also threw their arms around Peggy, prompting a new outburst of crying.

"What's wrong, Uncle Mike?" asked Lee Jr.

MJ helped Peggy to her feet. "Take the kids upstairs," he told her.

"I, uh, have to ask you guys a few questions," said the man with the glasses.

"Peggy--upstairs," MJ commanded.

She gave him a look of gratitude and climbed the steps, stifling sobs and dragging the kids with her.

He turned to the guy in the doorway, an ember of anger burning in his gut. "Who the hell are you?"

The man pulled out a badge. "Detective Felton with the YPD."

The cop looked vaguely familiar but MJ couldn't place him.

"You're Michael Shea, right?" the cop said. "I remember you. You spat on my partner at your brother's arraignment."

MJ remembered now. He was the guy that worked with Proferes, the slime who came to arrest Danny on possession charges when he was in the hospital. After the charges were dismissed at the arraignment, MJ had launched a hocker onto Proferes' nice shiny shoes to let him know what he thought.

"What happened to Danny?" MJ demanded.

The cop threw a look at MJ's mom, who was watching them anxiously but without comprehension from the couch in front of the tv.

MJ was pretty sure she didn't understand what was going on, but he sighed and motioned Felton to the landing outside. The rain had lessened to a fine sprinkle. He left the door ajar and turned to the cop. "I'll tell her later. Now what happened?"

"I'm not going to sugar-coat it. Your brother was murdered. Shot in the back of the head, then dumped in some weeds off Rayen."

MJ leaned his shoulder against the wall to steady himself, feeling the ember of anger flare up. "Which one of you cops killed him?" he said.

"Get serious," said Felton. "This was drugs."

Drugs. Of course. Stupid dumbass Danny, trying to get a score. The only question was...

"Who did it?"

"We're working on it," said Felton. "That's why I'm here. When was the last time you saw your brother?"

"Me? Sunday, I think. He was supposed to go into rehab."

"What about Margaret?"

Only a cop would call Peggy "Margaret."

"I don't know," MJ said. "Last week sometime."

"He lived with her?"

"Off and on."

"I'm going to need to talk to her."

"When she settles down, okay? Now I got my own questions, like, what are you guys doing to find out who did this?"

"Like I said, we're investigating."

"You said he was shot on Rayen. That's a busy street. Someone must have seen it go down."

"No, his body was on a side street, Watt. Pretty deserted but we're canvassing the area."

"You're *canvassing* the area. What the hell does that mean?"

"It's not like on tv. These things take time. Unless you know who did it."

"Would I be standing here if I knew who did it?" MJ said.

"Calm down," Felton said.

"It's my fucking brother, calm down! Whoever did it, they're going to pay. You saw my sister."

"I know you're upset but let's do this the right way. Would your brother want you to go to prison getting justice for him?"

MJ took a deep breath. "Where is he now?" he finally said. "The morgue?"

Felton hesitated. "He hasn't been transported yet," he said.

MJ felt the anger flare up anew. "You mean he's still lying out in the fucking street?"

"Like I said, we're investigating. The body will be transported as soon as we've finished. You can meet us later at the coroner's to identify him."

"I can identify him right now," MJ said. "Watt and Rayen, you said?"

"We don't allow that."

"That's my brother," MJ said. "I don't give a crap what you allow."

He clicked the front door shut and pushed passed Felton to the sidewalk, leaving the cop alone on the porch. If Danny was dead on the street, MJ wanted to see with his own eyes.

A few minutes later, MJ was turning onto Rayen, driving too fast and unable to shake his head clear of the anger he was feeling. The rain had filtered down to a cold mist that drifted from an indistinct sky, making everything wet and grey.

On the one hand, it was hardly a surprise that Danny had gotten himself clipped. As a confirmed crackhead he was in all kinds of scrapes, from burglaries to shoot-outs to accidents like the fire in Peggy's kitchen. He was on the street at all hours of the day and night, had been beaten and robbed more than once, and he hung around with other crackheads who thought and acted just like he did. He had even almost killed himself once with some bad dope, ending up unconscious in the hospital for three days. He *would* have been dead that time if Peggy hadn't come home to find him lying on the floor of the upstairs bathroom.

On the other hand, what the hell? Murdered a mile from the house on the day he was supposed to go into rehab? Danny had a lot of problems but he was smart. It wouldn't be easy to trap him. He was a beautiful human being. He could play anything on his guitar, from flamenco to Van Halen to soulful songs he wrote himself and which chicks dug enough to sleep with him when he turned it on. MJ had seen him in action, on the nights Danny would play at The Elbow Room, a fancy bar downtown by the courthouse.

Danny dead didn't make any sense. Whoever did it had to get what was coming to them, and quick.

MJ would have to be careful with the cops but he had to find out what they knew.

As he approached the bend where the street turned toward the river, MJ saw a cop car and an ambulance behind a line of orange cones which blocked off a small street on the left. MJ slowed and passed the scene, scoping it out more-or-less from habit. Then, around the bend, he made a U-turn and came back to park against the curb behind the yellow police tape strung between a traffic cone and a tree.

Watt Street was little more than a strip of asphalt running parallel up through some scrubby trees to merge with Rayen. A couple of fireman in lime green vests stood near the open back of the ambulance, chatting as if they were at a fish fry. The dickhead cop Proferes was there, Felton's partner. He wore a grey suit covered by a tan rain coat and was talking with a uniformed cop nearby, pointing to some trash in the street.

The trash, MJ realized, was Danny's Cincinnati Reds baseball cap--upside down and crushed. Nearby, toward the edge of Rayen on the wet pavement, was a smashed beer can, with a numbered marker beside it like the kind they gave you at Frisch's Big Boy. Now MJ noticed other markers--near a cigarette butt, beside a trashed umbrella, at a scorched tire mark on the wet road..

And to his right, on the weedy verge of the wood, lay a shape under a yellow plastic tarp. MJ stared at it uncomprehendingly for a moment, until he saw the bloody hand protruding into the weeds at the near end.

"Danny," MJ said, aloud to himself, somehow still not really believing his brother was dead but knowing in his gut that all the evidence he would ever need was right there, under that tarp.

ENJOYING THIS STORY?

Reader reviews are the lifeblood of any author's career. For an indie author like myself, getting reviews (especially on Amazon) means more readers can discover me and decide whether they might like my books.

Which means I can actually sell a few copies from time to time. And that keeps me writing and producing more novels for your reading pleasure.

So every review means a lot to me. Please take a moment from your busy schedule to leave a quick comment at Amazon, Goodreads, BookBub or your favorite book site. Help other readers—let your opinion be known!

Chapter Six

Big Boy Marker Number 7

Z ombie-like, he got out of the car and walked onto the crime scene toward the body.

Just as MJ was ducking under the police tape, Felton pulled up in the black unmarked car.

"Hey," he said, hopping out. He started toward MJ but Proferes, who was also watching MJ, waved him to stand back.

MJ could see the hand clearly now, the palm, blackened with blood, protruding from the covering. As he lifted the tarp, the rainwater collected and ran into the weeds at MJ's feet.

It *was* Danny, or some mangled version of him anyway. His head was cocked toward MJ, with one eye open and staring, but his face on his right side was shredded meat, with blood and grey matter tangled in his hair and a bulging puncture wound at the edge of his scalp. Blood dripped from the wound, from his nose, from the open eye--running down his chin and matting his navy-blue Mount Union college sweatshirt. His mouth lolled open, tongue black inside, and one arm was tucked unnaturally behind his back.

MJ's head began to swim, and for a moment he felt like he was looking down a tunnel.

Detective Proferes came up beside. He was in his 40s, with a pink-striped tie and greying hair brushed back dago-style. "My partner radioed you were coming," he said.

"Yeah, well here I am," said MJ.

"Let's try this time to get started on the right foot," Proferes said mildly. He looked at the uncovered body. "Is it him?"

MJ nodded.

"I'm very sorry for your loss," the cop said--but fake sounding, automatic.

MJ put the tarp back over Danny's face, while at the same time trying to cover the splayed arm without exposing the feet. Only then did he see the Big Boy marker: number 7.

MJ felt the anger rising up again, but swallowed it so the cop wouldn't see. "Who did it?" he said. "Who shot him?"

"You tell me."

"What do you mean?" MJ snapped. "You think I had something to do with this?"

"I don't know," he said. "Where were you last night?"

"I didn't come here to be interrogated."

"Do you want to play games like the last time or do you want to find out who killed your brother?" Proferes spat back.

MJ hated dealing with the pigs, they were all the same, all threats and tricks. "I was with some friends," he finally said. "And then at my sister's."

"So you weren't with Daniel at all last night?" the cop said, watching him closely.

"Hell, no," said MJ.

Proferes seemed to accept that. He pulled out a notepad. "Was Daniel a dealer, or just a user?" he asked.

"I don't know anything about that."

Proferes reached into his jacket and pulled out a plastic evidence bag. Inside was a glass crack pipe, a lighter, some foil, and a tuft of steel wool. "This was in your brother's pocket," he said.

"Okay, yeah, Danny used. But he was going to go into rehab."

"But he didn't deal?"

"He might have dealt a little too, on the side. Nothing big. So what are you saying? He was robbed?"

The cop slipped the bag back into his pocket, but not before MJ noticed it also contained one of Danny's guitar picks. He realized Danny's guitar was nowhere to be seen.

"There was no cash or drugs found on him," Proferes said. "Where did Daniel get his supply?"

"I don't know," MJ said. MJ had given him enough. Let the cop figure it out.

"How about his friends? Do you know who Daniel hung out with?"

"No."

"Know anybody who would want to harm him?"

"Everybody loved Danny," MJ said.

"Apparently not everyone," Proferes said, looking down at the tarp. "Did he ever get into arguments or fights?"

Danny's whole life was an argument or fight with everyone around him, including the only people who loved and cared about him.

"No," MJ said.

The cop gave MJ a hard look, then snapped the note pad closed. "All right," he said. "We're through here for now. The body is going to go to the morgue but someone will call you when it's ready for pick up."

"What? That's it? What about the person that did this?"

"We got some evidence here. We'll investigate."

"Investigate how? What kind of evidence?"

"It's pretty obvious what went down. Your brother got involved in a bad drug deal. He got shot somewhere, transported, and dumped. But you don't know anything about that."

The detective was eyeballing him, challenging him to deny it. "I sure as hell don't," said MJ.

"Fine," said the cop. "Here's my card. I'll be in touch."

"What about the car? When they dumped him here, someone must have seen it."

"Who?" Proferes snapped. "Look around."

MJ saw what he meant. Where Watt met Rayen was nothing but wet weeds on this side and, up the road opposite, a small office building that would have been deserted at night. The far end of Watt took a bend and disappeared into some scrubby trees.

"If your memory gets any better, call me. And I'm going to have more questions for you, so don't leave town."

***

Proferes walked away, back to his partner Felton who had been watching everything from near the cop car. MJ took a last look at the tarp covering Danny, then turned and got in the van. He backed out onto Rayen and drove away, not going anywhere in particular, feeling depressed.

Danny was always a fuck up, but he had really screwed the pooch this time, getting himself killed-- probably as Proferes had suggested--chasing his next high in some sort of sketchy drug deal. MJ had warned him many times that crack was going to kill him, and many other times to be careful of where he slept and who he dealt with when he was on the streets.

Looking back, maybe instead of bailing Danny out he should have let the court order Danny into rehab, or even have him committed like the one social worker said. Maybe MJ should have locked him up himself, chained him to the pipes in Peggy's basement until he was clean and thinking like a normal person again. But MJ hadn't done any of those things because Danny wasn't a normal person. He was MJ's little brother, one year younger. You didn't lock away your little brother no matter how screwed up he was.

The rain was coming down in a sprinkle again, and the wet roads glowered with a sullen silver glow. A warm tear squeezed from the corner of his eye and rolled down his cheek, then another. MJ found a stretch of road where nobody would bother him and pulled over, wiping away the tears angrily and feeling defeated and empty.

He thought of all the times Danny had gotten himself in trouble: Punching out Sister Mary Jeanne in 3rd grade. Getting arrested selling pot in high school. Fucking up his gig with Promo and having the crap beat out of him. The more MJ thought, the more pissed off he got. In his mind it became clear that Proferes wasn't going to do shit about Danny's murder. Hell, that prick could care less about Danny. That's the way the system worked if you weren't rich or didn't have connections. No one gave a flying fuck. That's why you had to help yourself and screw what anyone thought. Otherwise the world would just grind you down. No matter how charming and handsome and smart you were. The world just didn't give a shit.

MJ found himself remembering the incident with Kate Parknavy. MJ was 10, taking a short cut along Valley Street when he heard a scuffling in a basement stairwell. Kate Parknavy, a girl from his class at St. Paul's, was being attacked by a guy in a black motorcycle jacket. The man had Kate by the throat, her uniform hiked up and his dick inside her, pressing her to the wall.

MJ picked up a brick, intending to throw it at the man's back--but hesitated, afraid. Over her attacker's shoulder, Kate looked up to MJ with desperate, pleading eyes.

"MJ, help," she screamed, but still MJ stood frozen.

The man turned and lunged at him, grabbing his leg quick as a striking snake despite his pants being half-off. Their eyes locked and MJ recognized him as Jimmy Verduci, one of the biker guys who hung around the pool room near the Esso. Suddenly there was a knife in Verduci's left hand and MJ, never so frightened in his life, somehow kicked free and ran, hiding in some bushes across the street.

Verduci, yanking on his pants, took a few steps in MJ's direction, but when Kate tried to dart passed him up the steps, grabbed her instead and dragged her back screaming to the basement well.

MJ knew Verduci was hurting the girl--raping her, he suddenly under-stood--and knew he should go to help. Her screams and sobs, so helpless and pathetic, seemed to tear his own heart. He prayed to God for courage to return to the stairwell and defend his friend.

But he was afraid of the big man, afraid of the knife. Instead of defending Kate, he turned and ran and kept on running, arriving at home breathless and unable to explain what had happened to the groceries he had been sent to get. His father whipped his ass and sent him to his room.

The next day Kate Parknavy was found dead in the stairwell. MJ knew he was a coward and was too ashamed to tell anyone what happened. He didn't go near the pool hall again for two more years, until he learned Verduci had been killed in a gang fight.

All that bullshit the nuns taught in school--God is watching you, protecting you from harm, sorting out the good from the bad. What a crock of shit. The one time MJ needed God, he was nowhere to be found.

Kate Parknavy wasn't watched over. She was dead.

And now Danny was dead, too.

Where the hell was "God" for them?

God didn't exist, at least not in Youngstown. In Youngstown it was every man for himself.

He found himself passing Stambaugh Auditorium, where a large moving van poked half-way into the street, trapping MJ in his lane. He laid on the horn and eventually got around the truck, delivering a few choice words to the driver. What a joke life was, that Proferes would end up being the cop in charge of Danny's case. The same fucking cop who had hassled Danny for years, ever since the pot arrest, picking him up for minor offenses and trying to turn him into a snitch.

On the other hand, Proferes was a prick alright but he wasn't a dumb ass. And he had the whole Youngstown police department behind him so he ought to be able to find Danny's killer. But then what? Whoever killed Danny deserved the death penalty, but because Danny was a crackhead, the killer would probably get off with 20 years, and get probation in 10. Or his bullshit lawyer would make a plea deal with the prosecutor's office and the murderer would give up some supplier in exchange for a light sentence. Or maybe the lawyer would come up with some technicality and get the slayer off scot-free.

MJ's guts began to churn. It wouldn't come to that because MJ wouldn't let it. His brother was dead and MJ was going to find and kill whoever killed him--a gun to the guy's forehead so he'd know exactly why he was being offed.

After that MJ would have to disappear. Maybe it would be time for him to finally make his escape from Youngstown. There was a town he had discovered in New Jersey called Ocean Grove--small and old-fashioned but cheap and right on the water. He'd been thinking about it for a long time now. In fact, he'd been saving money to make the move. A few more good scores and he'd have enough.

Ocean Grove. The streets were narrow but clean and you could smell the ocean everywhere you went. He could rent an apartment with a view of the water and spend his mornings fishing off the ramshackle pier. No one would be looking for him there, and maybe even he could get Cassie to come if she would ever forgive him.

If. If. Screw the ifs. Right now there was only one thing needed to be done.

Kill the fucker who killed Danny, then get out of Youngstown. That was the plan.

He was going to need help. He turned the van around and headed over to Roma Restaurant to see if he could find his brother-in-law Lee.

Chapter Seven

Friends and Family

M J hadn't intended to try to see Cassie right away, but his daydreaming had put her in his mind. And it didn't help that on his way to Roma's he found himself near the hospital, not far from where Cassie was studying at Sacred Heart School of Nursing. He glanced at his watch--9:50 a.m.--then on impulse took a U-turn and circled around toward the school, which was located in an old stone building a block from the modern St. Elizabeth's Hospital Medical Center.

He found a space across the street and parked, staring at the gothic towers and gables of the school. The drizzle was still coming down, the grounds were deserted and Cassie would be in class somewhere inside, learning about chemistry and how to give injections. He felt an intense desire to see her, but all the ways he could think of to find her--pretending to be her brother, having her called out of class for some fake emergency--would just end up pissing her off.

He sat smoking a cigarette and trying to decide what to do, feeling more and more like a high school dumb-ass. He knew Cassie didn't want to see him, but he wanted to tell her about Danny. She had met Danny and had even tried to help him. She deserved to know.

But it was more than that. Somehow he hoped she could help him make sense out of his brother's bloody murder. Because just the thought of Danny ruined body lying on the wet street filled MJ with rage and frustration.

The cigarette burned down to his fingers and he flicked it out the window, then re-started the van, deciding to leave. But suddenly, at the school, a class let out and the covered portico began to fill with milling students--all girls, of course, and all identical in their blue student uniforms and ridiculous white hats.

And then there she was, pushing through the door with a friend, her long black hair neatly tied back and her slim figure making even the blousy uniform look good.

MJ jumped out of the van and started toward her without ever considering what he was going to say. Cassie stood against the wall out of the rain along with the other students, talking to her friend and cradling an armful of books.

Then she saw him, her dark eyes momentarily locking onto his with what MJ thought was curiosity and interest before the eyes hardened and she turned away. When he stepped up, her expression was all frost.

"What are you doing here?" she said.

The other students, sensing some impending drama, turned to watch.

"Cassie," he said. "I need to talk to you."

"Well, I don't need to talk to you. I told you to stay away."

"Please, can we just go somewhere and talk? It's important."

"What? Do you have some big 'business deal' you're working on," she said, making "business deal" sound like the lowest form of activity on earth. "Just go away."

"Cassie," he said, reaching out to touch her elbow.

She reacted as if he had poked her with a red-hot iron--whirling around and yelling, "Leave me alone!" before brushing through the students and disappearing back into the school.

Suddenly a stout, black-robed nun was standing in the doorway, a veil hanging half-way to her ass.

"What's going on out here?" she demanded, and then, seeing MJ, said, "Who are you?"

MJ looked past her to try to see where Cassie was going, but she was already out of sight. He could push past the nun to run after her, but what would be the point?

Bitterly, he turned and walked back to the van, feeling the glaring eyes of the nun on his back.

He should have known better than to come. Cassie had made it clear she would never forgive him, and by acting so needy he was just making himself look desperate. And anyway, what could she say about Danny's death? That Danny was resting peacefully now, his soul floating around in heaven?

He put the van in gear and pulled away. Actually, he realized, that wasn't what she'd say at all. She'd say that Danny was dead because he was on drugs, and that he was on drugs because of MJ.

The idea that Danny would do or not do anything because of MJ was ridiculous, but MJ's head was suddenly throbbing. The light ahead turned yellow, and MJ stomped on the accelerator and barreled through the intersection, scaring himself from thinking.

Lee would be over at the Roma Restaurant. He headed there.

***

Roma's was a place on Belmont Avenue where the Mafioso-types liked to hang out. Lee Messina, Peggy's husband, wasn't in the rackets (nor did he want to be, since he didn't like taking orders), but he had a lot of friends at the restaurant and liked the sausage strata. The Mafia's fingers were everywhere in Youngstown--numbers, prostitution, horses, hijacking big rigs--and Lee, as a *paisano*, was trusted as an extra hand on various jobs.

MJ knew Lee from high school. Danny was his friend first, helping jack cars for one of Lee's connections in Cleveland, and soon enough, Danny brought MJ in on the action.

Lee's father was a lifer in the highway department, and his mother a gray-haired Italian women who made pasta from scratch and embroidered an elaborate tablecloth every year to sell at the church bazaar. MJ sat beside them at Lee and Peggy's wedding. Lee's mother was all weepy but his father sat in silent disapproval of the whole ceremony, since Lee had just been dishonorably discharged from the Navy and didn't have any kind of a job to support a family. Mr. Messina's nickname for Lee was "Shit-for-Brains."

Using their profits on the stripped cars, Lee, MJ and Danny developed a little drug business together, supplying speed and 'ludes from Lee's sources to frat boys up at Youngstown U., no prescription required. Later, Danny branched off on his own selling pot, but Lee and MJ kept up the pill trade as a side line, selling out of a locker at the Janiro Boxing Club, where they trained together for Golden Gloves.

After graduation, Lee joined the Navy and MJ didn't see him again for a couple of years. MJ kept the pill trade going, but coke was getting big and he started picking up gigs with Waylay. Then Lee got a sudden discharge, reappeared as a nightclub bouncer and pretty soon started dating Peggy.

At the restaurant this morning, only a few cars were parked on the street, but sure enough, Lee's white '82 Camaro was out front. MJ entered through the glass door, scanned the counter and the tables, and found Lee sitting in a booth toward the back with a guy MJ recognized as Mike Longo, someone Lee did jobs with.

Lee caught sight of MJ at the door and waved him over. "Hey, MJ," he said. "What brings you here?"

MJ felt sudden relief; if anyone could help with finding Danny's killer, it was Lee.

MJ slid into the booth beside Longo, saying his hellos. Lee was a tall guy with boxer shoulders and a thin pencil mustache that would have looked ridiculous on anyone else, but on Lee it looked good--and he knew it. The table was covered with empty breakfast plates and copies of the *Youngstown Vindicator* and the *Yellow Racing Form.*

"Lee, something's come up."

Lee took a drag on his cigarette and gave MJ his trademark deadpan look. "Yeah? What?"

MJ glanced at Longo and hesitated.

Lee turned to him. "Mike, me and MJ got something personal to discuss."

"Yeah, sure," Longo said. "I was just leaving."

He threw a $5 bill on the table to cover his check, picked up his racing form and started edging out of the booth. MJ slid out to let him go, then sat back down again and stared at Lee.

"What is it?" Lee asked.

"I need your help," MJ said.

"What's going on?"

"It's about Danny..."

"Okay," said Lee, looking neither sympathetic nor surprised. Lee wasn't happy that Danny had started rooming with Peggy after the separation, and had even kicked him out on his ass the time Peggy caught Danny cooking crack in her kitchen.

"It's not what you think, Lee. Someone killed him."

Lee's cigarette, which had been on its way to his lips, paused in mid-air--about as surprised as Lee ever got. "What?" he said.

"Danny. Someone shot him, in the back of the head."

Lee looked at MJ, processing the information. "You're... You're kidding me, right?"

"No. I wish I was."

"When did this go down?" he asked.

"Last night sometime. The cops found his body this morning over off Rayen."

Lee looked down at the table. "I can't believe it. Danny."

"Yeah. Well."

What could Lee say? What could anyone say?

They sat there together looking at each other, until finally Lee took a drag from his cigarette and blew out a cloud of smoke. "Any idea who did it?" he asked.

"No," said MJ. "But that dick Proferes thinks it was a drug deal gone wrong."

"Proferes? The pig that arrested Danny?"

"The same. He's a detective now," said MJ. He filled Lee in on the conversation he had had with Proferes at the corner where Danny was dumped.

"He got any witnesses?" Lee asked.

"He says no. That place is kind of deserted. But someone must know something. That's why I need your help. I'm going to find the fucker that did this and shit in his fucking skull."

Lee clenched his jaw. Leaning back in the booth, he took another drag on his cigarette--more slowly this time--then blew smoke from the corner of his mouth. "That could be dangerous," he said.

"Like I give a shit. Whoever was in that car killed Danny, and when I get my hands on him I'm going to blow his brains out just like he did Danny. Except I'm going to shove the gun right the fuck up his nose so he can see what's coming."

Lee sat up and crushed his cigarette in the glass ashtray on the table. "We've known each other for a long time so I'm going to give you some advice. Leave this one to Proferes."

"That cop's an asshole. He couldn't find his way to the bathroom if he was sitting on the fucking john."

"Yeah, maybe. But he's got a lot of contacts on the street. Just wait and see what he finds out. If you run around shooting people, it'll be your ass that Proferes tosses in jail."

"I don't care. I just don't trust that guy. You know he tried to set Danny up to inform on Waylay."

Lee sat back and pulled another cigarette from his pack. "You sure he didn't?" he asked.

"Didn't what?"

"Turn Danny?"

"Hell, no. Danny wasn't no squealer."

"You positive? Because you know the cops are always recruiting junkies and crackheads, trying to bust down the coke business."

"I told you, Danny's no squealer."

"Okay," Lee said, leaning back. "But if he was informing on some big fish it would sure explain how he ended up with a bullet in his head."

At first MJ didn't get what Lee was driving at. Then he understood and felt a sick feeling in his stomach. "You mean Waylay?"

"You remember the trial."

When Waylay was up on trafficking and bribery charges, a bomb had taken out three State witnesses, literally blowing them up on the courthouse steps as they arrived from a secret location to testify.

MJ shook his head. "I don't believe it. Danny didn't know shit about Waylay's operation."

"Maybe, maybe not. That's what you need to find out."

MJ considered. Danny never forgot the roughing up he had received for the coke-skimming episode, and like a good Shea had vowed to "get even" with Waylay in some unspecified manner. MJ had dismissed the idea as an absurdity, but what if his brother had actually started working with the cops to help them bring down Waylay? The stash house *had* been raided not long after Danny's dust-up. Could his brother have had something to do with that?

It was at least possible. And it would explain the frosty reception MJ had gotten from Waylay at Big Man Donuts.

"All right," MJ said at last. "You got connections. Do you think any of your friends can find out if Danny was an informant?"

"I can sure as shit ask around," said Lee.

"Good. And I'm going to talk to Danny's dealer, Skeevy, see what he knows."

"I thought I just told you to leave that to the cops. Don't you hear right?"

Sometimes Lee annoyed MJ by trying to act like his big brother. "You know I can't do that, Lee."

"I don't like it. You know, if Waylay killed Danny, he won't hesitate to kill you too."

"Yeah, well--I'm not so easy to kill. If Waylay did it, I'll blow his fucking brains out."

Lee leaned forward and looked at MJ with narrowed eyes. "Play it cool, brother. You don't know what you're getting into," he said.

"Don't worry about me," MJ said.

Lee gave a dismissive shrug, then sat back, smoothing his mustache. "How's Peggy taking all this?" he asked.

Peggy. He still had to get back to her. She'd be worried. "She's probably completely batshit by now," MJ said.

"Peggy's always batshit," said Lee flatly. Both Peggy and Lee were bull-headed, and their marriage had been a drawn-out series of power struggles and fights until they had separated a year earlier.

"I better get back to her," said MJ. "You want to come?"

"No, ah, you go," said Lee. "Let me see what I can find out about Danny."

"Okay," said MJ, rising.

"Tell Peggy I'll call later, see how the kids are doing."

***

MJ found Peggy upstairs face down on her bed, the room reeking of pot. The kids were there, too, unsure of what was happening. They played with the kitten, which was tangled up in one of Peggy's Ace bandages.

He took a seat on the edge of the bed. "Peg," he said, his voice almost a whisper. "Peg, I know it's hard. But... we've got to talk. Can you sit up?"

Listlessly she turned and sat against the headboard. Her eyes were red from crying and her face looked haggard. "Was it bad?" she asked.

"Yeah," he said, thinking of Danny's blown-open skull. "Real bad."

"Did... did it look like he suffered?"

"He didn't have time to suffer," MJ said. Then lower, leaning in: "He was shot in the back of the head."

Peggy blanched and turned to the children. "Kids, go play downstairs," she said. "Mommy will be down in a minute."

Lee Jr. and Shannon climbed down from the bed, taking the kitten with them. When they were gone, she said, "What happened?"

MJ told her what he had seen, leaving out some of the gorier details of Danny's injuries, and giving Proferes' theory that their brother had been involved in a bad drug transaction.

"I warned him," said Peggy, in a voice both bitter and hard. "I told him to be careful who he fucks with."

"When did Danny ever take advice?"

Peggy lit a cigarette from a pack on the nightstand and sat up on the side of the bed. "I don't even know what he was mad about when he left," she said. "Something about a missing shirt. I should have gone out looking for him."

"It's not your fault," said MJ. "Danny did what he wanted to do. I just wish I could have gotten him into St. Elizabeth's."

Peggy inhaled and blew out a cloud of smoke. "I don't know," she said. "We tried that once, remember. I doubt a second time in rehab would have made any difference."

She was probably right but it still made MJ feel sad. They sat in silence for a moment, MJ's hands lying uselessly in his lap.

"So what are the cops going to do?"

"Who knows? They're not going to waste much time on Danny, that's for sure. Proferes is in charge, remember him?"

"The asshole who arrested him? I always hated that guy."

"Yeah, well, he's heading the investigation. He's probably going to come nosing around to talk to you, ask some questions."

"Well he can go fuck himself." Peggy had the same wariness of cops as everyone in the neighborhood, with special hatred ever since one showed up at the door with a case worker when someone reported her to social services.

She blew some smoke at the ceiling. "Who do *you* think killed him? That slime who sold him the bad stuff?"

"Skeevy? Hell no. Danny was too good a customer, so there's no reason he'd kill him, especially since it would bring down the heat. Danny must have been trying score from someone else."

"What if the cops don't find who did it?" said Peggy.

"Anyone who won't talk to the cops, I'll make 'em talk to me," said MJ. Then, abruptly, "I'm going to kill the bastard who did this."

A cloud of fear wisped across Peggy's face. She clamped MJ's wrist with an iron grip. "No, you're not."

"The hell I won't."

"No more killings!" she said. "I've already lost one brother. I'm not going to lose another. You remember what happened with you and Lee."

She was talking about when Paulie Colussi had shot Tom Ford after the liquor store hold-up. Lee was a friend of Ford and a witness, so when Marino came gunning for him, MJ had to help Lee out. Lee ambushed Marino at the Wal-Mart parking lot, killing him, but not before MJ got shot in the chest. He almost died twice, once on the way to the hinky doctor they had to use to keep the gunshot wound from being reported, and again a week later, from a bad infection.

"Don't worry, sis."

"No!" she said. "Isn't it enough that Danny's dead? Promise me you won't do anything."

He saw she was working herself up again. "Yeah," he said, to mollify her. "If that's what you want."

"That's what I want," she said. "Danny's dead, isn't that enough? No more killing."

She looked on the verge of tears again. He should have known to keep his mouth shut, not scare her. "Okay," he said.

She leaned over and hugged him. "I love you, MJ," she said.

"I love you too, sis."

She hugged him for a long time. When she finally drew back, she dabbed her eyes with a Kleenex from the nightstand and regarded him sadly. MJ felt a moment of relief. He could see that he had helped her over the worst and that from here on out she'd probably be okay.

As if on cue, she threw aside the Kleenex and sat up. "We're going to have to go over to Vlasik's, make arrangements."

Vlasik's was the Catholic funeral home which had buried their father.

"Yeah," said MJ, "Sure. You fix it up. Something small, like Dad's."

"Small, hell," she said. "We'll bury him at St. Paul's on, let's see, Friday, and tomorrow and Thursday we can have the viewing."

"Peggy, that's ridiculous. Let's just cremate him."

"You can't cremate in the Catholic church."

"As if Danny would give a shit."

"That's not the point. Dad's funeral was small because Mom wanted it that way. But Mom's not in charge now. We have to do right by Danny."

"Danny wouldn't want..."

"Don't you get it?" she screamed. "He's our brother! He's our brother and we have to bury him right. People have to know that us Sheas stick together."

MJ could see that Peggy was digging in her heels, and maybe she was right. And anyway, funerals were one of the things women took care of.

She plunged ahead: "Old man Vlasik, if he's still around, he'll put the notice in the *Vindicator* and can help pick out the casket, something nice, maybe silver like we did for Dad. I'll have to talk to Father Corkill about the funeral mass. You and Lee can be pall bearers, with cousin Gary and that friend of Danny's from the Music Shack, I forget his name."

"All right, Peggy," said MJ, giving up. "Whatever you want. You take care of it. And don't you worry about the cost. I'll pay for everything." *Pretty much the way it always was.*

"Don't be an ass," said Peggy.

"What do you mean?"

"You think I like taking your money?"

"What difference does it make, Peg?"

"I know you think I'm a leech."

"I never said anything like that."

"You never said it, but I know you think it. Yeah I take your money but only cause I have to, what with the kids and Mom. But this time, I'm going to help pay."

"Okay," he said.

"I mean it."

"I know you do, sis."

Mollified, she went to the window and took a last drag on her cigarette. "This is going to be painful," she said--but whether as a prediction or an order, MJ couldn't say.

Chapter Eight

Promises to Pay

As Tuesday bled into Wednesday, MJ lay in his bed thinking of Danny and listening to the sounds of barking dogs and distant police sirens. Despite being dead tired, he found sleep elusive. That next morning he was meeting Peggy at the funeral home to pick out a casket, and the first viewing would commence at 4 p.m.

Dawn came gradually. Through the window MJ could see the gray lid of the sky hovering over the city.

He gave up on sleep and threw off his blanket. If he was going to see Danny's supplier, now was the time.

***

Skeevy was a low-level drug dealer like scores of others across Youngstown, cashing in on the crack epidemic that was sweeping the city. MJ dismissed out-of-hand any idea that Skeevy might be Danny's murderer--he was too small-fry for that--but he had ears on the street and might know who the killer was. The problem would be how to extract this information from him. MJ took his Browning from the nightstand, and checked the clip. Then he chambered a round and slipped it into the pocket of his jacket, figuring Skeevy might need some convincing.

An hour later, MJ was parked a half-block from Grover's Kwik Stop, a convenience store on the South Side where Skeevy plied his wares. The street side of the store had a big window and a sign, "Bill Payments Money Orders," but the actual entrance was on the parking lot side, a glass door festooned with ads for Bud Light, Skoal and the Ohio Pick 4.

From his vantage point down the street, MJ could see Skeevy servicing his morning clients. A tall and thin black dude in his early twenties, Skeevy hung to the brick side of the building, greeting customers as they pulled up and palming bills in quick exchanges of product. Most of Skeevy's clientele arrived on foot, but a surprising number came in by car, and not necessarily crappy cars either. He even saw an official city tow truck in the mix.

MJ's pager beeped, displaying Peggy's number, and MJ remembered he was supposed to be at Vlasik's helping her look at caskets. But she'd have to make out on her own.

What Skeevy knew was more important. As MJ watched, Skeevy passed something through the window to the tow truck driver, then nodded to move him along.

MJ put the car in gear; he was driving his '84 Cutlass Supreme this morning, a car he used to tootle around town when he wanted something inconspicuous. With the tow driver gone, he drove up to Skeevy, rolling the window down on the passenger side as Skeevy came up.

"Hey, man, good morning, what can I do for you?" Skeevy said, with the fake good nature of a used car salesman.

MJ leaned forward so Skeevy could see his face. "We need to talk," said MJ.

A look of annoyance crossed Skeevy's face. "Talk? I ain't got time to talk. Can't you see I'm trying to do business here?"

"That's what this is about," said MJ. "Business."

Skeevy looked at MJ a little closer. "Wonder send you?"

"No one sent me," said MJ. "Get in the car."

"What are you, the fuzz?" said Skeevy, looking around nervously.

"I'm Danny Shea's brother, said MJ. "You know Danny, don't you?"

Skeevy took a step backwards. "I don't know nothing about that shit."

"Like hell you don't, you lying sack of shit," said MJ. He pulled the Browning from his pocket and thumbed the safety off, then rested the pistol against his thigh.

Skeevy saw it and froze.

"Don't make me use it," MJ said. "Get in the car. I just want to talk."

Reluctantly, Skeevy pulled the door open and slid inside. MJ kept his hand on the weapon just in case Skeevy got any ideas.

"How far we going?" Skeevy said. "I got customers."

"Not far. I just want some info."

"I told you already I don't know nothing about that killing," said Skeevy.

"Who said anything about a killing?"

"Hey, come on, man, I know why you're here. What happened to Danny, it's all over the streets. Everybody knows."

"Knows what? Tell me."

"Knows Danny got offed by some dudes in a big black Benz."

That was new. Proferes hadn't said anything about the car. "Somebody saw it? A big black Mercedes Benz?"

"That's what they say. Or a chromed-out Buick, I heard that, too. But I don't think the cops would drive something like that."

"The cops?"

"The cops who killed him."

"Why would the cops kill Danny?"

"I don't know man. It's just what I heard, that the cops burned him," Skeevy said. "Now can we maybe go back to where you got me? This is my busy time and I gotta make my quota."

MJ considered. YPD cops were trigger happy, known on the street for their "shoot first, ask questions later" policy. But MJ leaned more toward Proferes' drug-buy theory.

"How long was Danny buying from you?" asked MJ.

"I don't know. A year? Two?"

"When did you see him last?"

"I seen him every day. Up to Monday, that is.

"Monday what time?"

"Regular time, I don't know, around seven, eight a.m."

"Where were you Monday night?"

"Whoa whoa whoa, man. I ain't got nothing to do with that, you understand? I only seen Danny about 10 seconds a day, just like my other customers. Once in a while he'd hang and play guitar, share a blunt."

"So where were you Monday?"

"Hey, hey man, I never had no trouble with Danny. I liked your brother, he was a good customer, so I'll be straight with you. I was over church with my Aunt Wilodine for spaghetti night and then home with my lady Rochelle. You go check it you'll see. I ain't no gangster, going around icing guys."

Skeevy sounded sincere enough. MJ, who was still holding the Browning on his thigh, thumbed the safety and slipped the gun back in his jacket pocket. "Danny ever talk to you about doing a big score?" he asked.

"All the time, man. But it was all bullshit."

"He have any enemies? Anyone want to hurt him?"

"I know he had a beef with Waylay, told me about that. Something about getting the shit beat out of him and stealing Waylay's car."

MJ knew all about Waylay having Danny beaten, but had never heard anything about Danny stealing Waylay's car. "What did he tell you about the car?"

"It was one of those jacked-up Broncos. Danny said he took out in a field and burned it. He said Waylay owed him money."

MJ thought about this for one second and decided the stolen car story was bullshit. Even Danny wouldn't be stupid enough to burn up Waylay's vehicle, although he might lie about doing it to bolster his street cred.

"Can we go back now?," Skeevy said. "My customers' waiting."

MJ started the car and made a quick U-turn back towards Skeevy's turf. "What you said earlier, about Danny maybe getting cross-wise with some cops--you think Danny ever worked with them?" he asked.

Skeevy gave a skeptical snort. "No, man. He *hated* them dicks."

Satisfied that Skeevy had been straight with him, MJ pulled over a half-block before Grover's, reaching for his wallet and handing him a couple of twenties.

"What's this, man?"

"Keep your ears open. You hear anything about who killed Danny, I want to know."

"Well, alright then," said Skeevy. "You got money, I'm your honey."

MJ wrote his pager number on the back of a matchbook and gave it to Skeevy, who pocketed the bill and the matchbook, then opened the door. But before Skeevy slid out he paused and said, "Speaking of money, Danny must've needed some."

"Why do you say that?"

"He mentioned he was going to see this guy, Kidder, and that's what Kidder does, loan money."

MJ knew of Kidder. He was a mob guy, doing business as a union officer, who financed various criminal operations as a banker and a loan shark.

"When was this?"

"Monday, last day I saw him."

"Did he say why?"

Skeevy shook his head. "That's all I know, man."

*****

A half hour later, MJ was back in his apartment, a one-bedroom unit overlooking a now-dark Gulf Oil station not far from the college. MJ, suddenly starving, fixed himself a sandwich from some lunch meat in the fridge and sat at his little kitchen table to eat it, feeling wrung out and thinking about what Skeevy had said.

MJ was going to have to talk to Kidd, find out if Danny had borrowed money and for what. But Kidd wouldn't just talk to anyone who walked in off the street. With these mob guys you had to know someone.

Fortunately, MJ did.

Lee.

Lee could get MJ in to see Kidd and reassure the guy MJ was legit.

MJ looked up Lee's pager number from a slip of paper he carried in his wallet and gave him a page from the phone in the living room. A few minutes later the phone rang.

"Hey, Lee?"

"Yeah. What's up?"

"Were you able to find out anything about Danny working for the cops?"

"I put out some feelers. But it's going to take a little time."

"I got another favor to ask. Can you help me get in to talk to Kidder Kidd?"

There was a pause on Lee's end of the phone; MJ could hear dishes clanking in the background, so he was probably back at Roma's. "Kidd?" Lee said. "What's he got to do with anything?"

"Seems like he lent Danny some money. I want to know what for."

"Yeah? Who told you that?"

"Skeevy. He and I had a little talk after I left you."

"So you had to go and start digging around over there anyway? I thought you were going to leave things to the cops."

"I'm not waiting on that rube Proferes. Danny is going to get justice."

"And you're the one that's going to get it for him?"

"I sure as hell am."

"Listen, brother, you fool around with Waylay and you're wading in deep shit, and you ain't got the shoes for it. You think you're big enough?"

"Big enough if I have to be."

"Waylay don't take prisoners, you know that. He blows people up. I told you, remember the trial."

"We don't even know if it's Waylay."

"I say it is. And if it is, you better keep out of it. I need to keep you around so I have someone to shoot skeet with."

"Fuck skeet. Whoever was in that car murdered Danny. I'm going to find him and kill him, and that's it. Now can you get me in to see Kidd?"

"I don't like it, MJ."

"Look, Kidd wouldn't lend money to Danny unless he knew what Danny was going to use it for. If it had anything to do with Waylay, he'd know."

"You are going to fucking get yourself killed," Lee said, more of a statement than an exclamation.

Lee was right to worry about Waylay but MJ felt it was a chance he had to take. "Can you do it or not?" he said.

More dishes clattering on the other end. "Yeah, okay," Lee finally said. "Let me see what I can arrange."

"Thanks, buddy," MJ said, feeling like he was finally making some progress.

MJ hung up. Now he would just have to wait. He was dead tired and the viewing was starting in less than two hours.

He set the alarm for an hour's sleep and crawled under the cold covers of his bed.

He wasn't looking forward to the ordeal of the viewing, but he knew he had to keep his shit together and get the thing done.

Just as he finally drifted off, the phone rang.

It was Peggy. "Where the hell were you this morning? Leaving me alone to pick a casket."

"I got tied up with something," MJ said.

"You got tied up. You never do any fucking thing you say you're going to do. And it's Danny's funeral."

"I was going to call you."

"Yeah, right. Are you going to leave me all alone at the viewing, too?"

"I'll be there. Five o'clock, right? I got..."--he looked at his alarm--"..over an hour to get ready."

"You better fucking be there," Peggy said. And hung up.

***

MJ arrived at the funeral home lot a few minutes before five. With the overhanging clouds, the afternoon was dull, and the light grey and even. Peggy and the kids were standing in a group on the sidewalk, near the main building. He pulled up alongside her car and parked.

Peggy, looking morose, was wearing a grey cloth coat, and under that, a two-piece black outfit that did little to hide her bulk. MJ had never seen the kids so clean, with Lee Jr. trussed up in a white shirt and tie, and Shannon in a dark blue dress that looked brand-new. Peggy's hair, for once, was neatly coiffed and a green-pattered scarf hung around her neck. She was wiping Shannon's fingers with a Kleenex from her purse when he pulled up, apparently waiting for him.

MJ got out and greeted her.

"You look good, Sis," he said, giving her a hug.

"You, too," she said--relieved, MJ could see, that he had actually shown up. He was wearing a white shirt and a navy sports coat, the only jacket he owned.

"Ready to go in?"

"Wait," she said. "I want to show you something." She rummaged in her purse and handed MJ a white, unaddressed envelope.

"What is it?" said MJ, finding a folded wad of printed papers inside.

"Remember what we talked about?" said Peggy.

He unfolded the packet. *Mutual Benefit Insurance Company of Ohio*, it was headed in large type on the first page, with smaller headings further down--"In Consideration" and "Promises to Pay"-- separated by large amounts of fine print. His brother's name, "Daniel Patrick Shea," was typed in on a blank line, and on another blank line, toward the middle, was the amount, also typed, of "Two Thousand Dollars and 00/100 Cents."

A life insurance policy on Danny. MJ looked up. "When did you get this?"

"Last year," said Peggy. "After the thing with the hospital." She meant Danny's near-fatal overdose. "I was afraid... you know... something like this might happen and I wanted to be prepared."

MJ was impressed. The premium payments on a $2,000 policy wouldn't be large, but Peggy lived mostly on her welfare check and food stamps, so it must have been a hardship for her to keep up with the payments. MJ folded the papers up again and handed the envelope back to her, who took it hesitantly.

"I want you to know I'm going to use this money to help pay for the funeral," she said, stuffing the policy back in her purse.

"I told you not to worry about it," said MJ.

"I want to," said Peggy. "He was *our* brother."

"Just keep the money, Sis," said MJ. "Use it to fix some stuff around the house. Or use it for yourself. Hell, you deserve a break."

"No. I'm going to pay."

MJ could see that Peggy had made her mind up, so he decided not to press the matter further. He could handle the funeral expenses himself, but if Peggy wanted to pay something he supposed he'd best let her. A few hundred dollars for the flowers maybe, or food for the reception. Truth was she had already done more than MJ or anyone, having put up with Danny all through this last year when crack really took control.

Just then the glass door to the funeral home swung open and Dave Vlasik, Jr. emerged from inside in an black suit and tie. Now in his 40s, Vlasik was the pudgy younger son of old man Vlasik, who had run the funeral home since it first opened. It was five o'clock. He motioned them inside.

"I guess it's time," said MJ, his stomach beginning to churn.

"I don't know how I'm going to get through this," Peggy said.

MJ felt the same, but didn't want to say it. "Come on, kids, let's go in," he said, taking little Lee by the hand, as Peggy took Shannon.

Chapter Nine

The Viewing

In the burgundy-carpeted foyer, Dave Vlasik, Jr. offered his sympathy and shook MJ's hand, then turned to his sister. "How are you doing?" he said to Peggy, covering one of her hands with both of his.

That was all that was needed to set Peggy off, and she leaned on him and began to cry.

"It's okay. You'll be okay," said Vlasik.

Shannon clung to her crying mother while Lee Jr. took a step into the viewing room and stopped.

"Is that Uncle Danny?" he asked MJ, who had stepped in behind.

The silver coffin was elevated like an altar at the end of the room, with a kneeler in front and mounds of flowers at either side.

"Yes. That's him," said MJ.

"In the box thing?" said Lee Jr.

"Yeah," said MJ. "In the box thing."

The two of them approached the coffin while Vlasik continued to comfort Peggy in the hallway. The coffin was, of course, closed since any kind of reconstruction of Danny's face was out of the question.

Peggy came in, smoothing her outfit after hanging her coat. She stopped beside MJ and examined the arrangements. After a while she said, "It looks good."

"Super good," said MJ.

"I got the casket with the bronze handles," she said. "It was more but the wood handles looked cheap."

"Thanks for taking care of all this," MJ said.

"I ordered the carnations from Kraft's," said Peggy, moving closer and examining the floral bouquets. "They were Danny's favorite flower."

If Danny had any favorite flower, it was news to MJ, but if it made Peggy feel better to think so, he wasn't going to pop her balloon. Behind them, MJ heard Vlasik opening the door and greeting the first visitors.

Peggy heard them too and gathered up the kids. "We're going to say a prayer," Peggy said.

"Okay," said MJ.

"You should say one, too," said Peggy.

He drew the line at praying, although he would have liked to have a moment alone with his brother. "You guys go. There's not enough room on the kneeler for me."

He took a step back and watched as Peggy shepherded the kids to the kneeler, where they murmured their devotions.

Their cousin Rose came in from the hall and gave MJ a hug. "It's terrible, MJ. I'm so sorry."

Her husband Gary, a beefy construction worker who operated big cranes, also offered his hand. MJ shook it and murmured his appreciation.

Rose was gazing at the children, who, heads bowed, were praying beside the coffin. "Oh my God, the kids look just angelic," she whispered to MJ. "Are they okay?"

"They're confused."

"They are so darling," his cousin said, with a glance at her husband. MJ had heard from Peggy that Rose and Gary were desperate to have kids and had spent thousands on doctors without success. Now they were getting counseling with Catholic Adoption Services, hoping to adopt.

"How's your sister taking it?" Gary asked.

"Tough," he said. "It's been real tough on her... but she's been keeping her chin up, for the sake of the kids."

MJ was proud of his sister. In some ways Peggy was stronger than him--absorbing blows, able to roll with the punches and keep going. He could barely stand to look at the coffin. It felt like Danny was saying, "Look what they did to me."

He glanced at his watch. 5:20. Over two-and-a-half hours to go. Rose was talking to him and he forced himself to focus on her words. Like it or not, he had to stay to the end.

"Remember that time at the Kooky Castle?" his cousin was saying.

"How could I forget?" MJ said, smiling despite himself. The Kooky Castle was a haunted house at Idora Park, a turn-of-the-century amusement park on the South Side. Their families had gone there together when MJ and Danny were just kids, back in the 60s.

Rose explained to her husband: "MJ's brother hid in the building to scare people with his squirt gun, but their father freaked when Danny didn't come out."

"Dad made them close the ride and turn on all the lights so he could find him," MJ said.

"So where was he?" Gary asked.

MJ and Rose looked at each other and laughed.

"Dad found him hiding behind some scenery. He whipped his ass good."

"Danny screamed so bad I couldn't even watch."

"Idora Park," said MJ. "I loved that place."

"Everyone did," said Gary. "Too bad it burned down." A big fire had destroyed most of the park a few years earlier, forcing it into bankruptcy.

Feeling suddenly sad again, MJ looked at the coffin and tried to square his memory of Danny, the little boy pranking people with a squirt gun, and the reality of the body in the coffin. How did he go from there to here--from innocent to dead?

Maybe his Dad should have beat Danny a little harder?

Or maybe, like Mom always said, his Dad beat him too hard?

He thought of Cassie, and wished she were here to discuss it with him. Cassie had answers to things like that, unlike his other friends. It was one of the reasons he had fallen so hard for her.

He glanced at his watch again. 5:27. It was going to be a long night. Where the hell was Lee? MJ felt lost among all the sad remanences and wanted someone to talk to who knew which end was up. Plus maybe he had found out something.

For the next hour, a steady stream of visitors kept MJ busy. Peggy had spent the previous afternoon going through her address book and calling relatives, but MJ was surprised at how many friends Danny had: people he played guitar with, high school drinking buddies, and even a few newer crackhead acquaintances from the street. They looked straight enough, though their faces were drawn and clothes grungy. MJ carefully questioned them, thinking that someone would have a clue as to what his brother was up to, but he only got vague, contradictory stories about where Danny hung out and who with.

The one street person he expected might show up--Carnival Jane--was nowhere to be found, and no one seemed to have seen her lately.

Around seven MJ stepped outside for a minute to have a smoke with Tony Schnetz, a friend of Danny's from the Music Shack, a store where Danny had briefly worked. On his sister's instructions, he enlisted Schnetz as a pall bearer for the burial Friday. When MJ returned to the viewing room ten minutes later, the kids were sitting with Rose and his sister was gone.

Dave Vlasik, standing near the doorway, noticed MJ looking and motioned him over. "She's in there with the police," he said in a low tone, pointing to a room up the hall.

"The police?"

"A detective." He reached into his suit jacket pocket and produced a card, black on white. "Detective Edward Proferes," it said, beside the shield of the Youngstown Police Department.

MJ's first impulse was to march into the room and tear Proferes' face off--the nerve of questioning his sister with her brother lying in a coffin fifty feet away. Then he thought better of it. As Lee had repeatedly pointed out, Proferes was still a possible source for finding the killer, and maybe he could ask the cop a few questions of his own--find out if Danny was really a police informer.

He pulled back the sliding door and entered. It was a smaller, unused viewing room, lit with torch lamps along the wall. Peggy and Proferes sat side by side on some folding chairs. Proferes had his steno pad on his knee, and his sister--who had managed to compose herself for the last hour--was crying into a tissue, her makeup smeared and running.

MJ pulled up a chair of his own. "Hello, Proferes."

"Michael."

"Where's your sidekick?"

"He's off the case, we're spread too thin."

So it was just Proferes now. MJ's already low opinion of the Youngstown Police Department dropped another notch.

"You could have picked a better time to interview my sister," MJ said.

"I tried," Proferes said. "But I only got the answering machine and I have a job to do."

MJ turned to his sister. "He treating you right, Sis?"

"He's asking a lot of questions about Danny," she said.

"Just trying to get some leads on your brother's activities the last couple days," said Proferes.

"So, what have you found?"

"Not much. Did you live at the house with your brother and sister?"

"Me? No."

"Because Margaret says you were always over there, along with her husband."

"Everybody's over Peggy's house all the time. So what?"

"Did Daniel ever borrow money from either of you?" Proferes asked.

"No, but he stole money from me," said Peggy, more composed now that MJ had arrived.

"When was that?"

"A few weeks ago. I had $600 for emergencies that I kept in my jewel box. He said he didn't take it but I know he did."

"What did he want the money for?"

Peggy harrumphed. "What did he always want the money for? You ever live with a crackhead? Anything not chained down he stole and used to get high."

"I heard Danny made money in other ways," MJ suddenly interjected.

"You mean his drug dealing?" said Proferes. "We know about that."

"Not that. I heard he worked for the cops, selling information," MJ said.

"What?" said Peggy, looking surprised.

Proferes looked surprised, too. "He told you that?" he asked.

"What are you talking about, MJ?" Peggy said. "Danny wouldn't do something like that."

"He could and he would if he could turn a buck," MJ said. "Isn't that right, Proferes?"

"So you think your brother was a CI?"

"Yeah. And that's why he got killed."

"What's a CI?" said Peggy.

"Who told you that?"

"Sources," said MJ. "I got sources just like you got sources."

"What's a CI?" Peggy repeated more insistently.

"Confidential Informant," said Proferes to Peggy. "Someone who gives us tips. Did he ever say anything about that to you?"

"No, never," Peggy said.

"You're still trying to build your case against Waylay, aren't you, Proferes?"

"I'm a detective now," said Proferes. "I'm not in Narcotics anymore."

"Not you, personally, but one of your old pals. You guys have been trying to nail Waylay for years, and once Danny was a total addict, you found a way to squeeze him dry."

"Interesting," said Proferes. He made a note in his steno book.

"What's interesting?"

"It's something I'll check into. But I don't think the department has any shortage of crackhead informers."

Peggy checked her watch--the little gold watch with the tiny face that used to be their Mom's--and stood up. "If you're through with your questions, I have to get back."

"I guess that's enough for now," said Proferes, closing his steno pad. "Do you have any number that's not always busy or an answering machine?"

"No, just the one you have," Peggy said.

She went out.

"I need the names of the friends you were with Sunday night," Proferes said.

"So that's your theory? I killed my brother? Is that your big idea of investigating?"

"I have to check everything. You got something to hide?"

MJ sure as hell wasn't going to mention Waylay or Wonder, but he gave the cop the names of a couple guys he knew would vouch for him.

"Your brother, did he ever borrow money off of you?" Proferes asked.

"No."

"How did Danny get along with Margaret?"

"We're through here, Proferes," said MJ. "Go find my brother's killer."

"I'm trying," said Proferes. "But don't get your hopes up."

"Meaning what?"

"There's no witnesses and the forensic evidence is skimpy. If you know anything more than you told me, you need to step up."

MJ had had enough. "You step up and do your fucking job," he said, poking Proferes in the chest.

Proferes shoved his hand off and glared at him. "I'll let that one go out of respect for the situation. But don't ever touch me again, mother fucker, or I'll grass your ass and you'll wake up in a cell."

MJ didn't want Proferes angry at him and reigned in his temper. "I'm sorry," said MJ, swallowing it down. "My sister and me, we're kind of on edge, but we really do appreciate your help."

"Forget it," said Proferes. "And I'll follow up this CI lead."

They rose and went into the hall, and MJ watched Proferes through the glass door as he got in his car and drove away.

Back in the viewing room, the kids were playing with Matchbox cars on the parlor floor of the wake area and Peggy was seated along the wall, talking to their Aunt Laura. When Peggy saw MJ enter, she excused herself and came over.

"Is that creep gone? What a prick, showing up here. I thought you said he already talked to you?"

"Yeah, well, no harm, no foul if he can find out who killed Danny."

"What was that stuff about money? Danny didn't have any money," she said.

MJ thought it might be related to Kidder Kidd but didn't want to make his sister worry. "Maybe he owed someone," MJ said. "Proferes is just looking at things."

Peggy seemed to accept it. "And was that true--about Danny working for the cops?"

"If he was, Proferes didn't seem to know anything about it."

"What could Danny tell them? Was he spying on me? Maybe about the food stamps?"

MJ laughed. "What? No one cares about that." Peggy was the food stamp queen, having signed up herself, Lee, MJ, Anna and both kids. She traded the stamps with neighbors for pot and other services.

"It's not funny," she snapped. "He lived in my house. Who knows what he said about me?"

"I wouldn't worry about it. For starters it's the feds who investigate food stamps, not the local cops. Besides, it's just a rumor Danny worked for the police."

Peggy, who was facing the door, went rigid. "Oh God, there's Lee," she said.

MJ turned to see him standing in the doorway, in a narrow black tie that matched his mustache and a burgundy leather jacket like the one Michael Fox wore in *Back to the Future*.

He saw them and came over. "MJ, Peg," he said.

"You were supposed to call earlier," Peggy said.

"I got busy," said Lee, giving her a passionless kiss on the cheek. He stood staring at the coffin. "Too bad about Danny," he said.

"Too bad?" said Peggy. "That's all you can say?"

"What do you want me to say?"

"How about like, 'I'm sorry for your loss.' 'You have my sympathy.' At least to MJ if not to me."

"You're kidding, right?"

"You have no fucking class," she said.

"Hey, I'm here," said Lee. "I didn't come to fight."

Peggy walked off into the hallway.

"You see why we separated," Lee said.

"She's upset about Danny," MJ said.

"I bet," said Lee. "Hey, man, you do know I feel horrible about Danny, right?"

"I know," said MJ. "Any luck with Kidder?"

"I'm working on it. What was Proferes doing here?"

"You saw him?"

"He was leaving as I was coming in."

"He was questioning Peggy."

"Here? What an asshole."

"Yeah, they're all assholes. Hey, who do you know around here that drives a big black car? Like maybe a Mercedes Benz?"

Lee smoothed his mustache. "A black Benz?" he said. "No one."

"Or maybe a Buick?"

"No one," Lee repeated, a little more emphatically. "Why?"

"Word on the street is that Danny was seen in a big black Benz."

"Says who?"

"Says Skeevy. I forgot to tell you about that."

"You're a fucking dope," Lee said, out of the blue. "You make me sick."

Lee could be blunt, and MJ felt his anger rise. "Why? Because I'm not doing things exactly the way you would?

"You have a hard head. You come to me for help but you never listen. What do you expect me to do?"

Before MJ could answer, Dave Vlasik appeared in the doorway with Peggy. He had been hovering around in the background, available-but-not-too-intrusive, like the good funeral director he was.

"I'm turning off the outside lights now," he said. "But you folks can stay as long as you want."

MJ looked at his watch and realized it was eight. As if on cue, his cousin Rose approached, with her husband in tow. "We're leaving now, cuz," she said, giving MJ a hug.

Peggy came back over and Rose hugged her, too.

"Sad, sad, sad," said Gary, offering his hand to MJ, then to Peggy.

Their Aunt Laura got up from her chair as well, leaning her weight over her cane. She was actually their great-aunt on their father's side but still pretty lively for 86.

"I'm leaving with them," she said. "But I'll be back tomorrow."

"Thanks for coming," said Peggy, taking Laura's free arm with both hands like a politician; then, to MJ and Lee, "She was telling me stories about her and Dad on grandpa's farm."

"I bet that was pretty exciting," said Lee, dryly.

"Don't start on Aunt Laura. You make me so mad sometimes."

"Yeah, well," said Lee.

"Can you at least help get the kids to the car? I still need to talk to you."

"All right," Lee said to her.

He turned to MJ and, unexpectedly, gave him a hard hug. Lee wasn't the hugging type, and MJ realized he was more affected by Danny's death than he gave on.

"You're a stubborn fucking bastard," he said--a back-handed complement, MJ knew, meaning he was tough enough to survive his grief over Danny.

"Let's see Kidd tomorrow," said MJ.

"Yeah, tomorrow, for sure," said Lee. "Come on, kids. Let's go."

And just like that, the viewing was over and MJ found himself alone in the room with his dead brother.

Chapter Ten

Poor Captive Souls in Purgatory

N umbly, he approached the casket, silver with the bronze handles Peggy wanted, and surrounded on either side by the mountain of carnations she had arranged to make sure Danny got the proper send-off. MJ knew only too well what Danny's face really looked like under the closed coffin lid. The kneeler was cushioned with burgundy velvet, but MJ scoffed at the idea of praying to God for his brother because he knew for a certainty there was no God. Danny had had his chance on earth and now he was rotting meat.

MJ put his hand on the coffin and said, aloud but to himself, "You blew it, brother."

As MJ stood there, he became aware of a presence behind him and turned.

Cassie was standing in the doorway, looking poised and more beautiful than ever. She had changed from her nurse uniform into blue slacks and a long black trench coat with a double row of buttons and a wide belt cinched around her narrow waist. Her dark hair was pulled back neatly over her ears. She seemed more self-possessed than when MJ was dating her, more quiet and womanly.

Their eyes locked.

"Cassie," he said.

"MJ."

She took a few steps into the room, and looked sadly at the casket. "I can't believe about Danny. I felt so sad when I saw it in the newspaper. Is that why you came by the school?"

"Yes," he said. And then added, to be more truthful, "And I wanted to see you."

"I apologize for the way I acted. I didn't know."

"It's okay," MJ blurted out. "I'm just glad you're here."

She regarded him. "You look good, Michael," she said. And then, stiffly: "I see you still wear your 'business' jacket."

MJ shifted uncomfortably. He hadn't thought about it, but it was the same dark blue sports coat he used to wear when he would take her out on the town. She loved it then, said he looked so handsome in it.

"Well, you know..." he stammered out. "Funerals..."

She reached out a hand and looked him in his eyes. "I'm really sorry about Danny. Are you okay?"

"I'm all right," he said, his voice gruff as he tried to hold himself together, so she wouldn't see him weak. MJ felt Cassie's sincerity and was touched, as always, by this feeling that was so absent in his other friends.

"I know Danny had his problems, but to die like that--murdered..." Cassie shook her head in revulsion.

MJ felt his heart sink; she was so incredible, and he had screwed everything up so bad. When they had first dated, MJ had hidden his drug-running from her--pretending to be a big-spending businessman--never dreaming Cassie would ever mean more to him than any of his other girls. But Cassie, with her incredible kindness--despite having had a horrific childhood--and her Filipina good looks, turned out not to be like any other woman. There was something in her that seemed to be missing from the Youngstown girls--or indeed from Youngstown itself.

He watched as she turned to the coffin and closed her eyes. Her lips moved swiftly, sub-vocally, and even though she was not kneeling he realized she was saying a prayer for his brother. MJ knew that the orphanage in Manila where Cassie grew up was a hundred times worse than anything he had experienced in

Youngstown, yet somehow she could still pray, and that was like a spike to his heart. Not that the stupid, superstitious prayer itself impressed him, but the fact that, despite all her suffering, she still had the capacity to hope.

He had to have her back.

"Cassie," he said.

She opened her eyes.

"Cassie, you know I still love you. I never stopped loving you."

Cassie's face, smooth and beautiful in the yellow light, hardened. "That's all over now, Michael."

"I said I'm sorry for everything I did."

"Sorry isn't enough, MJ," she said. "Look at your brother."

"What? I had nothing to do with that. And you better believe I'm going to kill the bastard that did this."

"Oh, MJ," said Cassie. "Don't you see? That's exactly what I mean."

"I can't just let them kill my brother. I got to do something about it."

She took a step back, staring at him intently, then relaxed and shrugged. "It was good seeing you again, MJ."

"Can't you stay a little longer?" said MJ. "I want to hear about your school."

"I can't," Cassie said. "Someone's waiting for me in the car."

"Who?"

"Rob."

"Rob? Who's Rob?" MJ asked.

Cassie looked away from MJ's face and back to the coffin. "My fiancé."

A hand squeezed MJ's heart. "You're getting married?"

She looked at him accusingly. "Is it such a big surprise? You know how long I waited for you, hoping."

"But... you can't get married."

"Why not?"

"Because you still love me."

"I don't."

He took her hand, and she turned toward him reluctantly, as if powerless to resist. "You do."

"Even if I did," she said, hands trembling, "it doesn't matter now."

"But it does," said MJ, feeling more in control. He drew her to him, his lips touching hers. He felt them, soft and warm, yielding--before she turned her face away.

"No, Michael," she said--almost robotically, it seemed to MJ. "It's over with us. I'm marrying Rob. He's kind... and reliable."

A flicker of movement caught MJ's eyes and a man, short and stout, in a wrinkled white shirt and wearing a black beret, was standing in the doorway. He gave a loud guffaw. "Hey there, workers! Having fun?"

MJ released Cassie, who turned as the guy advanced into the room.

"This must be the ex- you were telling me about," the man said to Cassie, whose face was now bright red. "At least I hope it is." He extended his hand to MJ. "Hi, I'm Rob Appel. Cassie's fiancé."

MJ instantly disliked the man, with his hippie pony tail and phony good-nature. But he shook the outstretched hand because Cassie would want him to.

She moved to the guy and put an arm around his fat waist. "Michael and I were just catching up."

"I saw that."

"I'll explain later."

"No problem, no problem," Appel said. "To each according to his needs, right? Hey, you want I should leave you two alone?"

MJ didn't understand him. If *he* had found someone kissing *his* fiancée, he would have pounded the scumbag's face to a pulp.

"No," said Cassie. "Let's go."

"Okay, sweetheart," said Appel, kissing her on the forehead. Then, to MJ: "My sympathies about your brother. If you need help with the pigs, you come see me at the Workers House over on West Front Street, okay? I know a lot of public-interest lawyers."

When they were gone, MJ shook his head to clear it. How could Cassie even consider getting married to that asshole, with his stupid pony-tail and French beret? *I actually kissed her right in front of him, and the creep did nothing!* A pussy, MJ concluded. A total wuss. Just thinking about it made MJ want to pound Appel's mealy-mouthed face into the ground.

Yet Cassie was marrying the pussy. "Kind" and "reliable," she had said, as if that made any fucking difference in the real world. MJ knew he was in way better shape than Appel, and knew how to use his fists. He also knew how to use his hands in other ways, ways designed to drive Cassie crazy in bed--at least the one time he had managed to get her there. MJ didn't know exactly how much money he had saved, but there was about $10,000 in cash in a shoebox in his closet, and another $6- or $7,000 in the local Farmers & Merchants Bank. Of course $4,500 of that was going to go to pay for Danny's funeral, but he bet *Rob* didn't have as much money, based on the ratty, wrinkled clothes he was wearing. And when MJ saved $20,000, he planned to escape Youngstown and move to the beach in New Jersey. He'd be out of the drug business like Cassie always wanted, and when he'd done all that, maybe he could get her to go with him.

Except now she was marrying that beret-wearing fart.

MJ decided to do a little digging into this Appel guy. Not that he cared a shit about him, but to keep Cassie from making a big mistake.

"I locked the front door, but you take your time in here," said Dave Vlasik, who had magically appeared from the hallway. "I'll be in the office."

"That's okay, I'm leaving," said MJ. He took a last glance at Danny's coffin--*Rest in peace, brother,* came the ironic thought--and exited into the hallway.

"Have you seen these?" said Vlasik, handing MJ a Catholic holy card like the kind his Mom used for bookmarks. It had a picture of Jesus exposing his heart on one side, and a prayer on the back, "*In Loving Remembrance of Daniel Patrick Shea*":

Oh Gentlest Heart of Jesus, ever consumed with burning love for the poor captive souls in purgatory, have mercy on Thy departed servant, and be not severe in Thy Judgment.

MJ stared at the card in dismay. The musty piety and phony hope pissed him off. Danny would have hated it.

"Your sister chose the sentiment," Vlasik said.

Of course she did. MJ took the card and said his goodbyes, but as soon as he was outside he crumpled and stomped it, as if it were a burning cigarette butt. Dead was dead and Danny was no saint. Peggy was out of her mind with this religious crap and he was going to talk to her about it.

Except for a black Oldsmobile he assumed belonged to Vlasik, MJ's Cutlass was the last car in the lot, parked against a fence facing the road underneath a scraggly bare tree. MJ noted that the rain of the day before had left muddy streaks on the rocker panels that he would have to get washed off before Friday, when Danny would be buried.

He removed his suit jacket so it wouldn't get wrinkled, opened the driver's door and slid inside. Through the fence he could see the line of now-closed storefronts on the other side of the street.

A memory came back to him, from when his father was still alive. MJ and Danny were building castles out of playing cards at their Dad's feet while their mother and her church friends, in the dining room, clucked over the terrible story of Father Marchuk. Marchuk, a white-haired old man in a black cassock, was the last priest of Christ the King, the church that later became Danny's favorite crack house. As the church was being closed, a loose brick fell from some scaffolding and struck the old priest square on the head, killing him instantly.

MJ, who was frightened of Marchuk after being spanked by him, overheard and was glad.

Shortly after that came Black Monday, with the massive layoffs at Youngstown Sheet & Tube, and then more job losses at U.S. and Republic Steel. Their father, on unemployment, had his heart attack and died. Then Danny started jacking cars and selling pot.

The falling brick, apparently, was God's farewell card to Youngstown.

MJ laughed and shook his head to clear it. Overhead, the grey weather of the last several days was finally beginning to lift, with a large break in the sky showing an intense blue, washed clean by the recent rain. For the first time in the last few days, MJ felt something in him lift. He would find Danny's killer, get revenge for his brother, and go on with his life--like Danny would have wanted him to.

And he would stop that pussy Rob from marrying Cassie.

He turned the key in the ignition. There was a tremendous explosion and everything around him turned a deep, violet black--deeper and blacker than anything MJ had ever seen before. And in the black were thousands and thousands of sparkles of orange, like shimmering fireflies but faster, brighter, bubbling like the fizz in a drink. Then the sparkles were gone and MJ thought, *Cassie*--just before the darkness swept over him like a wave, tumbling him into the purple blackness.

Chapter Eleven

Good to Feel Bad

M J awoke face down on the pavement, a high-pitched ringing in his ears. He pushed himself to his knees. A mushroom cloud of smoke drifted overhead and MJ turned to see the smoke coming from his car, which sat smoldering on the asphalt, leaning at an angle and with the passenger door hanging half-off.

Whoever tried to blow him up had failed, but now, from around the back of the funeral home, a black-hooded figure started running toward him, shouting something MJ couldn't hear--coming, MJ figured, to finish him off.

He had to get out of there. He raised himself up, and staggering, ran toward the woody lot at the end of the parking lot, scrambling up a steep muddy bank twice his height and taking refuge up the slope behind the trunk of a big hemlock.

The hooded figure paused at the smoking car, then ran across the parking lot toward MJ, shouting words which MJ's still-ringing ears could not decipher. The figure stopped at the base of the embankment and shouted something--again indecipherable--before starting up the bank in MJ's footsteps.

There was a chain link fence at the top edge of the property--no place for MJ to run. He kicked himself for not retrieving his gun from under the car's front seat and braced himself for a fight. The only weapon he could find was a fist-sized rock. He scooped it up and watched the figure approach, slipping and sliding on the embankment. The guy was lanky, not very tall, and slight; if he didn't have a gun MJ ought to be able to handle him--surprise the pursuer when he came close and bash his head in.

MJ watched and waited. The man was having extraordinary trouble getting up the embankment, crawling up a few feet before sliding back. And when he did finally reach the top, instead of crouching for cover, he knelt upright on the edge--to catch his breath, MJ concluded--until he finally saw, in the fading light, the face beneath the hood.

It was Carnival Jane, and she was crying.

MJ, realizing he was safe, felt a wave of relief flow over him, instantly replaced by concern. If the girl had come by a minute earlier, she could have been caught in the explosion.

When MJ stood up and moved toward her, she rose and threw her skinny arms around him.

"Oh, MJ," he heard her say, directly into his ear. "I thought they killed you, too."

"What are you doing here?" he said, having to modulate his voice when he realized he was shouting; his hearing was coming back.

"Danny," she said, sniffling. "I came to see Danny."

The mention of his brother seemed to set her off her crying again, and she collapsed, jelly-like, in his arms. He sat down with her in the mud.

"It will be okay," he said.

"No," she said, "It'll never be okay. They killed Danny."

MJ held her and tried to calm her, surprised at the intensity of her emotions, particularly since he could see that she wasn't high on anything.

As if reading his mind, Carnival looked at him and said, "I loved him! I loved him so much and now he's gone and there'll never be anyone like him ever again."

She buried her head on MJ's shoulder, and MJ felt his heart squeeze and stay squeezed as if it would burst--because she felt the way he felt, hollow and hopeless.

Only he had to do something about it. He *had* to, because whoever killed his brother didn't deserve to live. And now, with the explosion, he had a pretty good idea who was behind Danny's murder. The thought made him sick with fear and anger.

Out of the corner of his eye, he saw another figure approaching the bottom of the embankment. It was Dave Vlasik, in blue jeans and a red cotton jacket. "Are you okay?" he shouted. "I'll call an ambulance."

"We're okay," said MJ. "Wait for us."

He helped Carnival up and the two of them slid down the slope toward Vlasik.

"You're bleeding," Vlasik said, when he saw MJ up close.

MJ looked down and saw that his shirt was bloody and peppered with holes. But he was still on his feet so he must be all right.

"I'm fine," said MJ, adding, when he saw Vlasik staring, "This is my brother's friend, Carni... ah... Jane Longman."

"Look at your car," she said, horrified.

His car was indeed a mess, with a mangled passenger door and a jagged hole in the floor where they must have placed the bomb. Somehow most of the force of the explosion had ended up on the passenger side or he would have been dead. An acrid odor hung in the air. MJ moved around to the driver's door and reached inside. His 9 mm was still under the seat. Vlasik's eyes looked big as MJ slipped the gun into his waistband.

"Can we go inside?" MJ said.

"Oh, I'm sorry, sure, let's go to my office," Vlasik said.

He led them back into the funeral home and turned on a lamp on his office desk. Carnival looked fatigued and shaken, with black circles under eyes rimmed-red from crying. MJ was surprised to realize she was wearing makeup.

Vlasik pushed a box of tissues toward her and nodded toward the bathroom. "You two clean up," he said. "I'll call the police."

He reached for the phone but MJ stopped him. "No police," he said.

"What do you mean, no police? Someone bombed your car in my parking lot."

"Come here a sec," said MJ, motioning Vlasik out of the office, away from Carnival. In the hallway he said, "Where do you live?"

"What? Over off Belmont, near the IGA."

"In a house?"

"Yes, a house, of course a house."

"Have the car towed over there and put it in your backyard, out of sight. I want to keep this quiet."

"No, no, no," said Vlasik, backing off. "I don't want to get involved in this."

"You're not involved," said MJ. "You don't know nothing. Just get rid of the car." He reached for his wallet, pulled out his last three fifties, and pressed them into Vlasik's hand.

Vlasik seemed to want the money but hesitated. "The police..."

"I'll take care of the police. Clean up your lot and add a little something to our bill. You're a full-service funeral director, aren't you?"

Vlasik hesitated a moment, then grinned and said, "Yeah, I guess I am." He smoothly pocketed the bills. "I can get Joe Kechter to tow it. He owns the Amoco down the street."

"Good, Dave," said MJ. "I won't forget it."

Vlasik went out and MJ took a deep breath. With the explosion, Lee had to be right about Waylay. He was going to have to have to find Lee again to plan what to do. But first he'd call a taxi, get home and change out of his bloody clothes. And he couldn't just leave Carnival. He hadn't realized she was so attached to Danny.

A few minutes later, in the cab, he turned to her and said, "Where do you live?"

"Downtown near the bridge," she said, adding quickly: "But I don't want to go there tonight." She had cleaned up in Vlasik's bathroom and re-applied her dark lipstick, making her face look almost doll-like in the passing headlights of cars.

"Where do you want to go then?"

"I don't know. Anywhere. Maybe by the Pepsi plant."

That was an industrial area on the south side of the river. It would be deserted this time of night, as well as damned cold, but maybe Carnival had crack friends there. He directed the driver to head over the bridge.

"So you and Danny--you were seeing each other?"

She gave a bitter laugh. "I was seeing him. But we weren't completely together."

"What do you mean?"

"I mean he treated me like a kid. Unless he was horny and wanted to fuck, and then he was okay to be with me. But he loved me though."

Her jacket was open and her fine tits were pressing against her dark tee. MJ could see why Danny would want to fuck her, but love? He didn't think his brother was capable. "You sound pretty sure," MJ said.

"I'm sure," Carnival said, turning her face away from him toward the window.

And she *did* sound sure. MJ thought achingly of Cassie and wished she could say the same about him.

"Let me show you something," Carnival said, reaching into her pocket and unfolding a tattered piece of yellow paper.

There were words on it in his brother's handwriting, but in the dark of the cab he couldn't make them out. "What is it?"

"A song. A song to me." She pointed to the scrawl at the top. "'You Stole My Thunder,' see?"

Now that he knew what it said, MJ could just make the words out. He held the paper up to a passing headlight and saw something about rain and the lyrics, "I know you girl/better than you know yourself."

MJ folded the paper up and returned it to Carnival. He had seen his brother seduce many a chick with a sweet melody and a special song.

"I'm glad for you," he said.

"Yeah."

"I am."

"I know Danny slept with other girls. I'm not stupid. But he really did write this song for me. And he really did love me. I told him he better, after what he did."

"What did he do?"

She turned her face toward the window.

"What?" said MJ.

She mumbled something MJ couldn't hear. He touched her on her arm and she turned.

"I said, he knocked me up."

"You're pregnant?"

She nodded her head and looked at him fiercely. "And I ain't getting no abortion. I'm having this baby no matter what."

Brother, brother.

They had reached the entrance to the employee parking lot of the vast plant, which was gated with a guard. On the other side was an abandoned storage yard, and beyond that the river.

"This okay?" asked the driver.

"We changed our minds," MJ said. He gave the man his home address and they turned around in the middle of the deserted road, Carnival looking at him quizzically.

Twenty minutes later they walked into MJ's cold apartment. MJ turned up the thermostat and came back from the kitchen with two Renners, handing one of the beers to Carnival. He sat across from her on the couch.

"When's the last time you used?"

"This afternoon."

"You know crack's not good for babies."

"I'm going to quit, starting tomorrow. Go to that place Danny talked about."

"St. Elizabeth's? They have a six-month waiting list."

"I know. But they'll take me because I got Danny's child."

MJ wasn't so sure but he let it drop. She looked okay right now, though--normal, not dope sick. He could see why Danny would like her. He wondered what she knew about his brother's activities.

"Ever see Danny talking to the cops?"

"Just that fat one that used to hassle him. He was always threatening to take him in."

If Danny was an informant, hassling him could be part of his cover.

"Do you know the cop's name?" asked MJ.

She shook her no.

"Did Danny ever mention he needed money?"

"That's funny, he had a lot of money that night in the church. He showed me a big wad. He said petty soon we'd be on Easy Street. I think he found a way to score. He wouldn't tell me though. It was a big secret."

Suddenly her eyes were tearing up again. "His sister was kicking him out. We were going to get a place together so I could have the baby."

The shack-up was more news to MJ. He got up for another beer, wondering whether Danny really meant to move in with Carnival or whether he was feeding her a line of bullshit. The wad of money was consistent with what Skeevy had said about Kidder Kidd. He could see Danny borrowing from him for a score, and if so Kidd would know who Danny was going to see that night. He and Lee would have to question him first thing tomorrow.

Carnival was in the bathroom when he came out, so MJ sat on the soft couch and took another sip of beer. Suddenly he was too tired to think.

Then he was sleeping on the couch and he heard Carnival's voice say, "Wake up. You're all cut."

He opened his eyes to find Carnival sitting there with a washcloth and a bottle of peroxide in her hands, ready to play nurse. He *was* all cut up so he decided to let her minister to him. She had showered and was dressed in his bathrobe from the hook behind the bathroom door. She unbuttoned his torn vest, then his bloody dress shirt and finally tugged on his undershirt underneath to expose the skin of his belly as high as his ribs.

The right side of his body was peppered with dozens of tiny black scratches and wounds, intermixed with whirling patterns of bruises and blood. It looked like someone had flailed his skin with a rusty chain.

"Jesus," said Carnival. "You're lucky to be alive."

"Jesus has nothing to do with it," MJ said.

"Well," she said, "your brother must be looking out for you then because anyone else that bomb would have killed."

He *was* lucky to be alive. Maybe Danny really was looking out for him, until he could get the murderer--like that ghost in the Classics Comics book he had found at the barbershop.

She began dabbing at his wounds with delicate hands, a butterfly tattooed on the back of one and a skull with a knife through it on the other.

"You really are messed up," she said. She dabbed at a particularly nasty wound. "Does that hurt?"

"No," MJ said, flinching.

"Sorry, sorry," she said. "I'll be more careful."

Clean and showered, her hair damp but neatly combed, Jane looked good in the dim light--tired maybe, but not haggard like that time at the church. The bathrobe was cinched tightly around her and her pregnancy didn't show. MJ found himself watching the mounds of her smooth breasts at the loose top of the robe.

Her hands fluttered about his stomach and he felt himself growing hard.

She laughed and said, "Just like Danny."

"You keep doing that, what do you expect?" he said.

She smiled and continued dabbing at his stomach gently with the washcloth. When she glanced up and their eyes locked.

"You're very pretty," MJ said.

"You don't have to lie."

"I'm not lying."

"Really? You really think I'm pretty?"

Her breasts were soft white curves, disappearing down her robe. "Take my word for it," he said.

She looked at him in the dim light. When she saw he wasn't joking, a smile crossed her face and she hugged him, her body warm against his. MJ put his arms around her and held her.

"I'm so lonely," she said. "What am I going to do without Danny?" Then she sat back and looked at him, her robe falling over the curves of her body, her eyes big. MJ hadn't planned to sleep with Jane but he wasn't surprised at the turn of events. He had slept with scores of girls, many on this very couch, and he never passed up a good thing.

Except...

...nothing. Their mouths found one another and it was on, a done deal. She reached down and opened his buckle and unzipped his pants. Her fingers felt good as she tussled with his underwear trying to free his cock. It was throbbing--life reasserting itself after his brush with death, his pain suddenly forgotten. He wanted nothing more than to get on top of her right then and there.

Certainly he would have done just that a week earlier, before all this started, but now something didn't feel right. Reluctantly, he moved his hands to her shoulders and pushed her away.

"What's wrong?"

"I thought you loved Danny," he said, wanting to hurt her for making him want her so bad.

She blinked, then sat back on the bed, her legs curled under her. "He's dead," she said.

"You're not wasting any time."

"Don't you get it?" she practically screamed. "He's *dead*. What difference does anything make now?"

MJ had no answer. He thought about zippering up and lighting a cigarette from the side table, let things cool down--but he didn't. Instead he tugged on the belt of Jane's robe until it opened, fully revealing her breasts--firm, soft and beautiful. Almost against his will, he reached up with both hands and cupped them, running his fingers across her already-firm nipples. She took a sharp breath and closed her eyes.

He was back in familiar territory.

He flipped her over and climbed on top.

***

Later, falling asleep again, MJ felt sick at his weakness, though he knew his brother didn't care. Hell, probably Danny would have laughed and egged him on.

But he still felt bad.

And, strangely enough, it felt good to feel bad.

MJ couldn't figure it.

All the men out of work, closed factories and ruined lives.

Weird.

Someone had to pay.

He dreamt he was holding a brick.

Chapter Twelve

The Social Problem and Its Solution

The next day at ten MJ was back at Roma's, this time driving his van. He found Lee at the same table as the day before, but alone.

Lee sat stock still, his face frozen in surprise, when he looked up and saw MJ, limping toward him with the right side of his face burned red. "Crap, what happened to you?" he said as MJ slid into the booth.

"You didn't hear?"

"Hear? Hear what?"

MJ thought, good, it wasn't all over the street, Dave Vlasik must have done his job with the towing and clean-up. But that didn't mean that MJ was home free; it would be best to keep his bomber guessing whether he was alive. "Let's go to your car," he suggested.

A minute later they were sitting in Lee's Camaro, its black-out window tint making it hard for anyone to see inside.

"So--what's up?" Lee asked.

MJ got right to the point: "Someone tried to kill me last night. When I was leaving the funeral home."

"What? How?"

"A car bomb."

"A car bomb," said Lee. He pushed in the dashboard lighter, waited for it to heat, then lit a cigarette from its glowing orange coil. "I told you not to tangle with Waylay."

"Yeah, if it is Waylay."

"Get real. Who else?"

In the war for control of the coke trade in Youngstown, Waylay's favorite means of execution was the car bomb, a method pioneered by his Mafia allies. In addition to the three State witnesses during his trial, he had already blown up Mike Killian, whose Irish gang had been one of his main rivals, and Sorcho Conti, his now ex-business partner.

"You could be right," MJ said, reluctant to face the possibility he might have to take out Waylay.

"Could be? That scumbag dealer you talked to must have gone directly to him."

It made sense. And if Waylay killed Danny, he wouldn't stop there now that he knew MJ was after him.

But why would he kill Danny?

"What did you find out about Danny working for the police?" he asked.

Lee took a pull on his cigarette, blowing the smoke upward toward the head-liner of the car. "Yeah, he was a rat--working for the Narco squad."

MJ was not so much shocked as hurt. He thought he had been pretty tight with his brother, but apparently Danny had secrets--if Lee's info was accurate.

"Are you absolutely sure?"

"We got a secretary, married to Tony Long--you know, that guy with the fancy tavern over in Boardman. She has access to the files on the inside."

MJ's spirit sank. He took a deep breath and lit a cigarette of his own. "Here's the way I see it. The narks are still trying to get Waylay and enlisted Danny as a fink. Waylay found him out, and had his goons lure him to a car with a fake drug deal. Then they killed him and dumped his body."

Lee nodded and blew more smoke. "What are you going to do?"

"I want to talk to Kidd. If he can tie Danny directly to Waylay..."

"What do you mean, 'if'? Who else would it be?"

"Well, Skeevy said maybe the cops did it themselves--to tie up loose ends."

"MJ, listen to me. This shit's getting too weird. You're lucky you're alive so you got a second chance. Get out of Youngstown, lay low somewhere for a while until things blow over. See how you feel then."

"Are you out of your fucking mind? My brother is dead. I can't lay low."

"All right, all right, have it your way," said Lee, not looking happy.

"Can you get me in to see Kidd, yes or no?"

"You know I can."

"Then let's go."

Lee smoothed his mustache. "Kidd never shows up there till after lunch."

"Okay," said MJ. "When?"

Lee crushed his cigarette. "Let's meet there at one. You know where it is?"

"I know." He had been there long ago with his dad.

***

Since he had some time, MJ decided to see if he could find Carnival Jane. He pulled out of the restaurant parking lot and headed over to the crack house church.

After he and Jane had screwed the night before, MJ had fallen into a dead sleep, not even moving from the couch to his bed. He was in truth totally spent after the toll of the vigil with his brother at the funeral home and the subsequent bombing.

He slept, his head a jumble of conflicting images--Danny's destroyed face, Jane's boobs, his sister's ceiling dripping water and the purple flash of the car bomb. He was aware of Jane sleeping with him, clinging, and then, later, her moving around the apartment restlessly, burning toast in the kitchen and flushing the toilet. Then it was quiet and he felt free again and slept deeply until some asshole's car alarm woke him around seven.

Jane was nowhere to be found, but the drawers in his bedroom bureau were open and the packets of coke--a half-dozen grams MJ kept around for his party girls--were gone. Panicky, he checked his closet, but his shoebox full of cash seemed undisturbed. His wallet, however, had been emptied of its last bills, maybe $30 or $40.

When he saw the money missing, he was pissed at himself the way he used to be pissed at Danny--surprised that he had yet again fallen for a crackhead's line of bullshit. He had actually believed that Jane was going to at least seek help at St. Elizabeth's, even if she weren't admitted. If he found her now, he was going to drive her to the hospital himself, figuring his brother's baby deserved at least a fighting chance against being born a crack addict like his Dad.

Once at the church, he parked his van in the alley behind and made his way into the crumbling inside. At this time of day it was deserted, its denizens out heisting car stereos or cadging money on street corners to get their next score.

The place was dank and musty, smelling of urine and strewn throughout with the detritus of dead-end drug users. The altar smelled like a sewer and the back room, where Danny had shared a crack pipe with Carnival, was pitch black and empty. A chill went up MJ's spine and he made his way back to the van quickly.

If Jane wasn't in the church she had to be somewhere in the neighborhood. He headed past the bleachers at Harrison Field, also deserted, and then in the general direction of the downtown, sticking to the seedier streets and cruising slowly in the hopes of finding her.

His route led down Oak and he pulled into a spot on the edge of Crab Creek, where he knew addicts congregated under the bridge. There were, in fact, a few bundled people seated on an abutment, and another further down the slope facing away from him--one, in a black hoodie--possibly Jane. But as he got closer he saw that the figure was actually a skinny teenage boy, hanging out with an older man who was holding a lighter to a pipe, not bothering to conceal it. The plastic-y burning smell of the crack assailed MJ's nostrils as he approached.

"You guys know Carnival Jane?" he asked.

"Carnival, yeah, I know her," said the man with the pipe, now feeling pretty good.

"Everyone knows Carnival," said the teenager, who must have been a recent entry into the crowd since his face was still clear of sores and abscesses.

"She been around here this morning?"

The older man shook his greying head. "No, not this morning, no," he said. "You see her?" he said to his companion.

"Yesterday, not today," the kid said.

"You see her tell her MJ's looking for her."

"MJ, okay, will do. You got any coin, help us out here?"

MJ hesitated, then gave the man a fiver from the wallet he had replenished from his stash. It was almost 11:30 and he had wasted enough time trying to track down Jane. She'd find him pretty soon herself, he figured, now that she knew where he lived.

He got back in the van and headed aimlessly toward downtown, thinking to stop somewhere and get a meal. He realized now he shouldn't have boffed Jane the night before. Not because she had ripped him off and would now be back poking around for more money and drugs. But because she had been Danny's girl. Thinking about it that way, he felt slimy to move in on her so fast--even though she had started it. Fucked up on crack and with Danny dead she didn't know what she wanted and if he had been thinking with his head instead of his dick he would have known it.

As he drove along the familiar, dirty streets, he was enveloped once again by the overwhelming sense of despair that seemed to reside somewhere between his heart and his stomach. Everyone thought he was strong but MJ knew he was weak. He didn't save Kate Parknavy, never got Danny to rehab, ruined his one chance with Cassie and even took advantage of Carnival Jane. He felt like he had been given all the responsibility for the people in his life, but none of the power to actually do anything.

Above all, he felt utterly and acutely alone. His father was dead, his mother a basket-case, and his sister a neurotic nag. They were no help in navigating the cold and dangerous world in which he seemed to find himself. Yes, he ran drugs for Waylay, but he didn't sell them and didn't use them and somebody had to make money to keep the family going. It wasn't his fault there was an endless supply of dope fiends buying up the product he brought in. He would be out of it as soon as he had enough to get started again in Ocean Grove. He would be alone there, too, but at least there was the ocean, and a lot of cute babes along the beach. He savored the image for a moment, then quashed it angrily, knowing that the whole lot of them could not hold a candle to Cassie.

He wondered if Cassie would be at the Workers House. If she had resigned herself to marrying Appel, had she also already slept with him? He supposed she had, having rejected MJ because he had lied to her and because she didn't approve of the way he made his money. When he was with her, he had liked to take her to fancy restaurants and to buy her expensive gifts. She was the only person who ever who made the aloneness go away. If he had kept on pretending to be a businessman, maybe he could have tricked her into marrying him and he'd have her today. But he didn't want to trick her. He wanted her to want him exactly as he was. And she didn't want him. Because she knew his strength was a front, a fake facade.

On impulse, he turned and headed over toward Front Street. He had the time and wanted to check out for himself the "Workers House" Appel had mentioned, see exactly what that guy was up to.

Five minutes later he pulled up before a run-down two-story house in an area of boarded-up shops and struggling businesses in a faded neighborhood on the edge of downtown. An iron fence ran around it, a remnant of former glory, with an open gate at the drive. A large billboard wired to the fence advertised a meal program, "Food for All," which--judging from the number of winos hanging around outside--currently was serving lunch.

MJ locked the van and entered the building, looking for Appel but hoping he might see Cassie. On the entrance wall, a fake wanted poster showed front and side views of President Reagan with the headline, "Wanted for International Terrorism." Another poster--much larger and in color--featured a scowling guy with a pointy beard and the slogan, "Power to the People." MJ followed cooking smells to a big room in front--the former living room, now converted to a dining room with three rows of long tables. One woman and a half-dozen men sat in scattered knots at the tables, toying with plates of sad-looking spaghetti and sipping coffee from Styrofoam cups.

Just then Rob Appel, dressed in jeans, beret and white apron, emerged from the kitchen carrying a basket full of sliced white bread, which he placed before the bums at the table. He caught sight of MJ standing in the entrance and came over. "Hey, MJ, welcome. What happened to your face?"

"Sunburn," MJ said.

Appel knew he was being punked but only said, "You're just in time for lunch."

MJ glanced at the offerings on the table and said, "No, thanks." He wasn't here to cadge a crappy meal, but to check this guy out--figure out his angle.

"If you came looking for Cassie, she's gone. She works the six to nine breakfast shift."

"I came to talk to you."

"To me, comrade?" Appel said. "All right, then. Let's go to my office."

He led MJ across the room into a hallway and then into a tiny room in the corner. The place was jammed with stacks of papers on every surface. Appel sat at a crowded desk under a hammer-and-sickle flag, pulling a bottle of vodka out of a desk drawer and pouring two shots in paper Dixie cups.

"To Cassie," he said, offering one to MJ.

MJ had to drink to that. He took the cup and knocked it back.

"Let me ask you a question," MJ said.

"Shoot."

"What does Cassie see in you?"

"Ouch," said Appel, sitting back. "You mean, what is she doing with a slob like me, instead of slick street hustler like you?"

MJ didn't think of himself as a slick street hustler, though Appel was definitely a slob. He let it pass and said, "I just don't get it, you two."

"It's pretty simple, really, and I believe she's already told you. There's justice and there's injustice in this world. Cassie prefers the side of justice."

MJ wanted to punch his face. Instead he nodded at the hammer-and-sickle flag. "The commie side? This commie bullshit?"

He could see that annoyed Appel. "You can call it bullshit if you want. But"--he waved his fingers in a circle in the air--"take a look around."

MJ saw a guy in an apron and a cramped, dirty office overflowing with old books. "Doesn't look like you're doing so good to me."

Appel laughed. "I don't mean look around my office. I mean, look around this town. The capitalists chewed it up and sucked it dry, and now they left the proletariat to deal with the garbage they left behind."

Proletariat, capitalists--MJ didn't see what that had to do with Cassie. He looked at the books closest to him on the desk: *The Social Problem and Its Solution* and *The Religion of Social-Democracy*.

Suddenly MJ got it.

"You're one of Cassie's professors, right?" MJ didn't know they taught philosophy at nursing school but he did know professors liked to sleep with their hot students.

"Professor, hell," Appel said. "They're part of the problem. I'm an activist and organizer."

He was so full of crap. "Is that how you met Cassie? Holding signs at some peace march?"

"In a way, yes. Engaging in revolutionary activity, anyway. She helped get blankets for our homeless outreach and we worked together on the street. Now she volunteers in Food for All. So that's how we got to know each other."

MJ tried to wrap his mind around it. "So you're saying Cassie's a communist now?"

Appel grinned. "She's getting there. She got a first-hand taste of American imperialism in the Philippines, and now Youngstown is finishing her education."

"With your help."

"Yeah, with my help," he snapped. "Look, let's cut the shit. I know why you're here. Cassie prefers me to you because I'm an agent for social justice and you're a tool of the ruling class. We're helping the people and you're enslaving them. The right and wrong side of history, see? So you will never, ever get Cassie back--no matter how much you come nosing around."

MJ stood up. He had gotten what he had come for. What a clown. MJ couldn't even feel angry. Appel was a fucking commie with an ego as big as his ass. Cassie, missing a father and coming from the slums of Manila, must have gotten sucked into his feel-good homeless projects and snowed under by his fancy words. A few vodkas in his office, plus some bleeding heart bull crap from his pinko playbook and he had her hooked.

Fucking phony. "Kind" and "reliable" Cassie had said. He really had her snowed. MJ would have to set her straight about this guy.

"See you later--comrade," MJ said. "Let the best man win."

"He already has," said Appel.

MJ left.

Chapter Thirteen

Stop Saying Murder

At one MJ found Lee's Camaro parked across the street from Kidd's union hall, where a sign outside announced, "Teamsters Vending Machine Service Employees Local 110." Having crushed out competition all over Youngstown, the mob, through the Teamsters, now controlled every machine in Mahoning County that took a coin--candy, cigarettes, laundromat washers and dryers, even condom dispensers in bar bathrooms. The coins added up, providing an easy and reliable source of hard-to-trace cash for the union and hence the mob. Isaac "Kidder" Kidd, as the Teamster Treasurer, skimmed a big portion of the profits for himself and for other illegal enterprises, including loan sharking.

"I just want to know if he lent Danny money and for what," MJ explained to Lee as they crossed the street toward the entrance. "If Waylay was involved, that clenches it."

"Okay, but these guys, they don't like outsiders," said Lee. "You better let me do the talking, okay?"

"That's what you're here for," said MJ.

A surveillance camera hung over the corner of the heavy metal doorway, which was locked. Lee pushed the button on the intercom box.

"Yeah?" came a voice from the speaker.

"It's Lee Messina here to see Kidder," Lee said into the intercom. "I'm a friend of Joey Russo."

A buzzer sounded and the door clicked open. MJ followed Lee inside to a room full of card tables and stuffed chairs, with some pinball machines along the back wall.

A single guy, dressed in blue overalls, sat in a sagging sofa under a chalkboard, playing solitaire. "He's in there," the guy said, nodding toward the hallway.

They walked down the hall and found Kidd sitting at a desk in his office, writing in a big accounting book. He was a heavyset man, bald with a grey fringe, and brown-framed glasses that magnified his eyes as if underwater. A small black-and-white TV monitor in the corner showed the view from the front security camera. As they came in, Kidd flipped the ledger closed and sat upright.

"Friend of Joey's, huh?" Kidd said to Lee. "How do you know him?"

"I did a little work on that airport job last year. And see him now and then over at Roma's."

Kidd looked at MJ. "And how about you? You a friend of Joey's too?"

"I'm a friend of Lee's. They call me MJ."

"He's okay, Kidder," said Lee. "We went to high school together."

Kidd relaxed. "I hope you learned more than this dufus," he joked to MJ.

"At least I graduated," MJ said.

"Yeah, but I whipped your ass in Golden Gloves," Lee reminded him. In their last tournament before Lee went into the navy, he and MJ and had been matched and Lee had knocked him out with a crafty left hook.

Introductions out of the way, Kidd sat back. "What can I do for you boys?"

"We got a couple questions for you," Lee said.

Kidd frowned. "Questions?"

"About my brother," said MJ.

"About your brother, huh? And who's your brother?"

Another smart ass like Proferes. But MJ held his tongue. "Danny Shea."

"Oh, Christ. You're Danny Shea's brother?" Then to Lee: "Why didn't you tell me?" And back to MJ. "Hey, sorry man. I didn't know. Danny, he was a good customer here. I liked him."

"Yeah," said MJ. "Everybody liked him. Except the bastard who killed him."

Kidd's eyebrow arched. "Why you coming to me? I didn't have anything to do with that."

Lee jumped in. "Nobody's saying you did. We were just wondering if you lent Danny some money last week. That's all."

"Yeah, sure, I lent him money, like I lend everybody money. Danny was always in here for a fifty or a hundred and he always paid back, no trouble."

"Is that what you lent him?" asked MJ. "Fifty or a hundred?"

Kidd turned to Lee. "You know Joey don't like Teamster business getting around."

"I told you, MJ's okay."

Kidd sighed, picked up a half-smoked cigar from a tray on the desk, and re-lit it. He blew some smoke from the corner of his mouth. "All right," he said. "Because you're Danny's brother and a friend of Lee's. But this is just between us, okay?"

"Okay," said MJ.

"I mean it," said Kidd. "The cops have already been here once."

"What did they want?"

"The same thing you do. But them I didn't tell." He took another puff on his cigar, blew out the heavy smoke, and sat back. "Yeah, your brother was in here last week all excited. But instead of his usual front he was looking to borrow $9,000. I asked him for what and he said he had a bead on a half-kilo of coke, which he was going to turn and flip to some buyers in Dayton, double, maybe triple his money."

"So Waylay was going to sell Danny a half-kilo of coke?" Lee said, glancing at MJ.

"Not Waylay. Some dago with a connection in Pittsburgh, he wouldn't say who."

"So some stranger," said Lee.

"Danny was sure the guy was legit, who am I to argue? I get my money back one way or another no matter what happens, you know that, what do I care who it is?"

"So you lent him the $9,000?"

"Not right away. I had to check with Waylay first."

"Waylay," said Lee.

MJ felt the hairs on his arm rise. "What did Waylay have to do with it?" he asked.

"Hey, I do big business with Waylay. I'm not going to queer that deal over some small time dealer trying to sell in his territory."

"And what did Waylay say?" MJ asked.

"Waylay said, okay."

"He said okay?" MJ asked. Surprised because Waylay had the coke business in Youngstown wrapped up tight. As Kidd pointed out, why would he let someone from Pittsburgh horn in on his turf?

"He was setting Danny up," Lee said.

"Look," said Kidd. "Waylay said okay and I didn't ask why, all right? I fronted Danny the dough and that's the last I heard of him until I read about what happened in the *Vindicator*."

MJ felt his anger rising but sat stock still. Lee was right. Waylay must have found out Danny was informing and set him up to take him out. The money was just bait to keep Danny from getting suspicious.

"Thanks for being upfront with me," said MJ.

"Not a word of this to anyone--especially Waylay, *capisce*? What Waylay does is none of my business. You boys gonna find that Pittsburgh guy?"

"Maybe," said MJ.

"So far as I'm concerned he stiffed the Teamsters $9,000. So let me know if you need any help."

A minute later, MJ was sitting in Lee's car, steaming. "God-damned Waylay killed my brother," MJ said.

"That's what I've been saying."

"Hell, I'm a dope. Why else would Waylay tell Kidd to lend Danny money if he wasn't setting him up? And when he heard I was talking to Skeevy he hit me with that car bomb." Waylay was a crafty one, though, MJ thought, thinking back to the way he had sat in Big Man Donuts with that totally poker face.

"What are you going to do?"

"What the fuck do you think I'm going to do?" said MJ. Taking Waylay on, that was going to be tough. He hardly ever came out of the bar that was his headquarters. Attacking him there would be a suicide mission. He had a house in Austintown, a fancy suburb, but with a fence and security. About the only other place Waylay ever went was one of his stash houses, when there was a big delivery, and always with plenty of muscle.

But he did travel between places in his pride-and-joy BMW--sometimes chauffeured, sometimes alone at the wheel.

"You still have that Mossberg 12 gauge?" MJ asked. It was a pump action shotgun that held the legal limit of three cartridges. Lee bragged it would turn a trio of attackers into a trio of wet puddles in three seconds.

"Yeah."

"Bring it tonight to the funeral home. And don't make any plans for afterwards."

After first checking the van's undercarriage for explosives, MJ hopped in and drove back to Peggy's, parking on the street behind for caution and cutting through the neighbor's yard to let himself in the back door. He both wanted to lay low for a few hours and to retrieve a box of 12 gauge shells left over from a target shooting junket the year before.

"Peggy?" he said, hearing her voice in the kitchen along with a whole lot of noise.

She poked her head out into the hallway. "MJ, oh, hi, you're just in time. I thought you were going to meet us at the funeral home."

"Yeah, well, I thought I'd come visit." A crash came from the kitchen. "What's going on?"

"The guys from Sears are here," she said. "Come see."

Curious, MJ moved up the hallway to the kitchen door. Inside, two men in Sear's overalls were ripping out the water-damaged cabinets, one on a ladder with a crow bar, the other wiggling the cabinet box from underneath.

"What is this?" MJ said.

"Let me show you," said his sister, all excited. She plucked a hefty Sears catalog from the counter and opened it to a place she had marked. "See? It's going to be these honey birch cabinets with the dark brass pulls. Aren't they pretty? The counter's going to be Formica butcher block, and the floor looks like stone but it's really vinyl--everything super-easy to clean."

She was like a little girl with a new doll house. "Peggy..."

"What?" she asked, anticipating an argument and becoming defensive.

"Why are you doing this... you know, now--what with the funeral and everything?"

"I'm not 'doing it now'. I've had this planned for months--for years, actually. And if we're going to have people over after the funeral, don't I need a working kitchen? It's just that, since we have to fix the water damage, now seemed the logical time to do it."

She regained her previous enthusiasm. "And since we have to fix the plumbing anyway I'm going to finally get the dishwasher I've been begging for all these years. By the way, what do you think of this lighting?" She flipped to a different page in the catalog and pointed to a florescent fixture. "They can put these under the ceiling and make a kind of fake skylight. I'm sick of it being so dark in here."

"Peggy, really? We've got to be at the funeral home in a few hours."

A flicker of anger crossed her face. "Don't start," she said.

"I'm not starting anything," MJ said. "But can't this wait?"

"I can't live with a falling-apart kitchen!" Peggy said, exploding. "It's not my fault the plumbing blew. How the hell am I supposed to make meals and wash dishes with pipes hanging from the ceiling and no water? I can't even plug in the refrigerator with the wires all wet, and look!"--she threw open the refrigerator door to reveal a crowded, disorganized interior--"All this food is starting to go!"

The Sears guys had stopped what they were doing to listen to his sister's outburst, joined by Shannon and Lee Jr. at the hall door. The fridge *did* smell rank so maybe she had a point.

"Okay, calm down," MJ said.

"Calm? How can I be calm? What am I supposed to do, wait for the ceiling to cave in? Besides, you told me to do it."

"*I* told you? Just when the hell did I tell you?"

"Didn't you say, use the insurance money? If I waited for you or Lee to help I'd never have a working kitchen. Thank God for Sear's installment! You guys expect me to cook and clean and do everything for you but you never lift a finger to help."

MJ had heard that groove before and took a step back. "You're right," he said. "It's great, sis.

"You never listen to me. How long was I saying the kitchen water wasn't running right? But no, you wouldn't listen. So now we have this mess, and if it happened in the middle of Danny's funeral, well, I'm sorry, but what can I do about it? And that's another thing. I'm taking care of all this *and* all of the funeral arrangements. What have you done?"

"Okay, okay," said MJ with a sigh.

"Well, it's just that I'm tired of living in a dump. And it's not for me. It's for the kids. And Queen Anne in there too. And like I said, how are we going to have a reception if I don't have a kitchen?"

"You're right, sis. I'm sorry." Peggy was always stressed out, but Danny's death seemed to have pushed her over some invisible edge of anger. Best to just back off. He had more important things to worry about than his sister's kitchen.

He pushed past the kids and retreated to the basement. The leftover shells were on the top shelf above the workbench. There was a half box of #4 birdshot and maybe a quarter-full box of double-aught buckshot he and Lee had been messing around with the previous summer, out past the junkyard in North Jackson.

MJ ignored the birdshot and chose the buckshot for its better penetrating power. He crammed his jacket pocket with a handful of shells. It still wasn't clear what sort of shot he was going to get at Waylay, assuming he was able to get a shot at all, and if he had to shoot through a windshield, he wanted to make sure the bastard ended up dead.

Upstairs, the Sears men were still banging away in the kitchen and he could hear the TV blaring cartoons in the front room. Having gotten what he came for,

MJ had second thoughts about spending the afternoon at Peggy's. Instead, he let himself out the back door and made his way through the neighbor's lawn back to his van.

From when they had dated before, MJ knew that Cassie often spent her afternoons studying at the nursing school library. If he could find her there, they could talk, alone, and he could try to straighten her out about this guy Appel.

He drove across town to Cassie's campus, then followed the curving roadway around back to the new addition. The four story brick annex had expanded the school in the 50s, with more modern classrooms and a library. MJ parked, then entered through the annex doors, thus evading the school's minimal security. He took the elevator to the third floor. The library was in the southeast corner, overlooking the grounds.

A librarian--a nun in one of those modernized habit that looked like a dinner napkin pinned to her head--sat at a desk near the entrance, busy helping a student check out a towering load of books. MJ headed in the other direction, toward the card catalog against the wall. He pulled out a drawer at random and pretended to be flipping through the cards inside, then closed the drawer and moved off into the book stacks.

Against a windowless wall at the far end of the shelves stretched a series of wooden study carrels, largely deserted. MJ walked along them and spotted Cassie sitting at the last carrel, her back to him. Even in her baggy school sweatshirt she was a true beauty, her long, glossy black hair cascading over slim shoulders. He paused for a moment to watch her as she studiously consulted an open text book and made notes in a three-ring binder.

"Hey," he said, softly so as not to startle her.

She turned and saw it was him. "What are you doing here?" she asked in an annoyed tone. But she couldn't hide the fact that she blushed.

"I just came by to visit. Isn't that okay?"

"No," she said. "They don't allow visiting here--and, anyway, I'm busy."

He pulled up a wooden chair from a nearby carrel and sat at an angle beside her. "What are you studying?"

"Keep your voice down, this is a library!" she hissed. Then, maybe hearing her own tone, she relented and flipped the book cover over so MJ could read, *Principles of Psychiatric Nursing*.

MJ, who was never good at books and hated school, was nonetheless impressed. "Psychiatric nursing, what's that--crazy people?"

"Mentally ill. People's minds get sick, too, you know. Someone has to take care of them."

MJ thought for a moment. "Is that what you want to do? Care for mental cases?"

"It's a possibility. Something I have to learn anyway." She gestured toward her notes. "I have to do a care plan for a hypothetical 67-year-old female schizophrenic patient."

Cassie was beginning to sound like a real nurse. He was amazed at how much she knew, and it made his confidence falter. Even when they were dating, he had never been able to talk with her without starting to feel like a dope. An unsettling thought that maybe she *was* too classy for a guy like him wormed its way into his head, but he smacked it down by reminding himself that he was worlds better than Appel.

"Why is your face all red?" she asked.

"It's nothing. Sunburn."

"Michael, your eyebrows are singed."

"I had an accident with the stove."

A flash of anger crossed her face, but she let it pass.

"Anyway, you look tired."

"I am," MJ said.

Cassie stared at him intently. "You worry me," she said.

"I can take care of myself."

"It's okay to be sad about your brother," she said. "You can drop the hard-ass attitude around me."

Is that how he came off to her? The same way MJ saw Appel--some kind of posturing blow-hard? "Cassie," he said. "I got to know. Do you really love that guy?"

She looked at her textbook.

"You don't, do you?" MJ pressed.

"There are many levels of love," Cassie said. "It's not just feeling all swoony and starry-eyed. You can make a lot of really bad mistakes if you see love as just a feeling you have about someone."

"That's bullshit, Cassie. Didn't you tell me you loved me once? That was real, wasn't it?"

"What do you care? You ruined it all with your lies."

"Cassie, I told you, I never meant to lead you on like that. I wanted to tell you the truth. But I was just afraid you wouldn't like me if..."

"If I found out you were a drug dealer?"

"If you found out who I really was," said MJ, an image of Kate Parknavy flashing in his head. He felt trapped and overwhelmed, and bitterness rose in his throat.

She sensed his suffering and touched her fingers to the back of his hand. Then, reconsidering, withdrew them. "But you're still involved in all that."

Miserable, but unable to lie to her, MJ reluctantly nodded his head yes. "But only until this thing with Danny is over. Then I'm getting out. I'm moving to Ocean Grove, New Jersey, and going legit."

"Really? And what will you do there?"

"I have plans. I got in this business with a goal, and I'm going to make it."

"And what is your goal, MJ?"

"Construction."

She was looking at him skeptically. "Are you serious?" she said.

"Yeah, maybe I'll do roofing to start. Then I'll get my construction license and make my own company."

"Not about construction. About getting out of the drug business?"

"Yes," said MJ eagerly. Then, to be completely honest with her and put everything on a new footing, he said, "Well, not exactly yet."

"Not exactly yet."

"Well, there are some things I have to clear up first, about my brother."

Cassie pulled her hand away. "Do you know how crazy that sounds?"

"What?"

"You're going to go murder the person that killed Danny, isn't that what you mean by 'clearing things up?'"

He should have realized she wouldn't get it, but there was no point in sugar-coating it and he wasn't going to lie to her anymore. "I'm going to do what I have to do," he said. "Wouldn't you want me to do that if someone killed your brother?"

"No," said Cassie with a shudder. "Just the thought of that disgusts me. I can't believe you're even thinking about it. The police will find and arrest the murderer."

He had to make her understand how things were in Youngstown. "The cops won't do squat," he said. "To them Danny's just a piece of dirt. They'll pretend to investigate for a day or two, then drop it. They already took one of the cops off his case.

"And this guy who killed Danny, he'll get away scot-free. I'm his brother so I'm the one who's got to do something, you see?"

"No, I don't see. Didn't you just tell me you want to start a new life? How is murdering someone starting a new life?"

"Stop saying murder," MJ said. "It's not murder if it's the right thing to do."

"You'll murder him and then one of his friends will murder you," she said, a note of despair tinging her voice. "Then you'll be dead--just like Danny is dead--and where would that leave me?"

Her eyes began to brim with tears, which she brushed away angrily. But to MJ, the tears were a sign that she still did care for him.

His heart began pounding in his chest and he had to force himself to breathe. So this marriage to Appel, whatever it was, was crap. But he had to be very careful now to not scare her off, and he couldn't lie to her either.

"Cassie, listen, please. I know Robert is a very smart guy, just like you're a very smart woman. And that stuff he does with the homeless, that's good, I see that. And he's not just a bunch of gobbledygook talk, he's *do*ing things that are helping people. I can see how you'd like that."

He held her eyes in his, wanting to emphasize his next words. "But I know one thing. You don't love him, you love me. Wait, don't say anything. You love me and you've got to give me a second chance. A real second chance. Don't marry him, don't sleep with him, just wait. Will you do that for me, Cassie? Please."

"And if I do all that, you'll go to the police? You won't try to kill anyone?"

"Cassie. This man who killed Danny, the police can't touch him. They've been trying to get him for years for things a lot worse than Danny and they can't lay a finger on him."

"So you've already identified the man," Cassie said bitterly, "and you'll go on with your vendetta."

"It isn't like that, Cassie, it's what has to be done. Listen, this guy has already tried to kill me once--with a car bomb."

"What?"

"So I have to get him, or he'll get me."

"You have to go to the police. You *have* to. They'll..."

"They'll do nothing. Nothing. If I rely on them, I'll be dead within a week."

Cassie sat in horror for a moment. Then her demeanor hardened. "You see, this is exactly why I can't be with you."

"But it will all be over very soon, I promise. And we can go to New Jersey together and I'll never have anything to do with drugs again, I swear."

"You swear," she said skeptically.

"Yes, I swear. I swear to God."

"Oh, Michael," she said. She called him Michael in moments of tenderness, but this time her dismissive tone was like a stab in the heart.

"Don't you believe I love you?"

"Yes," she said. "But I can't love you. I can't allow myself to love you."

"What do you mean, 'allow yourself'?"

"I'm engaged to Robert," she said. "That's what has to be." But the tears were back in her eyes.

"Cassie..."

"Just go," said Cassie, wiping her face with the back of her sweatshirt and turning back to her books. "And stop bothering me."

Chapter Fourteen

Pleased to Meet You, Mom

B ack in his apartment to get ready for the funeral home, MJ couldn't shake the cold anger he felt at Cassie, at Appel--and at himself, for fucking everything up.

MJ knew Cassie could be hard and unforgiving once she had made her mind up--a quality she had earned as a runaway on the streets of Manila. Her father was unknown, her mother a prostitute, and Cassie had told MJ of her decision to leave the concrete hut where she had grown up when one of her mother's johns had drunkenly tried to rape her.

She ran and kept on running, living on the streets, sorting through garbage looking for food. Once, to quell hunger pains, she ate stuffing from a discarded sofa; another time she scraped the remains of a jar of petroleum jelly.

The jelly, she said, was the worst.

She was 7 when rescued by a kindly shopkeeper, who saw her looking into the window of his restaurant and invited her in for a bowl of soup. When Cassie wouldn't say who her parents were or where she lived, the stranger took her to the police station and the police delivered her to a Catholic orphanage--thereby, she said, saving her life.

From the nuns she got her sense of right and wrong, and the strength that had kept her alive was gradually channeled into a stubborn desire to excel in school. At first she thought the nuns were kind, but found the house matrons less so--they beat her entire dorm when a sick girl vomited on a newly cleaned floor. As Cassie grew older, she began to understand that the house matrons took orders from the nuns, who looked the other way when their charges were abused. This hypocritical behavior--and the nuns' kowtowing to the wealthy American visitors who occasionally adopted from the orphanage--disgusted Cassie and she lost her faith in the Catholic Church. She began to misbehave, talking back to the sisters and refusing chores. One by one her friends were adopted while Cassie remained, increasingly depressed and unhappy.

Fortunately, one particular nun, Sister Tala, her science teacher, took a special interest in her. Through friends in her order, she arranged a scholarship for Cassie at the Sacred Heart School of Nursing School in far-off America. Cassie jumped at the chance.

Given her early years on the streets, MJ could understand why Cassie was wary of people who dealt drugs, although the situation in Youngstown was far different from that of Manila. What he couldn't figure out was why she would decide to marry Appel when she so clearly was still in love with him. She couldn't allow herself to love him, she had said. But love was a feeling and a desire you had, not something you could decide to have. The nuns might have saved her from starvation, but they had screwed up her mind somehow with the same sort of Catholic bullshit that his mother got from the priests in the parish. In Cassie's mind, MJ was "bad," some sort of sinner. She couldn't deny her strong sexual feelings for MJ, but she could push them down and convince herself that the "right" thing to do was marry that asshole Appel, the smarmy, dickhead communist who fed the homeless.

He would have to have a long talk with her about that guy, show her what a phony he was, just as soon as he took care of Waylay.

***

And then it was 5 pm, time for MJ to put in his obligatory appearance at the funeral home. MJ--not wanting to drive around in his van--had taken a thousand dollars from his box and bought a brown '79 Nova that a neighbor was selling. As he drove to the funeral home, his mind was awash with thoughts about Cassie, interspersed with an evolving plan of how best to take down Waylay.

He parked the Nova a block down the street, then made his way to the funeral home--looking for, but not finding, any evidence of Waylay's goons. He slipped in a back door and saw, from the hallway, that Rose and Gary were back again, along with two women MJ recognized as friends of Peggy's from her diet club. Peggy's kids were nowhere in sight--probably she had left them with a neighbor--but she had dragged along their mother instead. She sat in a folding chair against the wall near the flowers, a look of blank incomprehension on her face. Keeping her company was a short, stout 50-ish man with a ring of grey hair around his balding head--Father Corkill, a priest from St. Paul's, a long-timer at the parish. Peggy had got him to say Danny's funeral mass on the basis that Danny had been baptized in the parish.

Cassie of course was absent, as was Carnival Jane.

But Lee. Where was Lee with the shotgun?

Dave Vlasik, seeing MJ in the hall, came up to him, looking haggard and a bit nervous. "Are we, uh, expecting any more problems here tonight?"

"Not that I know of," said MJ.

Vlasik licked his lips nervously, unconvinced. "I took care of that tow," he said. "The car's in my backyard, under a tarp."

"Good man. Did the cops ever show?"

"No. And the tow guy, Joe, he'll keep his mouth shut."

"Have you seen my brother-in-law? Tall guy with a mustache? He was here last night."

Vlasik shook his head. "I know who you mean, but I didn't see him. I can check the guest book," he said.

"Don't bother," MJ said. He doubted Lee would have come by and left, and wouldn't have signed the book anyway. He'd have to wait for him to show up.

In the viewing room, Peggy was still talking to the diet ladies, so MJ approached his mother.

"Hi, Mom," he said. "How are you doing?"

She looked up at him with a blank stare--trying, MJ supposed, to figure out who he was.

"It's your son, Anna," said Father Corkill, helping her out.

"Danny?" she said, squinting at MJ.

"Your other son," the priest said. "Michael."

"Michael," she said, offering a hand. "Pleased to meet you."

"Pleased to meet you too, mom," said MJ, mockingly, for the priest's benefit, since the disease that took his mother proved there was no God.

"Where's Danny?" she asked.

"Danny's in the box, mom," MJ said.

The priest shot him a dirty look.

"Danny's with God in heaven," he told Anna.

Right, thought MJ, grinning. But where the hell was Lee?

He went back into the hallway and found Vlasik in the office.

"Can I use your phone?"

"Sure," Vlasik said, waving him to a seat and leaving to give him some privacy.

MJ needed that pump action if he was going to take on Waylay. He dialed Lee's home number.

The phone rang and rang--no answering machine. He looked idly at a pile of bills stacked neatly on the desk. He could page Lee to the funeral home number, but Lee already knew he was here.

Screw it, he'd have to wait to see if Lee showed up. He went back into the viewing room. His cousins had left, but the diet club ladies were still there, along with a few of their old neighbors he would eventually have to talk to.

To buy himself some time alone, he stood by the coffin and stared at it, avoiding an impulse to kneel and say a prayer. Poor, dumb Danny, picking a fight with the biggest kid on the block. And poor, dumb MJ, who was going to have to pick that same fight--hopefully with a better outcome.

Peggy came over. "Let me see your face," she said. "Why didn't you tell me they fucking blew your car up?"

MJ, annoyed, figured Lee must have told her. "When did you talk to Lee?" he asked.

"Huh? Last night. You were here."

"I mean, today? I'm supposed to get something from him. Do you know where he is?"

She shook her head. "I thought he was coming tonight." She looked again at MJ's face and said, in a lower voice, "Do you think it was the same guys that killed Danny?"

"I know it was. Because I know who killed him."

Her eyes went wide. "You do?"

He looked around the room. "Let's go out in the hall a minute."

When they were out-of-earshot of anyone inside, MJ went over what he had learned about Danny being a police informant and Waylay setting him up with a loan to lure him into an ambush. "And that's why I need to find Lee," he said. "He's going to help me take Waylay out."

Peggy screwed up her face, looking uncertain, as if many competing thoughts were rushing through her head. "Oh, MJ," she said at last. "I don't like it. You are going to get yourself killed."

"Not before I take out Waylay."

"Can't you just wait and see what Proferes does? Maybe it will all take care of itself."

MJ harrumphed. The cops had never been able to touch Waylay, and that wasn't going to change because of Danny. "Sis, that's not going to happen."

Dave Vlasik approached them. "It's ten to eight," he pointed out. "Your guests are going to be leaving."

"We better get back inside," said Peggy.

"You first," said MJ reluctantly.

***

A half hour later--after again checking for explosives--MJ sat in the driver's seat of the new Nova trying to decide what to do. He was puzzled. It definitely wasn't like Lee to duck a fight, but he had failed to show at the funeral home and MJ was starting to get worried. Maybe something bad had happened to him.

He would have to look for him.

Decision made, MJ started the car and headed east, thinking about the fun he, Lee and Danny used to have together as kids. Once on a dare, Lee jumped 60 feet off the top of the Republic Steel Rail Bridge into the Mahoning River, forcing MJ and Danny to follow suit. Another time they released the brakes on a police cruiser and sent it careening down the road and into a telephone pole.

As they got older, of course, the pranks edged into crime--everything from extorting smaller drug dealers to smash-and-grab store robberies. Sometimes MJ would join the rotating cast of characters that revolved around Lee, sometimes not. And of course MJ was glad to be Lee's best man when Lee married Peggy--even as he had his doubts about how well two bull-headed people would get along.

A few blocks from YSU, MJ turned onto Madison Street and drove past Lee's apartment. Lee's car wasn't anywhere around and his apartment was dark, but MJ parked and knocked on the door anyway in case he was just asleep. No answer.

At Roma's he found Mike Longo sitting at the counter chowing down on a plate of ravioli. "Mike, hi, have you seen Lee?"

"Lee? Yeah, he was here a couple of hours ago with some college chick."

Lee liked to sleep around, which was one of the reasons he and Peggy had separated.

"Any idea where he went?"

"That chick, she was pretty cute, I'd say Lee's place, or maybe her's."

"Do you know where she lives?"

"No idea," Longo said. "I don't even know her name. She was majoring in business, though, if that's any help."

Frustrated, MJ made his way back to the car and cruised along Federal Street, where the college bars were, hoping maybe to see Lee's car parked out front.

Fucking Lee, blowing him off for a hot date, if that's what had happened. How long would it have taken him to drop off the shotgun at the funeral home--and pay respects to Danny, who was, after all, his brother-in-law. The college strip was pretty calm this Thursday night and soon MJ found himself dead-ended at the Greyhound Bus station.

Without the shotgun and Lee as a driver, there was no way MJ would be hitting Waylay tonight. About the only thing he could think to do was to head over to Waylay's bar, and try to scope out his movements. Maybe he could find some pattern of weakness that would leave Waylay vulnerable to an attack once MJ got everything properly set up.

***

The Pig Iron Bar, Waylay's headquarters, sat in a row of bankrupt and empty store fronts on River Street, not far from the entrance to the old Liberty Metals. The mill was still in operation, barely, with a skeleton work force scaling and fabricating steel plate for whatever manufacturing business was left in Youngstown. As he drove down the street, MJ caught glimpses beyond the row houses of a line of black metal buildings, with glaring yellow lights illuminating an empty industrial yard. He pulled up in front of an abandoned music shop ("Custom Accordions") at a point where he could observe the Pig Iron's entrance and side parking lot.

Right off, MJ saw Waylay's BMW parked under a floodlight near the back of the building. In the shadows nearby, a stocky guy in a hooded jacket leaned against the building with his hands in his pockets--obviously one of Waylay's soldiers, keeping an eye on the street. So Waylay was probably inside.

But, even if MJ had the shotgun, it would be foolhardy to attempt a hit on Waylay at the bar. MJ slouched low in his seat and waited, hoping he would emerge.

At 11 p.m. the shift changed, with the few dozen men still employed at the mill moving in-and-out of the gates--getting into waiting cars or stopping at the Pig Iron or its competitor down the street, Daley's Lounge. The guard in the hood went inside. The storefront of the bar was glass block, curving into a recessed entrance with a red door containing a single small window.

With no one watching the street, MJ decided to chance a look inside to see if he could spot Waylay. He grabbed his corduroy jacket from the passenger seat and pulled his watch cap low on his forehead. Then he hopped out of the car and walked toward the bar, ducking into the entry alcove under the pretense of getting out of the wind to light a cigarette.

Through the window in the door, he could see a half-dozen workingmen sitting in booths along the wall, and more drinking at the bar serviced by a bartender MJ recognized as another of Waylay's men. The Stones' tune "Brown Sugar" was playing on the jukebox.

While he watched, a figure emerged from the door behind the bar--Waylay, tonight dressed in a soft black sports jacket over a black shirt. Waylay put a hand on the bartender's shoulder and said something into his ear, then turned and started for the entrance.

MJ ducked back and ran down the street to the next doorway, hiding himself just in time to see Waylay's BMW pull up to the front of the bar. The stocky guy in the hood was driving, and Waylay stepped smoothly from the bar into the car, his slicked-back hair glistening under the illumination from the overhead bar sign. MJ flattened himself against the wall as the car sped past, daring a peek just in time to see it turn right at the next corner.

A minute later he was back in the Nova and on Waylay's tail--or sort of on it because the little car had no acceleration and leaned in corners like it was going to roll over. But the BMW wasn't speeding, merely moving along smoothly and in-flow with the traffic, giving the cops little reason to pay it attention. MJ slowed and followed the E32's distinctive rectangular lights, which were a little bigger and a little brighter than the other cars on the road. The BMW looped up and onto Mahoning and then Tod, crossing the Mill Creek Bridge and continuing along Price Road.

MJ followed, allowing the Nova to drift even further behind when he realized that Waylay was heading toward Schenley, the neighborhood where he had his stash house. Waylay's car went right onto Chaney Circle, a neighborhood of respectable homes purposely chosen to be far from any drug activity. MJ, having been at the stash house and knowing its location, slowed even further, and when the BMW turned into the driveway, he pulled over and turned off his lights.

Waylay and the driver got out of the car and the driver headed up the sidewalk toward the front door, which opened to admit him as soon as he set foot on the porch. Waylay started around the front of the car, but instead of following into the house, climbed into the front seat and backed out of the drive, turning straight back toward MJ.

Shit, thought MJ, slouching under the dashboard as the BMW's extra bright headlamps approached. This was the moment he had been waiting for--Waylay was alone and vulnerable. But without the shotgun, and Lee as a driver, MJ was screwed. No way could he get a good shot through Waylay's windshield with just his 9 mm.

Frustrated, he watched as Waylay's headlights burned into the Nova's upholstered roof liner and passed by. Thank God he wasn't in his van, which Waylay would easily have recognized.

MJ was going to kill that goof-off Lee when he found him.

In the mirror, he watched as the BMW turned the corner and proceeded uphill, further into the West Side.

MJ sat up. It might be a long time before he caught Waylay alone again. Danny was dead and the 9 mm could do the job he had come to do--if he got up close and personal. It was riskier but as long as Waylay was off his guard MJ thought he could make it happen.

He took the Browning from under the seat, checked the clip, flicked the safety on, chambered a round and slipped it into his waistband. Then he turned the little Nova around in the street, mowing down a flowerbed in the process, and followed Waylay.

Wherever Waylay was going, MJ was going too. The BMW moved slowly through the street of darkened houses, turned onto Oakwood, then merged onto the I-680 ramp heading west. MJ followed, keeping a car or two between himself and Waylay. A few minutes further on, 680 merged with the old Ohio Turnpike, now re-badged Interstate 80 but still charging tolls. Waylay stopped at a booth for a ticket, with MJ behind an 18-wheeler in an adjacent lane. MJ laid his jacket across his lap--to make doubly sure the Browning was concealed--and took the ticket from the bored toll booth attendant.

The BMW continued west, its tail lights easy to follow even from a half-mile back. MJ lit a smoke and tried to keep alert in case the car made a quick exit, but it rolled west for miles at a steady 60. Just as MJ was wondering whether Waylay intended to drive on to Akron or even Cleveland, the BMW edged into the right lane and got off at Exit 216, Lordstown.

MJ knew Lordstown from Lordstown Assembly, the GM vehicle plant where some of his Dad's friends used to work. In a few minutes Waylay was skirting along the edge of the complex, passing enormous grey buildings which housed the assembly lines, then parking lots crammed full of hundreds of Chevy Cavaliers, each parked identically and each glowing the same shade of red under the glaring overhead lights. Built in the mid 60s, the huge plant had been churning out Pontiac Astres, Oldsmobile Starfires and Chevy Monzas by the train load for the last two decades. TV commentators always referred to Lordstown Assembly as a "bright spot" in the Youngstown economy--even though the complex wasn't really in Youngstown and even though it frequently operated at a third of its capacity.

If everything had gone by his parent's plans, both Danny and MJ would be working at the plant now--Danny as a mechanical engineer for GM and MJ as a machine operator and sullen member of UAW Local 1112.

MJ sighed and crushed his cigarette. The BMW turned off onto a boulevard filled with fast food restaurants and motels, then turned again onto a two-lane road that led onto a bridge over railroad tracks to a development of neat new ranch houses surrounded on either side by empty farm land.

MJ warily followed the BMW into the development, turning his headlights off and hanging back as far as he could. Ahead, Waylay pulled into the driveway of a house with a maple tree in the front yard, waited for one of the two overhead garage doors to roll up, and pulled inside. The garage door closed, taking with it its slice of yellow light.

Waylay had arrived. But where?

Chapter Fifteen

An Involuntary Sigh

Puzzled, MJ for some minutes sat in the car and watched the house, which appeared to be dark and quiet. It wasn't Waylay's house--he lived in Austin-town--but it could be a new stash house, in which case there would be eyes on the street from inside. It was exactly the kind of neighborhood Waylay liked for his operations, and the garage, with its automatic door, offered perfect concealment for his precious car.

MJ forced himself to sit patiently, carefully watching for movement at the windows or in the dark shadows on the side of the house. If guards were present it would be foolhardy to attempt anything. But, as his night vision slowly improved, MJ failed to detect anyone. The only movement was a faint flickering from a tv inside, and the shadow on the porch that MJ thought might be a man turned out to be a hanging flowerpot with a tricycle underneath.

And suddenly it clicked. Waylay was known to like the ladies, but was scrupulous in keeping business separate from pleasure. The house, with its flower pot and tricycle, wasn't a stash house. It was the home of one or the other of Waylay's girls.

MJ's heart suddenly began beating more quickly. If he were right, this was it, the moment he had been waiting for. For sure Waylay wouldn't take any of crew with him on a visit to a girlfriend, so this was a chance to take him out before he even knew what was happening.

He pulled his watch cap low over his forehead and clicked off the safety on the 9 mm. Then he ducked between two houses and made his way through several back yards until he reached the rear of the home where Waylay was parked.

MJ's movements had set off a chorus of barking dogs, and he was forced to wait some minutes for the commotion to die down. The back of the house was a long wall of vinyl siding, with two windows on the left and a pair of sliding patio doors on the right. He could see the bright screen of the tv inside, high up along an inside wall, and as he slowly moved closer he realized the sliders led to the master bedroom, with the tv sitting on top of a bureau.

He waited and watched. White vertical blinds hung like curtains on the inside of the sliding doors, but they weren't entirely closed. Inside, he could make out the shadowy form of figures in the room, moving. MJ crept across the lawn and edged closer to the house along the far end of the lot, until he finally reached a position where the angle of the blinds gave him a better view.

Now he could see clearly into the room. A girl, slender but with huge breasts, lay naked on the bed. Waylay, also naked, stood on the floor over her, holding her legs in the air and giving her a pounding she definitely seemed to be enjoying, based on her gasping screams.

From where MJ was standing, her cries seemed loud enough to wake the neighbors, and suddenly he realized that the slider door was open by six inches.

Do it, he heard Danny's voice say to him clearly. *Do it now.* Waylay's back was to the slider door and MJ knew he would never get a better chance.

He sprang up from where he was hiding and ran toward the door, the Browning in his hand. As he crossed the patio, a motion-activated floodlight above the door flicked on, practically blinding him with its glare.

MJ continued to run forward but the element of surprise was lost. The girl saw him, screamed and pushed away from Waylay. She scrambled off the bed and fell, almost comically, off its far edge.

Waylay, meanwhile, had whipped around and seen MJ. The sight of the gun made his eyes open wide in fright.

MJ felt a rush of emotions--fear, satisfaction, victory--all rolled into one as he shoved the slider open with his left hand and fired at Waylay with his right.

The explosion was deafening in the small room, but the shot missed. Waylay was already moving, spinning around and darting for the hallway door.

MJ fired a second time as Waylay disappeared into the dark hall, this time sending a shower of splinters into the air as the impact of the slug blew apart the door frame.

The girl screamed and--MJ saw from the corner of his eye--cowered with her hands over her head.

MJ dashed through the door and headed down the hall the direction Waylay had run, toward a living room. A glimpse of movement at the end of the couch gave away Waylay's position, and MJ raised his arm to fire.

But... *blam!* MJ felt a tremendous jolt in his arm, and the 9 mm flew away backwards up the hall. Waylay had literally shot the Browning out of MJ's hand; instinctively, MJ threw himself to the ground and dove after it.

The pistol was lying on the floor near the threshold of the hallway bath. MJ crawled toward it.

Another round, going far wide, exploded into a mirror on the wall above and beside him, raining the hallway with shards of glass.

MJ had almost reached his gun when suddenly a naked foot kicked it out of the way. It was the girl, a Mac 10 machine pistol in her hands, aimed straight at his head.

"I got him, I got him," she yelled.

MJ snaked out his hand and grabbed the girl's foot, knocking her off-balance.

A fusillade of 9 mm rounds rent the air, pulverizing the wall and ceiling as she fired wildly.

Then Waylay was on top of him and a gun barrel poked straight into the side of his neck.

MJ, numb, lay very still as Waylay grabbed his hair and twisted his face sideways.

"What the fuck?" Waylay exclaimed, when he saw who it was.

Then he jabbed the revolver barrel in harder, and MJ knew Waylay was an instant from pulling the trigger.

So this was it, MJ found himself thinking, his spirit already detaching from his body. He had failed Danny, failed Kate Parknavy and above all failed Cassie.

"Wait!" he heard the woman shriek.

A little girl, wearing pink polka dot pajamas sporting a picture of Minnie Mouse, had pulled open the bedroom door opposite and was staring at the scene in fear and confusion.

"Not in front of Cindy!" the woman said. Still holding the machine pistol, she grabbed her daughter and dragged her back into the bedroom.

The door slammed, and MJ tensed, expecting his life to flash in front of him but seeing only dirty carpet.

Then he felt the pistol release from his neck as Waylay climbed off his back. "Get up, you piece of shit. Keep your hands where I can see them."

MJ's spirit snapped back into his body as he realized he had been granted a reprieve--at least temporarily. Holding his hands high, he rolled over onto his back, feeling the mirror shards dig deep as he did so. Slowly, he got to his knees.

"That's far enough," Waylay shouted, his chest--with its scorpion tattoo--heaving. The sight of his thin naked body would have been hilarious if he hadn't been pointing a .44 magnum directly at MJ's heart.

MJ was swept with the same gut-sick, cowardly feeling as when Jimmy Verduci pulled the knife on him.

"Who sent you?" Waylay barked.

MJ's mouth felt like it was stuffed with cotton and his head began to swim, as if he were going to faint.

No, he thought. At least die like a man.

"No one sent me. I'm here for Danny," MJ said.

"We're not playing games, here, asshole," said Waylay, taking a step back and cocking the Magnum's hammer to drive home his point. "Now, who sent you?

"I told you," MJ spat. "I'm here for Danny."

"Danny? Danny who?"

"Danny Shea."

"Don't fuck with me, man," Waylay said. "Your brother is dead."

"You should know. You killed him."

"*I* killed him? What the fuck are you talking about?"

"Or one of your guys if you didn't do it yourself."

Waylay blinked. "Are you fucking nuts, man? You think I killed your brother?"

"I know you did."

The .44 dropped by a fraction of an inch. "You crazy, fucking Mick. Why would I kill Danny?"

"Because he was going to blow your organization apart. Send you to jail."

Waylay huffed. "Yeah? And how was he going to do that?"

"Gathering evidence for the D.A. Working for the cops."

Waylay's brow furrowed. "Stand up."

The cotton-mouth returned and blood pounded in his ears. MJ's one chance would be to jump up and wrestle the gun from Waylay. He tensed himself, looking for an opening, but Waylay's gun didn't waver.

"Just cool it, man. If I was going to cap your ass you'd be dead already," Waylay said. "Now stand up, real slow, and sit over there on the couch. You need to get your head straight about a couple things."

MJ's mind whirled. Was Waylay going to shoot him on the couch? He still held the gun on MJ, but more loosely. And he was taking a seat opposite. What was Waylay up to?

"I didn't kill your brother," Waylay said. "But I know who did."

Of course Waylay would try to put it off on someone else. "Yeah?" said MJ. "Who?"

"You're right about Danny working for the cops. But what you sure as shit don't know is--he was working for me, too."

"What?"

"He was on the payroll. Feeding back to me what the pigs were up to. So I didn't have any reason to kill him, you understand?"

MJ considered. It could be. Playing both sides of the street would be right up Danny's alley. "So what are you saying? The cops killed my brother?"

"Not the cops."

"Who, then?"

"Your buddy."

"What do you mean, my buddy? Who?"

"That dago that married your sister. Lee Messina."

MJ felt a sharp shock, as if he had been plunged into a lake of icy cold water.

Lee. Fucking Lee.

It was crazy, but MJ knew instantly in his gut that it was true. If it weren't, Waylay--like he said--for sure would have capped him by now.

Lee and Danny had never got along, and Lee had a hair-trigger temper. If Danny got in his way...

But still.

MJ's stomach churned. "What makes you think it was Lee?" he demanded.

"Promo saw it."

"Saw what? Lee kill my brother?"

"Saw him dump the body anyway, over on Watt."

That seemed suspicious. "What was Promo doing there?"

"Following your brother."

"Why?"

"Because I sent him. Even though my boys were taking care of Danny, I got word he was going make a big coke buy with some guy from Pittsburgh--right here in my territory. I figured it was a scam, nobody would be that stupid, but just in case I sent Promo along to check it out."

What Waylay was saying explained why Promo wasn't around at the donut shop to take delivery of the package. It also lined up with what MJ had learned from Kidd--and even explained why Waylay had told Kidd to lend Danny the money. "So you used my brother as bait."

"Not as bait, man. I just let Danny do what Danny was going to do. But I had to make sure no one was fucking with my territory."

"All right," said MJ. "But where does Lee come into it?"

"That's just it. There wasn't any guy from Pittsburgh. Danny met Lee in the parking lot of the Tote'm Out over in Landsdowne. They talked for a few minutes and Danny got into the car. Promo followed along pretty far back, but close enough to see Danny's body get dumped."

MJ sat silent a moment, trying to wrap his mind around his brother-in-law blowing Danny's brains out.

"If it means anything," Waylay said. "Danny was dead by the time Promo caught up and checked him. Of course, by then, Messina had gotten away."

"And he was sure it was Lee?"

"He says yes."

"What kind of car was he driving?"

"Car? I don't know. Ask Promo."

"I can talk to him?"

"Yeah man, why not?"

A little ball of white-hot anger throbbed at the base of MJ's brain.

He didn't know why Lee had offed Danny, but at least he knew what he had to do next. If Lee killed Danny, Lee had to get what he had coming.

MJ massaged the back of his neck.

"We're good then?" Waylay said.

"We're good," MJ said. He had come close to making a huge mistake. "I guess I owe you one."

Waylay picked up MJ's Browning, emptied the clip and chamber, and handed it back to MJ.

There was an oblong streak of lead on the Browning's slide. "That was pretty fancy, shooting the gun out of my hand like that," MJ commented.

Waylay laughed. "Fancy my ass. I was aiming for your gut," he said.

"Then I guess I'm glad we both missed," said MJ.

***

MJ arrived home at 2:30 a.m., wrung out and exhausted. He had a thousand questions about Lee but he couldn't think clearly and had to get some

sleep. Plus his brother was being buried in a few hours and he had to steel himself for that.

Wearily, he climbed up the stairs to his second floor apartment, but at the door he paused.

The TV was on inside, and he never watched tv.

He had reloaded the 9 mm with ammo from the car and he now pulled it out and chambered a round. The door was locked and, gingerly, he inserted his key and pushed the door open.

Carnival Jane, in the same hoodie as the night before, sat on the couch in front of the tv, listlessly watching some old black-and-white movie.

Disgusted, MJ lowered the Browning's hammer and tucked the gun back into his waistband. She hadn't turned herself in to rehab, so she must be nosing around for more drugs.

He couldn't deal with her tonight, though. She had to go. He stepped up and turned off the tv.

"You can't stay here," he said.

"You didn't say that last night."

"How did you get in?"

She nodded toward the bathroom. "The window," she said.

The bathroom window overlooked the building air shaft. He left it open an inch because no one would ever be crazy enough to try to climb between the air shaft window and his bathroom window over the 25 foot drop.

"If you're here for coke, I don't have any more."

"Maybe I came by to see you."

"Did you?"

"Yes," she said.

If she did it was the last thing he needed.

"I thought you were going to St. Elizabeth's?" he asked.

"They're full. You said so yourself."

"Did you even try?"

"I didn't need to."

Of course not. She had left his house that morning with three or four of his dime bags of coke, which she probably cooked up into crack and smoked with her crackhead friends. But now that was over and now she was withdrawing.

"You have to leave," he repeated. "Get up."

"What about the van?" she asked. "You must have something in there."

"You got the last bag. Now get up."

Instead she put her face in her hands. "I'm a worthless piece of shit," she said.

"No you're not," said MJ, even as he knew not to argue with a crackhead, no matter how crazy they were being.

"Yes I am," she insisted. "That's why Danny hated me."

"Danny didn't hate you."

She began to cry. "He only loved me when he wanted something. He didn't care that he knocked me up. That song was a lie, just to get in my pants."

Maybe it was, maybe it wasn't, but MJ felt exhausted and just couldn't deal. "Come on, get up," he said.

"I want to die," she said.

"You've got to leave," said MJ, pulling her up by her arm.

"Let me go," she said.

He marched her to the door and pushed her outside.

She stumbled and let herself collapse on the landing. "No one loves me. I want to die."

He reached into his wallet and handed her a $50 bill. "Get yourself a room," he said.

She turned to him with a look of hatred. "You're a prick," she said. "Just like Danny."

"A room," he repeated. "And something to eat. You'll feel better in the morning."

"Fuck you," she said. But she stuffed the money in her pocket and stumbled off down the stairs.

He slammed the door and locked it. At the kitchen window, he watched as Jane walked past the gas station and around the corner into the darkness, hunched over with her hands in her pockets.

MJ's body ached for rest, but there was one thing left to do before he could sleep. He needed to hear what happened to Danny from Promo's own lips--to see if there was maybe any small piece of information that Waylay had left out. He dialed Promo's pager number from the phone in the living room, then lit a cigarette and waited.

Five minutes later, the phone rang.

"Hello," said MJ.

"Hey, MJ," Promo said. "Waylay told me you might call."

"Is it true what he said? That you saw Danny get whacked?"

Promo sighed. "Yeah, it's true," he said. "We figured Danny was working something on the side, so Waylay had me following him."

"Tell me what happened."

"Danny spent most of the afternoon under the bleachers at Harrison Field, hanging around smoking pot with those guys who sleep there and playing his guitar. When it got started to rain, he and some sorry-ass girl ate at the Taco Bell before heading over to that crack church in Sleepy Hollow. A lot later, like 1 a.m., Danny came out alone and hiked all the way over in the rain to the Tote'm Out at Garland and McGuffey. And that's where he met Lee Messina."

"Lee Messina? You're sure?"

"Yeah I'm sure. He got out of the car to use the pay phone, so I got a real good look. Yeah, it was him."

"Okay," MJ said, accepting it for the moment. "Then what happened?"

"Lee was only on the call a minute, then he nodded at Danny and the two of them got in the car."

"What kind of car?"

"A black Buick LeSabre with a white Landau roof. Pennsylvania plates. I've got the number written down at home if you want it."

"Yeah, for sure," said MJ. A black LeSabre matched up with the description of the car Skeevy had given him, and the P.A. plates might lead back to the dealer Danny was supposed to meet, if there really was a dealer.

"Any idea who Lee called?"

"I assume the guy they were going to meet."

"Anyone else in the car?"

"Not that I could make out," Promo said. "It was raining but I was just up the street on my Suzuki so I think I would have seen."

So Lee with Danny, alone. MJ almost didn't want to hear the next part, but he forced himself to ask, "Then what?"

"The car headed over toward the college, I thought maybe they was going back to Harrison Field, but they turned away into a residential neighborhood there. I was hanging pretty far back, but after they turned off at the end of the block I thought I heard maybe a shot, so I sped up. When I turned the corner, the car was stopped along the woods there, the passenger door was open and then Danny's body got shoved out."

MJ let out an involuntary sigh, and Promo stopped. "Hey, man, I'm sorry about your brother. He was an okay guy."

MJ said nothing, and after a moment Promo continued: "So anyway--Lee, he must have seen me, because just then he peeled away. I stopped for Danny but, you know, he was already dead. You got to believe me, there was nothing I could do for him."

MJ remembered back to the gaping wound in his brother's head. "I believe you," he said. "And you're absolutely sure it was Lee in the car with him?"

"Listen, I worked with that mustachioed prick a couple years ago, jacking trucks for Joey Russo. I told Waylay and now I'm telling you, it was him."

MJ thought back to when Lee was jacking trucks, the summer before he went into the Navy. "Any idea where Lee went after he dumped my brother?"

"No," said Promo. "I cruised around the area for a while, but he was gone."

MJ, exhausted, couldn't think of anything else to ask. He said his goodbyes, hung up, and bee-lined for the bedroom, where he threw himself on the bed.

Chapter Sixteen

Why Am I Still Alive?

B ut as soon as he closed his eyes, his mind was a jumble of conflicting thoughts and emotions. It was obvious now that Lee had set the car bomb. Bombs were a favorite Mafioso tactic, and Lee had plenty of mob friends to help him get explosives and tell him how to wire them up. It wasn't Waylay who wanted MJ to stop poking around Danny's death. It was Lee.

Danny's burial was that morning and he would have to be careful what he said to his sister. She was already a bundle of nerves. Learning that Lee had murdered their brother--shit, it didn't take much to imagine how she was going to react to that.

Peggy, though, was close to both Lee and Danny. If anyone would know what was going on between them, it would be her.

One thing was certain. Danny was supposedly meeting Lee to make a big purchase of coke. Was the coke sale just a ruse to get Danny in the car and kill him? Or were there actually drugs, and something went wrong between Lee and Danny? But what the hell, MJ thought angrily--what difference did it make whether there were drugs or not? The important thing was that Lee had killed Danny.

The clock ticked and ticked and Danny was dead and not coming back. His body was in the coffin, but the real Danny had somehow evaporated, like water from a shallow puddle.

The world just made no sense, MJ concluded. There was no order or justice, and the only possible plan was to do unto others before they did unto you.

If Danny had remembered that, he would be alive to see his baby born and Lee would be burning for eternity in hell--or at least be as dead as Danny was.

Peggy was going to be torn up when she learned what Lee had done. When he thought about it, she had a right to bitch about her life--with two kids, their senile Mom, a murdered brother and now a husband who had killed him.

What the hell kind of a person was Lee that he could kill Danny? Surely it couldn't have been for the nine thousand bucks Danny was carrying. They had all been friends in high school, drank together, jacked cars together and even dated the same chicks. Yeah, Lee had a short fuse and Danny had gone off the deep end with coke and then crack. But if Lee had a beef with Danny, he should have come to MJ to make it right.

The clock ticked and MJ ached. What was he doing here on earth anyway? Where the fuck did people come from and what the fuck was their purpose? What was *his* purpose? To kill Lee and exchange Ohio for New Jersey?

And when he killed Lee, what was MJ going to tell Cassie? Being from the Philippines, she just didn't know how it rolled in Youngstown. Danny was dead and that meant his killer had to die too. It didn't matter who did it, Lee or anyone, MJ couldn't just walk away. Danny was his brother. His brother would do it for him, so he had to do it for his brother. That was just the way things were. He had to make her see that. Then he could take his money, go legit and find a place to live together.

The weakness returned, washing over him like some suffocating gas. Listlessly, he curled himself on his side, his limbs heavy, waiting for sleep.

He ached.

The clock ticked.

Cassie. Cassie. Cassie.

She loved him, that was clear. Maybe she was the only woman who ever really did love him--or maybe even ever could. She seemed to understand him on a deep level, better than he understood himself.

MJ couldn't stand the thought of her marrying Appel.

Was she going to be at the funeral? After their argument in the library, he wasn't so sure.

MJ looked at the clock. 5:20 a.m.

It was still early, but according to Appel, Cassie would soon be cooking up breakfast at the Workers House. He decided to pay her a visit.

***

It was still dark when he reached the big house on the South Side, though a small crowd of bedraggled panhandlers were already gathering at the front gates, awaiting their free communist breakfast. In the back, a door opened and some bearded jackass in an apron dragged a trash can to a dumpster in the corner. He emptied it noisily, then banged down the dumpster lid with an ungodly crash before disappearing back into the kitchen. Cassie would be in there.

MJ swallowed hard. Feeling nervous and tense, he made his way to the small gate in back. He knew it was pointless to try to get Cassie's approval for what he had to do, and she had already shot down his arguments about why she should leave Appel for him. But he felt compelled to be there. Somehow he had to make her see how right they were for each other, and how happy they could be together in the future, and most of all, why that wuss Appel was so wrong for her.

He stepped up to the kitchen doorway. Inside he could see a big steel sink and a couple of mismatched refrigerators. A thin black woman stood scrambling eggs at a gas stove while the bearded guy who had emptied the trash was rinsing a bus tray at the sink. Robert Appel was nowhere to be seen, but neither was Cassie.

His heart sank. Maybe she wasn't working this morning. He was about to step inside to ask when a voice came from behind.

"MJ?"

He whirled around to find her standing on the path not six feet behind him, dressed in an outfit casual almost to the point of frumpy--jeans, a loose white tee and, on her head, a UAW baseball cap.

In his mind he had intended to play it cool, but instead he rushed up to embrace her.

She stiffened and turned her face but her attempt to push him away seemed feeble and lacking conviction. Finally she gave up and stood limply, a wet fish, purposely unresponsive.

MJ let her go. "Cassie," he said.

"I asked you to stay away."

"I can't do that, Cassie. I love you."

Hearing those words, her features momentarily softened, and it gave him courage.

The sun was rising now and the treetops on the hillside above were suddenly illumed with orange flame, throwing a warm glow into the ugly yard and onto Cassie's face--that lovely face he could not tear his eyes from.

"You've got to go," she stammered. "I'm cooking this morning."

"Just give me a minute."

"Rob will be here soon."

"I don't give a crap about him," he said.

"But I do," she snapped. Then, more calmly: "We're getting married next Tuesday."

"What!"

"There's no reason to wait. There's a peace demonstration Saturday in Minneapolis and our honeymoon will be that."

"Are you kidding me?"

"We're going to take turns driving the Communist Youth bus."

It was so crazy, he had to laugh.

She reddened. "You think that's funny, huh? That's your problem. You never take me seriously."

"That's not true, Cassie."

"Robert is good. Robert is decent. Robert is trying to build up the world instead of tearing it down with drugs and killing like you."

"I told you I'm quitting all that."

"You told me, but you're not doing it."

"I am, Cassie. After the funeral. Danny is being buried today, remember?"

Her expression softened once again. "I know. I was going to come to the funeral mass."

"I miss him so much," said MJ.

"I'm sorry," Cassie said, her voiced tinged with sadness. "He was so talented. What a waste."

MJ had the feeling she was also talking about him.

There was a bench at the edge of the building, away from the kitchen door. "Sit over here with me a little while, Cassie."

"But Rob..."

"Forget Rob for a minute. Please?"

She let him take her hand and lead her to the bench.

"Cassie," he said. "I almost died last night."

A worried expression crossed her face.

"But I'm okay," he hastened to add. "Don't ask me what happened, it's not important, I made a mistake."

Her worry changed to skepticism. She said nothing and waited.

"It made me think, though. I had to ask myself, why am I still alive when Danny's dead? Yeah, he was stupid, he should have known better. But he was tricked. And I'm not tricked so I'm still here. But maybe I'm tricked too. You always say I'm fooling myself. Well, maybe you're right. Maybe I *am* fooling myself."

"I don't know what you're talking about," said Cassie.

"Yes, you do! I'm a liar like you said, and I've hurt a lot of people. I've hurt you, that's for sure. I've hurt so many people. But I'm still here. And why?"

"Why?"

"I don't know," MJ said, anguished. "Except..."

"Except what, MJ?"

He shook his head in confusion.

"What?"

"Maybe I'm still here to... to take care of you..."

"That's very gallant," she said. "Except maybe I don't need anyone to take care of me. I made it to the States on my own, and next month I'll have my nursing degree. And if I need any protecting if the future, Rob will do it."

"Don't take it that way, Cassie. Maybe I'm not saying it right. I didn't mean you need my protection. What I mean is--you were put on earth for me. And I was put on earth for you. Can't you feel it?"

Cassie's features softened.

"You know I'm right, Cassie? Only the two of us, it's the only thing that makes sense."

She turned her face from him. "Rob..."

"Rob might be a nice guy. But you know he's the wrong guy for you."

He took both her hands in his. They were small and delicate.

She looked at him, anguish on her face.

He raised her hand to his lips and kissed it.

Tears suddenly glistened in her eyes. She reached up and touched his cheek, so gently he shivered.

"Michael. Are you serious about quitting the drug business?"

"I already told you I am."

"And you, what? Want to move away and live in New Jersey?"

"Or wherever you want."

"And marry me?"

MJ jumped at the chance. "Yes, marry you, and be with you for the rest of our lives. It's what I want more than anything--just to be with you and make you happy."

Just then a voice called from the open doorway: "Cassie?"

It was Robert Appel, in his black beret, tying a white apron around his waist. He stopped when he saw them, then came over.

Cassie stiffened and pulled her hands from MJ's.

"This is getting pretty tiring," Appel said to MJ. Then to Cassie: "Are you okay?"

"Yes," she said.

"We're getting married Tuesday," Appel said to MJ.

MJ wanted to jump up and punch the smug smile off Appel's face, but instead said, "I heard."

Appel smiled at the sour note in MJ's voice. "Best man wins, remember?" To Cassie he said, "Invite him to the ceremony if you want."

"Oh, Rob," said Cassie.

"Sorry, sorry," Appel said, backing off in mock apology. "Some fiancés wouldn't be so understanding. But you guys take as long as you need. I'll start the pancakes myself." He touched his beret in a farewell salute. "Comrades."

When he was back in the kitchen, Cassie turned to MJ. "If you really meant what you just said, then... it has to be now."

"Now?"

"Yes. You said you were serious. Let's get in your car and leave."

"You mean, for the funeral?"

"Not the funeral. New Jersey. You said that's where you wanted to go, right? What's the town called?"

"Ocean Grove? Right now?"

"Yes, please."

MJ's heart leapt as he realized what Cassie was suggesting. After he was done with Lee, he had planned to clear out for a few months anyway, lay low until the heat died off. He never expected to be going anywhere with Cassie. But he wasn't going to muff the opportunity again.

"Really, Cassie? What about your school?"

"There are schools in New Jersey, aren't there?"

It would be a huge sacrifice for her. He was almost ashamed to take her away. "You're sure?" he said. "May is only a few weeks. We can wait until you graduate."

"Didn't you hear me? I said now."

There was a strange note of stridency in her voice. She was going to make a fearsome nurse.

Just then in the kitchen, a pot clanged to the floor. MJ nodded toward the open door. "What will you tell him?"

"Nothing. He'll figure it out. Let's go."

Wow. Now that she had made up her mind, she was all in. A warm glow enveloped MJ as he realized how very much she loved him. "All right," he said. "I'll drop you at your dorm and come back for you in an hour. How's that?"

"No. You can just wait. I can pack in five minutes."

"Pack? You mean you want to go *now*? *Right* now?"

"That's what I've been saying."

"I can't go right now. My brother's being buried. Didn't you say you were coming?"

She turned to him abruptly. "Do you love me, MJ?"

"You know I do."

"Then forget the funeral. Forget Youngstown. You want to quit this drug business, quit. Let's just go."

"It's not that simple, Cassie. I can't just snap my fingers and leave. I need a few days at least. Bury my brother, say goodbye to my sister--that sort of thing."

"Oh, so you want me to put my life on hold whenever you snap you fingers, but when it comes to your life--well that will take a few days. Is that how you see it?"

"Of course not, Cassie."

"Well, if that's not the issue, then what is?"

He hesitated, uncertain.

Anger crossed her face. "This isn't about your brother's funeral, and it's not about saying goodbye to you sister."

He knew immediately what she meant. And she was right. He couldn't leave Youngstown until he had settled things with Lee.

"Cassie..."

"Don't 'Cassie' me."

"We've been over this before," said MJ, his own anger flaring up, not wanting to argue and frustrated that she was trying to make him choose between her and getting justice for Danny.

"You said yourself, last night you almost got killed. How do you know the next time you won't be?"

"It's my life," he said. "That's a chance I've got to take."

"Not if you're with me," she said.

"Cassie, why are you doing this? Just give me a couple more days and then we can go."

"No. You'll be dead."

"Don't worry about me."

"Or worse than dead, you'll be a murderer. And I can't live with a murderer."

"Stop saying murder. My brother has a hole in his head like this"--he made a gesture with his fingers the width of an apple--"and Lee? He gets to go free, with Danny lying dead in the street?"

"Lee? Your brother-in-law Lee?"

He hadn't meant to name any names because the less she knew the better. He looked away and said nothing. Let her think what she wanted.

"You're going to kill your sister's husband, aren't you? Not only is that murder, but have you thought about what that will do to her? She'll hate you for the rest of your life."

The happiness he had felt just a few minutes ago was already ebbing away, leaving a raw shelf of bitterness. He could see how this was going to go. "I don't care," he said.

"MJ," Cassie said. "Go to the police."

"I thought communists hated the police," he taunted.

"Not if they do their job and serve the people."

"And anyway tell them what?" he said. "I don't have anything they would call evidence."

"Then what business do you have killing Lee or anyone?"

"I know what I know. If I don't take care of it, no one will."

"Leave it, MJ. Let the police investigate."

"Investigate and do nothing," said MJ.

"Even if they do nothing!" said Cassie. "Come right now with me, and live your life."

MJ thought of Kate Parknavy--watching her get raped in the stairwell by Jimmy Verduci. He had run away then but he was a man now. Why did Cassie expect him to just roll over?

Cassie looked at him sadly. "All right, Michael," she said.

She stood up, and MJ, in shocked disbelief, knew that he had lost her.

"So that's it," he said, his voice wavering.

Tears sprang to Cassie's eyes, but she wiped them away angrily. "That's it," she said. "Good bye."

She turned and ran into the kitchen, still crying, leaving MJ alone in the empty yard on the empty bench.

He felt leaden inside. His one best chance with Cassie and he had blown it.

But what the hell could he do? His brother was going into the ground in a few hours and Lee was somewhere walking around free.

He swore he was going to kill that prick before the day was out.

But first he had to take care of Peggy, help her get through the next few hours. Peggy was family. He could at least do that.

Chapter Seventeen

In for What?

St. Paul's was an undistinguished, modernistic brick building that had replaced a much older church sometime in the 60s. Formerly much-used by the families of the neighborhood, the church now looked dated and shabby, with peeling paint on the white trim and overgrown bushes along its front wall.

By the time MJ had put on his suit jacket and driven over to the church, the hearse was already at the front stairs, with his cousin Gary and the other pall bearers waiting. As MJ pulled into the nearby parking lot, Peggy rushed out to intercept him. She was dressed in an outfit MJ had never seen before, a black overcoat and black pillbox hat with veil.

"Where the hell have you been? Everyone's waiting and Father Corkill is ready to start."

"I'm sorry, sis. But we still got ten minutes, right?"

"Ten minutes? That coffin should already be inside."

She was, as MJ had expected, all worked up. But that was understandable, given the circumstances. He was feeling pretty dragged out, himself--running on adrenaline. "How are you holding up?" he asked.

"You don't know what I've been through. The kids won't shut up with questions and Mom didn't want to get dressed."

"It will be okay."

"I should have known you'd be late. And I had to get Dave Vlasik to fill in as pall bearer because Lee won't be here."

"Lee? You talked to him?"

"Well yeah, yesterday."

"Did he say where he was?"

She must have read something on his face, because she reacted strongly. "Why?" she demanded.

"Sis, we need to talk."

She glanced over at the steps, where the other pallbearers--his cousin Gary, Danny's friend Tony Schnetz from the Music Shack and the funeral director Dave Vlasik--were waiting. "Now?" she asked.

"Just sit in the car with me a minute," MJ said.

"We're already late as hell. Are you drunk or something?"

MJ's face went dark. "Do I look like I'm drunk, sis?" he said.

Peggy could see that he meant business. Reluctantly, she came around and joined him on the front seat of the car.

MJ decided to plunge right in. "Peggy," he said. "Lee killed Danny."

Her face went blank with shock. She sat a moment in stunned silence, blinking at him uncertainly. Then she seemed to regain herself, and her anger flared.

"Shit, you *are* drunk. Why the hell would you even say a thing like that--and, now, before the funeral?"

"Peg, this is real. You've got to listen." MJ explained how Waylay had Promo following Danny, and how Promo had seen Lee push Danny's body from the car.

He could see that Peggy was thinking furiously, trying to reconcile his words with her feelings about Lee.

"Shit," she said at last. "Give me a cigarette." Then, when she had taken one and lit it, said, "This guy Promo, he says he actually saw it?"

"Yeah, he saw it."

"How do you know he's not lying?"

For a second, MJ considered telling her about what happened between him and Waylay, but then thought better of it. "Sis, you know the kind of people I run with. On something like this, a guy don't lie.

She was silent a moment, absorbing what MJ had just said. "And he says for sure it was Lee, no one else?"

"Just Lee. Promo got a good look at him at the Tote'm Out, and it was just the two of them in the car."

Peggy's face twisted and she leaned back against the head rest, squeezing her eyes closed. "My God, that mother fucker," she cried.

"Peggy, I'm sorry," MJ said, reaching out to touch her hand.

Her body sagged. "Did they... do the cops know? Are they going to arrest him?"

"The cops don't know shit, and no one's going to tell them. This is all in the family."

"But if Lee killed Danny..."

"I'll take care of it."

She turned and looked at him, her expression uncertain.

"You live here, you know how it is," MJ said, his voice hard. "It doesn't matter that Lee is married to you. He has to pay. You understand?"

At the hearse, Dave Vlasik was beginning to pace as he and the other pall bearers waited. The back door to the vehicle was open and Danny's silver coffin was visible inside.

Peggy shuddered, but gave the slightest nod, her eyes filling with tears.

"I'll make it up to you, I swear."

She sat up, suddenly alert, and looked around. "Where is he? Do you think he'll show up here?"

MJ shook his head. "He's probably laying low. Disappeared. He must know what he's got coming to him."

"I mean, the kids, and, ah, me--do you think he might try...?"

MJ opened his jacket to show the handle of his 9 mm. "Let him try," said MJ.

Dave Vlasik, in his dark suit and tie, broke off from the group at the hearse and approached the car where MJ and Peggy were seated. "Michael, Margaret, we need you now," he said. "It's time."

Peggy burst into tears, a handkerchief MJ didn't know she had suddenly in her hands.

"Go on inside, sis. Leave everything to me."

He climbed out of the car and joined the other pall bearers waiting at the coffin.

MJ's relief at his sister's understanding was short-lived, because as soon as the service began, Peggy fell apart.

They were seated in the front pew, with their mother between them and the kids on Peggy's other side. As the coffin was draped and Father Corkill began sprinkling it with holy water, Peggy let out a loud groan and began sobbing, unable to even watch.

The kids looked useless and bewildered, the way MJ felt. There was nothing he knew to do that would heal Peggy's grief, but somehow her anguish seemed to break through their mother's Alzheimer's. She reached out and put comforting hand on Peggy's arm--causing her to bury herself on their Mom's shoulder with even more wrenching sobs.

MJ glanced around. There were maybe a dozen mourners in all in the big church--mostly neighbors and friends of his sister, along with his Aunt Laura and cousin Rose. None of Danny's crack friends were in attendance, and neither were Carnival Jane or Cassie.

MJ had never felt so alone. The homily he heard in bits and pieces--"loving savior," "merciful judge," "trespass," "eternal," "kingdom of Christ." MJ remained in the pew with his mother while a sniffling Peggy and the kids took communion.

"In peace let us take our brother to his place of rest," intoned the priest, and the service was over, except for Peggy throwing herself atop Danny's coffin with more loud wails and weeping.

"Let's go, sis," said MJ, lifting her up and hugging her.

Her mouth was against his ear. "Fucking Lee," she whispered through her tears. "You're right, he has to pay. I'll kill him myself if you don't."

Then she pulled herself together and escorted their mother and the kids out of the church.

MJ followed a few minutes later, helping to carry Danny's coffin to the waiting hearse.

He was going to have to talk to his sister later, see if she had any ideas about Lee's whereabouts.

But that would have to wait until after the burial.

***

St. Paul's cemetery was a green rectangle of rolling land off Wickliffe on the way to Schenley. When MJ's father died, his mother had bought plots for the entire family, "so we can all be buried beside each other together," she said.

At the time, MJ didn't see what difference that could make and thought she was having her pockets picked by the priest that sold her the idea. Now he was glad she had done so. Danny would be buried with his father, and, if Mom got her wish, MJ himself would be in the dirt with them all, sooner or later.

The burial itself was, mercifully, short. The grave had already been dug, stretched over by a metal frame with wide web straps to hold the coffin suspended. MJ took a seat in a folding chair while Peggy cried and the priest intoned prayers. Only their cousins Rose and Gary had followed the hearse out to the cemetery, so in the end Danny only had a handful of mourners.

It was then that MJ noticed a grey LTD parked along the cemetery roundabout. For a moment, MJ feared that it was Lee but, squinting, he could make out the familiar round face of Detective Proferes.

MJ fumed. What the hell was he doing here? He was just about to get up, say something to him, when Father Corkill raised his hand in the sign of the cross and loudly proclaimed a blessing. Then he came over and squeezed Peggy's hand.

"You have my sympathy," he said.

"Thank you, Father, thank you," Peggy said, dabbing her face with her now limp handkerchief.

Next the priest tried to give the same treatment to MJ, but MJ pulled his hand away. "That's it?" MJ said. "Aren't you going to bury him--lower him in the hole and throw dirt?"

"We, ah, don't do that anymore," Corkill said. "Out of consideration for the family."

"Well I'm family and I want to see him go in the ground."

"Oh, MJ, don't ruin it," said Peggy, her veil turned up from her face to reveal red, swollen eyes.

"Ruin it? How am I ruining it?"

"It's not Catholic," she said, tugging him away from the priest. When they were out of earshot she added, "And if you stay, I have to stay. And I don't think I can take any more. The kids are exhausted and Mom's peed her Depends. Plus I've got to get home and put the food out."

MJ relented. "All right, Peg."

What difference did it make, really? He already felt limp, like he was sleepwalking through an unreal world of churches, coffins and graveyards. And he still had to deal with Lee--but first, Proferes, who was leaning against the car, his arms folded.

"I'll see you at the house, sis."

She followed his gaze up the hill. "What's he want?" she asked.

"That's what I'm going to find out."

"And then you'll be over, right? We need to talk about Lee."

"Don't worry about Lee," MJ said.

MJ left her and walked up the hill to where Proferes stood against the car smoking a cigarette and watching below, where the mourners were dispersing and the groundskeepers folding up the chairs. He wore the same grey suit he had been wearing that day on Watt Street, but with a different colored tie.

"Hello, Michael," he said, as MJ approached.

Whatever he wanted, MJ wasn't going to give it him. "What are you doing here, Proferes?"

"That isn't very friendly. Maybe I came to pay my respects."

"Yeah, well, you did, now get out of here and leave us alone."

"Listen, smart ass, I'll show up where and when I have to, and if you don't like it, we can continue this conversation down at the station. I'm doing you a favor showing up here."

A favor. They always wanted to take you down to the station so they could pull their cop tricks and record you. MJ looked at him, trying to read his face. In the sunlight, MJ noticed for the first time that the Proferes' sideburns were going grey, and that there were lines at the corners of his eyes.

"All right," MJ said. "What do you want?"

"I want the truth. I have some questions for you and no more jerking me around, you understand?"

MJ said nothing and Proferes took that as compliance. He reached into his car and pulled out his little spiral bound notebook. "Who do you know drives"--he looked in his book--"a black 1981 Buick LeSabre, two door coupe, P.A. plates but I'll spare you the number since it's stolen."

MJ looked away, down to where the pair of groundskeepers now emerged from a little hut and walked over to Danny's grave. A black LeSabre lined up with what Promo had said about the Buick, and with Skeevy's rumors about a dude in a black car.

"I don't know nothing about that," MJ told Proferes.

"Oh, you don't, huh? What about Leo Messina? You know him?"

"He's married to my sister."

"Is he really? Wow. Why wasn't he here today?"

"I don't know. Ask him."

"Was he driving the Buick?"

"What Buick?"

"I told you, no jerking me around," Proferes said, his voice getting hard.

But just then the groundskeepers down below turned a crank and Danny's coffin, supported by the web straps, began descending into the grave. MJ couldn't take his eyes off it. When it disappeared completely into the hole and the men withdrew their cranks, MJ felt his knees begin to buckle. He sagged down and sat on the curb before he fell, tears stinging his eyes.

Somehow, until now, the reality of Danny's death hadn't entirely hit him. He waited for his head to stop swimming.

A hand appeared in front of his face holding out a pack of Winston's. MJ had forgotten all about Proferes. He took the cigarette and lit it with the offered lighter, then sat smoking until he could stand up again.

Proferes looked at him. "You okay?"

MJ nodded. "Look, this really isn't a great time."

"I get it," Proferes said. "I buried my mother last year. But you understand I've got a job to do. We're on the same side here. We both want to get whoever killed Daniel, right?"

MJ nodded again. Thinking of what Cassie had said, he was almost tempted to tell Proferes what he knew about Lee. He could see Proferes watching--pretending to be his friend, waiting for him to weaken and spill his guts.

MJ kept his mouth shut.

"I got something in my trunk I want to show you," Proferes said.

"What?" said MJ.

"I think you'll know when you see it."

He opened the trunk. The interior was perfectly clean and empty except for a black plastic garbage bag, loose and wrinkled.

MJ knew what it was as soon as Proferes picked it up, before he even peeled back the bag.

Danny's guitar, the neck broken and all swollen up with water damage.

"Is it his?" Proferes asked.

Proferes cradled it in the bag like a baby, and pulled the instrument away before MJ could touch it and mess it up with his prints. But the fancy inlay around the sound hole was a dead give-away, and Danny's silver marijuana sticker was still attached inside.

"It's my brother's," MJ said. "Where did you find it?"

"In the back of the Buick I was asking about," Proferes said. "At the bottom of the Mahoning River."

MJ was pretty sure he knew just the spot, off the old storage yard at the abandoned Brier Hill Works. That's where he and Lee used to dump stripped cars, pushing them off the embankment into the river.

"If you know anything, tell me now," said Proferes. "Because if I find out later you've been holding out on me, I'll charge you with obstruction of justice."

The threat raised MJ's hackles. Lee would run circles around this clumsy motherfucker. "I already told you everything I know," said MJ.

Proferes looked at him through narrowed eyes--tinged, MJ suddenly realized, with sadness. "Okay," he said. "If that's the way you want it. If you see Leo Messina tell him I want to talk to him.

"You're free to go."

Free to go my ass, MJ fumed as he climbed back in the car. A hundred feet in front of him, Danny's grave stood unfilled--a gaping muddy gash in the green landscape.

One of the groundskeepers, now wearing a hard hat, stood beside it with a shovel, but for the first time MJ realized there was no mound of dirt. His puzzlement only lasted a moment, however, for just then from behind a shed came a yellow construction loader--like a bulldozer but smaller and riding on wheels--its bucket, held high, piled with the missing earth. It dumped the dirt unceremoniously into the grave before backing out the way it came with a series of loud, discordant electronic beeps. The guy with the shovel smoothed down the pile, breaking up a few of the bigger dirt clods, then tossed the carnations, brought over from the funeral home and already starting to wilt, onto the grave. Then he headed off between the tombstones and disappeared into the shed.

Well, MJ had wanted to see Danny put in the ground and now he had.

He sat staring numbly through the car's insect-splattered windshield. Danny was good and buried now, suffocating under a ton of cold, wet dirt and a dusting of his supposedly-favorite flowers.

It wasn't right. It should be Lee under the dirt, not Danny. Crazy fucking Lee, with his stupid mustache and slick clothes, always scheming something or picking a fight, so cool, one chick after another, why didn't MJ see it sooner, the greed, the anger? He had let Lee sucker punch him over and over, and now Danny was dead because of his, MJ's, stupidity and desire to be "in." In for what? No wonder Cassie was disgusted. MJ was disgusted with himself, and there was only one way he could fix things now.

He put the car in gear and headed for Lee's place. If he were there, MJ would use the Browning to finish him. If not, he could at least search inside, see if the place held any clue as to where Lee might have gone.

***

MJ parked down the street from the ugly World-War-2-era apartment building where Lee lived. From the space, he could see that Lee's car wasn't at the curb in its normal spot, nor in the side yard in the red dog gravel lot under the trees. Lee's apartment blinds were drawn and the cheap tin mailbox nailed near the door was filled with mail.

He wasn't home.

Time for Plan B. MJ fished the tire iron from the back of the Nova and, his Browning tucked into his pants, approached the unit on foot.

Feeling very conspicuous in his funeral jacket and tie, MJ walked boldly up to the entrance and, using the screen door for cover, inserted the tire iron into the frame between the knob and the dead lock and pried the door open. He moved quickly inside, his gun drawn just in case Lee was there to greet him. But the apartment was empty--no one in the corners of the rooms or the closets, but the bed unmade and smelly dishes in the sink. It was obvious that Lee hadn't been there for days.

Satisfied he was alone, MJ tucked the 9 mm back under his belt and closed the front door. Now he just had to toss the place--find an address book or papers or anything else that might give him an idea where Lee was hiding.

The apartment was railroad style--a long narrow hallway with rooms strung out on the left and right. The entry let into the living room so he started there. On the stained coffee table were some old copies of the *Youngstown Vindicator* and a half dozen empty beer cans, some used as ash trays. A phone directory lay on the floor beside the couch, but it looked like it had never been cracked open--no turned-down corners or numbers written on the cover.

The kitchen had more beer cans and a stack of junk mail and flyers. The freezer, an inch thick with ice, contained a single package of mixed vegetables. The sink was full of stinking dishes, and the drawers to the left and right contained silverware, take-out menus, Scotch tape, scissors and assorted other crap. The small bedroom opposite held a bicycle, a set of dumb bells and some old picture frames--no bed. In the bathroom was the usual toothbrush, razor and aspirin, and--in the grooming section (Lee was always fussy about his hair)--a burgundy bottle of Crew Grooming Spray and a curling brush like women's hairdressers used.

The last room was Lee's bedroom, with its window to the street. MJ tugged back a corner of the pull-down shade, saw nothing suspicious, and turned his attention back to the room. The dresser held socks and underwear, along with an empty envelope that MJ suspected might once have contained cash. In the nightstand was, in the top drawer, a half-empty tube of KY Jelly and a box of Extra Safe, Lighter Weight Durex Condoms, also half empty. The discovery gave MJ pause. It was no secret that Lee liked to fool around--that was one of the reasons he and Peggy separated--but could he be shacking up with a girl?

He pulled open the bottom drawer. It contained a green box of Winchester .45 caliber ammo, 50 count but empty. That would be for Lee's Glock 36, which he loved for the sleek looks even though it constantly jammed. The only other thing in the drawer was some Hoppe's No. 9 solvent, so Lee probably had the Glock with him.

On the closet shelf, MJ found a box with more gun cleaning supplies and several boxes of 12-gauge shells, but no Mossberg--so he probably had the shotgun with him too. There were plenty of clothes in the closet, but whether that meant Lee hadn't packed anything or that he simply had a lot of clothes, MJ couldn't tell. In the corner was an old Adidas gym bag. MJ pulled it out and unzipped the zipper. Gym clothes.

There was nothing under the bed, between the mattresses or under the pillows. MJ pulled the drawers all the way out of the nightstand and found nothing. He repeated the operation on the chest of drawers, where he found also nothing. He kicked through the pile of dirty laundry in the corner and came up with carpet.

If there were any clues to Lee's whereabouts in the house, MJ couldn't find them.

He gave up, defeated. Peggy already said she didn't know where Lee was, but he'd have to grill her some more, particularly about Lee's past girlfriends. Otherwise his best bet would probably be staking out the Roma, waiting for Lee to show his face again there. That might be days or weeks and could get dangerous, with Joey Russo and his mob friends hanging out there.

As MJ turned to leave, the gym bag again caught his eye. So far as he knew, the last gym Lee belonged to was the Janiro Boxing Club, where they trained for Golden Gloves. He picked up the bag and emptied the contents to the floor--shorts, tee-shirts, towel, and leather workout gloves. At the bottom, to help the bag hold its shape, was a fabric-covered cardboard stiffener, and under that, a bulky manila envelope.

He opened the clasp and emptied the envelope onto the bed, spilling out a dozen or so bundles of folded paper. He opened one. It was a contract from the Associated Underwriters Guaranty Company--a life insurance policy similar to the one Peggy had taken in case something happened to Danny. But this one was "payable on due proof of the death of ***DANIEL P. SHEA***," the amount of $4,000, "to Leo M. Messina, his executors, administrators or assigns." The premium was $51.08 per annum, "payable quarterly on the sixth day of January, April, July and October."

MJ understood why Peggy had taken insurance on Danny's life in the aftermath of his near-fatal overdose--but why had Lee? Especially since the policy had been issued in October of the previous year, after Lee and Peggy had already separated.

With a sick feeling is his stomach, MJ opened another bundle. It was also a life insurance policy, for $5,000, also payable to Leo M. Messina but from the Freedom Life & Health Insurance Company. A third policy, for $2,500, was from the improbable Afro-American Protectors Insurance Company. A forth, for $8,000, had been issued by the United Labor Life Insurance Company of Boston.

There were many more, all on Danny's life and all payable to Lee. Each was for a relatively small amount--$2,500, $5,000, $7,500--but altogether added up to a huge amount, something over fifty grand.

MJ plopped on the bed. He hadn't found Lee, but he had found Lee's motive, and it was a stunner. Fucking *money*? Lee had killed Danny for *this*, a pathetic fucking insurance scam?

He tried again to look at the papers, but his hands were shaking and his eyes no longer able to focus. Lee had known Danny since high school, raced stolen cars with him, smoked weed with him and even lived with him for a while when he was still with Peggy and Danny would crash in the basement. So how could Lee even think about offing Danny? What kind of a shit was he?

"No," MJ exclaimed, slamming his fist down hard on his thigh. No way was this going to stand. Lee had to die. No, not just die. He had to see it coming, and die painfully. And it made no fucking difference what Cassie would think, because she could never understand.

Lee would know MJ was coming for him--that was why he had disappeared--and he had his Glock and his shotgun. MJ only had the .9 mm, but Lee wouldn't know when and where he would be hit.

Surprise was MJ's hole card. He had to find Lee fast, before the bastard could plan some counter attack. And he had better do it street style--from behind--so that Lee had no chance whatsoever to react.

He stuffed all the papers back into the manila envelope, got back into the car and drove straight to his sister's. The policies were the final proof that Lee killed Danny and he wanted her to see them, to erase any doubt in her mind about what had to happen next. Plus maybe she knew something about Lee's girlfriends and could help him find Lee.

Chapter Eighteen

Goombah

Peggy had done up the house for the post-burial reception, with a black-ribboned wreath hanging on the front door and a big tray of hors d'oevres from State Market in the middle of the living room, where she had also moved a half-dozen chairs. A spray of drooping carnations adorned the top of the tv, and a pile of Danny's holy cards, along with the funeral home guest book, sat on the entrance table at the door.

Nobody was around, however, and there didn't seem to be any fresh signatures in the guest book. MJ heard dishes clinking in the kitchen, where he found Peggy serving lunch to the kids.

"Eat it," she was telling Lee Jr., whose plate held a variety of meat slices and cheese, apparently from the tray in the living room. Both she and the kids were still in their Sunday best. She went to the refrigerator and began rooting about on a shelf. The Sear's guys must have been worked hard because the new cabinets were in and so were the fake-butcher-block Formica counters.

"Hey, sis," said MJ, standing in the doorway.

She turned, startled, a carton of orange juice in her hand. "MJ. You scared me, creeping in like that."

"I wasn't creeping," MJ said. "Where is everyone?"

She relaxed and poured the orange juice into two paper cups for the kids. "Can you believe all this work I did and practically nobody showed? Just Rose and Gary, and Father Corkill, and Becky and Sue from down the street. Oh, and Dave Vlasik brought the holy cards."

"I saw them," said MJ.

"I want a hot dog," Lee Jr. said, pushing around a piece of salami with a plastic fork.

"Me too," said Shannon, who had an identical paper plate.

"Eat it and shut up," Peggy said, leaning against the new Formica counter. She lit a cigarette, looking strung out and exhausted. "And where were you? You could have called at least. I was worried."

"I had a stop to make," MJ said. "At Lee's."

Her eyes went wide. "Did you...?"

MJ shook his head *no*. "He wasn't there," MJ said. "But I found something I want to show you."

For the first time, Peggy noticed the manila envelope in MJ's hands. "Oh, God," she said, intuiting something bad about to unfold. She plopped herself down at the table.

MJ took a seat beside her and lay the envelope out flat. Peggy stared at it like it was a snake, probably wondering what new bad news MJ was going to dump on her.

"You kids go watch tv," MJ said.

"But I'm still eating," Lee Jr. said.

"Take your plates and go," Peggy snapped.

They watched as the children carried their food out of the room. When they were gone, Peggy turned to MJ. "Did you get that at Lee's? What is it?"

MJ opened the envelope clasp and slid the bundles of paper out onto the table. "These are insurance policies. On Danny's life. Eleven of them and all made out to Lee."

Peggy seemed to stop breathing for a minute as the import sank in. "Made out to Lee?" she repeated.

"Every single one," said MJ.

Peggy drew a policy at random from the pile and read through, tension and dismay on her face. She repeated the process with another contract, then a third, her brow furrowed.

"You see what this means, don't you?" MJ prompted. "It wasn't a drug deal like Waylay thought. That was just a setup, so Lee could kill Danny. For the insurance money."

She looked up from the paperwork, letting her anger flare in her eyes. "That slimy fucking bastard," she said. "That asshole! That money grubbing pig!"

"Take it easy, Peg."

"Fuck taking it easy," she said, lurching upright to the kitchen counter, where she supported herself on two arms over the new stainless steel sink, as if she were going to throw up.

"Peggy, I know this is hard, but I've got to ask you some questions. Do you have any idea where Lee might be hiding? With an old girlfriend, maybe?"

But Peggy was wound up. She fumbled for a cigarette from a pack on the counter and turned. "I should have known that's what he was up to," she said. "Remember that policy I showed you? The one I took out on Danny? No wonder Lee was so interested in it!"

"Peggy..."

"He wanted to know how much it paid and how much it cost, and then took it with him, to show his lawyer friend he said. At the time, I didn't think that was all that strange--like maybe he was just looking out for me. But now. Now I see what he was doing. And then the next day he wanted to know where I got it, so I showed him the ad in my *Woman's Day*, and another in *Redbook*, and he took the magazines and said I had done the right thing, because if Danny were to OD again or something, there could be a lot of expenses.

"He said that?"

"God, I was so stupid!" She looked at MJ in dismay. "How could I have not seen this coming? They had a big fight when Danny moved into the basement, and then when Lee's cassette player got stolen from his car, he blamed Danny and broke his nose."

Carrying her ashtray, Peggy sat back down at the table. "They were always arguing, fighting. And..."--she put a hand to her mouth--"Oh my God, I think I know when Lee decided to kill him. The time when Danny was cooking crack in my microwave and caught it on fire. Lee had moved out by then, but I called him up and, ah, asked him to talk some sense into Danny--just talk! But Lee went and beat him unconscious. He just went wild and I couldn't stop him. I had to call the police and an ambulance."

MJ thought back to the incident, a year or so back when Danny really started to go downhill. Lee had worked him over good, too, breaking several of Danny's ribs and rupturing his spleen.

"Was that before or after you talked with Lee about the insurance?" MJ asked.

"It had to be after, because Danny OD-ed in the spring, and Lee moved out in the summer," Peggy said. She gestured at the policies on the table. "He must have started buying these after we separated."

MJ picked up a few of the contracts and reviewed the purchase dates. They all seemed to have been bought in the summer and fall of 1985, lining up with Peggy's theory.

Which meant Lee had been planning to kill Danny for almost a year.

As if reading his mind, Peggy suddenly said, "Lee, Christ, I hate him! Danny was a pain in the ass, but he didn't deserve to die like that."

"That's why I'm going to take him out."

Peggy looked at him and took a deep drag on her cigarette. "MJ, she said. "I'm worried about you. Yeah, you talk the talk, but--do you really think you can handle Lee... kill him?"

"What?" said MJ. "You think I can't?"

"He beat you in boxing like a thousand times," she said.

"This isn't boxing," he said, annoyed.

"And your car. He must have been the one that blew the crap out of it. He's dangerous."

"I'm dangerous too," MJ said. "All I have to do is find the bastard."

She took a final puff of her cigarette and stubbed it in the ashtray. "I think I can help with that," she said.

"You know where he is?"

"No," she said. "But I might be able to find out." She rose and went to one of the new cabinets and brought back a pint bottle of Jack Daniels, three-quarters full. She poured both of them a shot in a paper cup.

"There's a woman Lee used to see, back before we separated," Peggy said. "She was a stripper at the Palace Lounge near the school. I'm pretty sure he might be with her."

MJ knew Peggy was trying to be helpful but the lead was pretty thin. "What makes you think so?"

"I told you, Lee called here last night."

"Lee called you? When?"

"After the viewing. Maybe 10 o'clock. He said he got busy and that's why he wasn't at the funeral home, then he asked a lot of questions about where you were and what you were doing."

Lee asking questions about him. That would mean he still intended to try something but was looking for the right opportunity. "And what did you tell him?"

"Nothing, I told him nothing, except that you would be at the funeral--but he already knew that."

"What's this have to do with the stripper?"

"Her name was Mindi. And last night on the phone, I heard a woman talking in the background and I think it was her."

MJ's hackles went up. "Do you know where this Mindi lives?"

Peggy shook her head no. "But she worked at the Palace Lounge. And if you give me a few hours I think I can find her address."

"How?"

"I have a friend who used to tend bar at Rutter's. She was the one that told me Lee was cheating on me with Mindi. She knows where Mindi lives because she's been to parties there."

MJ felt energized. If Peggy could get an address, he could scope out the situation and set up Lee. And--he looked at his watch--even though it was early he might be able to talk to someone at the Palace Lounge, which he knew was one of the strip clubs downtown along Wick.

"All right," he said. "See what you can find out and beep me. I'll check out the club where she worked."

"To Danny," his sister said, lifting her cup with the whiskey.

MJ did the same and they knocked down the toast. Then MJ picked up the pint and poured them both another shot.

"To payback," he said.

His sister hesitated, then touched her cup to his.

They drank. Peggy could be moody but he should have enlisted her help much earlier instead of trying to do everything himself.

***

The strip club was across from the defunct Rayen School in a nondescript three-story building of yellow brick. A large rectangular sign announced, in bright red letters, "Palace Lounge," and below that "Girls Girls Girls." A strip of incandescent light bulbs, with a few missing, lined the bottom of the sign but were unlit in the afternoon sun. The twin wooden doors were closed.

MJ parked in a space across the street and approached the club on foot. He was hoping to find someone who might know Mindi but the door was locked. He knocked and waited, meanwhile admiring the silhouette of a perky stripper on the Totally Nude sign on the wall.

When no one answered, he walked through the alley at the side of the building to the back, where--wedged between a dumpster and a barred window--he found another entrance. The metal door was open a crack so he let himself in to what proved to be a small kitchen, with a hooded stove, a long prep table and a big insulated freezer door. No one was around but MJ could hear a radio playing further inside. He moved down a hallway past a tiny dressing room and emerged alongside a mirrored dance floor in the main area of the club.

A fat man in a loose white tee shirt was sitting at the bar, smoking a cigarette and going through a pile of paperwork. MJ took him for the owner.

"Hey," the man said when he caught sight of MJ. "What are you doing in here? We're closed."

"Relax," MJ said, opening out his hands to show that he was not threatening. "I'm looking for somebody."

"Yeah?" said the man. He was mid-40s, with his hair combed back and reading glasses dangling from a cord around his neck. "Who?" he asked.

MJ sat at the bar a few stools down from the man. "A girl named Mindi. A dancer."

The owner blew out smoke and returned to his paperwork. "We don't give out information on our girls," he said. "You can leave the way you came." He scribbled some notes on what looked like an invoice and waited for MJ to go away.

MJ sighed, reached into his wallet, and pushed two twenties across the bar.

The fat man looked at them through his reading glasses and turned to MJ. "You're kidding me, right? Let me guess--you want her number so you can ask her out."

"Not her number. Her address," MJ said.

The man gave MJ a closer look. MJ had ditched the jacket and tie but still wore his pressed white shirt, neatly tucked into his slacks. "I'd say you were a cop if you weren't throwing around your money. So what are you?" he said. "Jehovah Witness? Bill collector?"

"I'm trying to find a friend of mine," MJ explained. "And I think he might be staying with Mindi."

"And why do you want to find this friend?" the owner asked.

"I have something to give him," MJ said, feeling like he had told the fat man enough.

The man stood up and went around the bar. "You got a name?" the man said.

"MJ," he said.

"MJ what?"

"MJ Shea," said MJ. "Why?"

"I don't know what you're up to, MJ Shea. But whatever it is, count me out."

"I told you," MJ said. "I'm just looking for Mindi's address."

The man reached under the counter and pulled out a baseball bat, which he held across his fat belly with both hands. "Get out of here," said the fat man.

"Whoa, whoa, whoa," said MJ, rising and backing up.

"I had it with you goombah punks messing with my girls."

"Goombah? You stupid fuck, can't you tell an Irishman from a dago?"

"You're a goombah because you act like a goombah," the fat man said. "Now get out before I knock your goombah block off."

MJ almost wished he hadn't left his gun in the car, but instead he took a step backwards.

"Don't forget your cash," the owner said.

MJ was not feeling stupid enough to put his hands on the counter in front of a crazy man with a bat. "Shove it up your ass," he said, then turned and left.

Only when he reached the sunlight of the back lot did he suddenly think it was funny, the fat guy with the dangling glasses and a bat in his hand. He laughed to shake off the tension but was pissed he had failed to get Mindi's address. The money had been a mistake. He should have played it dumb like the fat guy thought, a love-sick schmoe trying to hook up with a dancer. If Peggy didn't come through, he was going to have to return later that night and try to meet this Mindi in person--avoiding the fat man with the bat.

He was almost to the car when his pager went off. *Peggy*, he thought. *She found Lee*. But when he glanced down, the number was unfamiliar. It took him a second to realize it was Skeevy that had beeped him, Danny's dealer.

There was a phone on a post in front of the drugstore at the intersection and MJ crossed to it and slipped in a quarter.

The phone rang and rang and then a voice answered, "Yo."

"Skeevy? This is MJ."

"Oh, hey, man, you gotta come down and get this chick out of here."

"What chick? What are you talking about?"

"That Jane chick that hung with Danny--Carnival Jane. She's high, super-high, and she's freaking out my customers singing and acting crazy. And she keep asking for you."

"For me?"

"Yeah for you. And just now she tried to cut herself with some glass I took off her so you better get here quick before she do something or someone call the law."

He didn't want to deal with Jane right now but it didn't sound like he could leave her.

"Where are you?"

"Where am I always? Grover's Kwik Stop, where you was the other day."

"I'll be there in a few minutes," said MJ. "Just keep her calm until I get there, okay."

"I'll try," said Skeevy. "But this bitch is fucked up."

She must have taken the money he gave her to keep the party going. Danny's death hit her hard but maybe now it was just an excuse to get even higher. She was going to keep rolling downhill for sure unless she got some help. MJ doubted he could get her into rehab but he could let her stay at his place for a day or two until she came down enough to have a rational talk.

Chapter Nineteen

Rat in the Handkerchief

G rover's Kwik Stop was a white concrete block building plopped down in the middle of a cracked parking lot near the 422 on-ramp. MJ scoped it out as he waited for an opening in the opposing traffic to turn into the lot. Skeevy was at the far corner near the pay phone, conducting some business with a bearded guy in a red sweatshirt, but Jane was nowhere in sight.

MJ finally managed to cross traffic into the lot and parked near a sandwich board advertising Newports for $12.50 a carton. He waited for the bearded guy to walk off, then approached Skeevy.

"Man, where you been?" Skeevy said as MJ came up.

"I came as soon as I could. Where is she?"

"Ain't you got eyes? She's right there," Skeevy said, indicating the end of the lot.

"Where?"

He pointed. "There. Right there on the ramp."

MJ looked past the lot in the direction the dealer was pointing and saw Jane in the weeds at the edge of 422 on-ramp, bent over with one of her hands on her ankle, like she was going to puke.

"She look calm now, but she all chalked up," Skeevy said. "She been down here for an hour hassling my regulars and trying to score a ten from me."

"Did you sell her anything?"

"You got money, I'm your honey. But she ain't got no money," said Skeevy. "She did offer to blow the love whistle, but I told her I don't need no crack whore, I already got a girl."

MJ shook his head. A crackhead would do anything with anybody for a crumb of crack, no room for self respect. He had bought her story about being in love with Danny, but suddenly he wondered whether she was even pregnant. Maybe she was just playing on him for sympathy, the way Danny would come at him for cash with some sad story that later proved to be a lie.

He studied her more closely. She was still bent over with a hand on her ankle, but now she was stumbling forward, scuffing through the weeds.

He should fucking get back in the car and leave her. He had better things to do than babysit a crackhead. She wasn't his responsibility.

Just then she woozily reached for something in the dirt and fell down. He waited but she did not get up.

Shit. He wasn't any doctor but she needed help. For a moment he thought about calling Cassie--she would know what to do--but he doubted she would even take his call. No. He would take Jane to the hospital and dump her at the emergency room door.

"Come on," he said to Skeevy. "Help me get her in the car."

"No man, I'm doing business here," Skeevy said.

"You want her gone, don't you?"

"I'm through with that crazy bitch," Skeevy said. He rolled up his sweatshirt to reveal a big scratch mark on his forearm. "Look what she did," said Skeevy. "You're on your own, brother."

MJ, pissed, was about to argue but decided it was pointless. What did he need Skeevy for anyway? Without another word, he turned and walked toward the highway on-ramp, crossing the small street at the end of the parking lot and clambering up the weedy embankment to where it leveled out the guard rail.

Jane was lying on her side in the dirt, her grey tee shirt dirty and ripped at the collar and one of her sneakers missing. A wadded-up, bloody handkerchief poked from her jean pocket, and she writhed on the ground with eyes closed, lolling her head and talking to herself under her voice.

Man, she was in a bad way.

"Jane? Come on. Get up. It's MJ."

Upon hearing his name, she opened her eyes and looked at him, then pushed herself onto her knees and recoiled as if in fear.

"What's wrong? It's me, MJ." He extended a hand. "Come on. Get up. Let's go."

She mumbled something.

"What?" he said, his hand still out.

"I JUST WANT THIS ALL TO END," she screamed, getting to her feet and balling her hands into fists. Then, like a mechanical doll, she bent over to her side and dug her right hand into her pocket.

"What did you take?" MJ asked.

She popped up and looked at him, uttering something unintelligible, then twisted back into her former position, standing there like a mannequin dummy.

"Jane," MJ said. "What did you take?"

Again she popped up, in the same strange mechanical manner, as if the real Jane was trapped inside the body of a puppet--a really high puppet.

"Do what I tell you!" she said. She mumbled some more unintelligible words and then said, shouting, "Now what do you want? I'm dead, listen to me mother fucker! What do you want to know?"

Holy shit. She didn't even seem like the same person. She needed to get detoxed, and quick. "Jane, my car's right there. Let's go for a ride."

Another stream of gibberish gushed from her mouth, and then, "Don't play with me! I am fucking dead!"

"Okay," said MJ, trying to get her to calm down.

Some yellow flowers were sprouting from a weed bush and Jane lurched toward them. "I am eating flowers," she announced. "I AM EATING FLOWERS."

She tried to break off a woody stem but failed. She was barely standing.

"Let's just go down and get in my car," MJ said.

More gibberish and then, "I just got here, what do you want?" Jane said. "I am dead, really dead. No one will do what I tell you. Here."

She took the bloody lump of rag from her jeans pocket and placed it in the dirt with elaborate care, then got distracted and said, "Look at my foot there."

She wasn't making any sense and MJ realized she wasn't going to come voluntarily. He'd have to drag her back. He grabbed her arm but she yelled and twisted.

"Help! Help!" she screamed, as if he were going to rape her. She pulled and jerked away with surprising strength. "Call the cops you fucking piece of shit!" she said, turning on him with full fury. "You are garbage! You are trash! LEAVE ME ALONE!"

She turned and started to run. MJ tried to tackle her but only managed to trip her up. She scrambled to her feet, ran twenty feet along the berm and turned to scream: "HE PUSHED IT IN I COULDN'T HOLD HIM!"

Then she turned again, leaped the guardrail, and ran straight across the on-ramp--right into the path of a Cherokee 4x4 accelerating to get onto the highway.

MJ saw it in slow motion.

One second she was sprinting wildly across the ramp, the 4x4 heading straight for her.

Then she was smashed against the front hood, her body bent backward into an unnatural C.

Then the 4x4 swerved and braked, too late, carrying her body with it. The Cherokee turned a donut as it ground to a halt, but Jane's body continued to roll and tumble, finally coming to a halt, legs splayed, against the ramp's far guardrail.

The body was not moving and MJ knew without a doubt she was dead. No one could survive an impact like that. But he ran to her anyway.

She was lying face down, one arm above her bloody head, her tee shirt rolled up to her tits and her legs spread like broken twigs.

Then a man was standing there, an older guy in a pressed denim shirt with an embroidered nametag that said *Frankie*. "Oh my God, is she okay?" the man said, looking down.

"She's dead," MJ said.

"Dead?" said the guy, recoiling and taking a small step back. "Are you sure?"

MJ, still in shock, wanted to grab the old man and smash his face in, make him pay for what he did.

"It was an accident," the man said. "She ran right out in front of my car. I tried to stop."

MJ stood up and looked at the man, his fists in a tight clench.

Fear sprang into the old man's eyes. "It was an accident," he whined.

He was just an old guy, a workman like all the other old men in Youngstown. MJ swallowed down his anger and said, "Yeah, I saw it. She ran in front of you. It wasn't your fault."

Traffic was already stopped on the ramp and other drivers were getting out of their car to gawk. Then, down on Wick, a cop car put on its lights and sirens and pulled a U-turn to come back to the accident scene.

MJ didn't want to hang around and answer questions. He stood up and, as the police car tried to pull up the ramp past the stopped cars, walked back the way he had come, hopping over the guard rail and almost landing on Jane's bloody handkerchief. It looked strange--something was wrapped in it--and on impulse, he picked it up. A bag of pot maybe, or some blow? He threw it on the passenger seat when he got back in the car.

In the rear view mirror, he could see a crowd of people around Jane's body as the cops came up. One looked over the railing, maybe having seen him go. Slowly, MJ pulled the car through the Kwik Stop's empty Drive Thru and turned onto the residential street beyond.

After a few blocks, when he was sure no one was following him, he pulled over and unwrapped Jane's dirty handkerchief.

He was right. There was something inside.

A baby rat, MJ thought at first, slimy and repulsive. Why the hell was Jane carrying around a baby rat?

Then he saw the little arms, wrapped around the bloody torso and he knew it wasn't a rat at all, but a little tiny baby, two inches long, grey, helpless, dead.

Jane must have miscarried sometime in the night.

MJ, shaking uncontrollably, wrapped the baby back up again and put it on the passenger seat.

He drove ten yards and stopped. He didn't want the thing around him in the car. He wound down the window, and picked up the tiny parcel to toss out the window.

Then he hesitated, thinking maybe he should get out and give it a decent burial. It was his brother's baby, after all, with a big head and tiny little fingers.

But it was dead, just as stupidly and uselessly as Danny was dead. So what difference did it make anyway.

With a shudder, he threw the bloody mess into some roadside weeds.

Danny forgive me.

He drove another ten yards, stopped again, and this time cried--sobbed really, great big convulsive gasps that squeezed out of him one after another, howls of pain which he couldn't stop.

It wasn't just the baby, or Jane, or even his brother (buried now under a ton of dirt). It was life. *His* life. The ugliness of it, the futility. He had tried to help Danny, getting him involved in the coke-running business, only to watch him become just another corpse, like Jane. She was screwed up, too, but maybe more screwed up because he, MJ, had slept with her one night and kicked her out of his apartment the next.

A sudden thought intruded--a thought about Cassie. She literally was the only un-screwed up person who had ever entered his life. It was true. Danny, Jane, his Mom and Dad, Peggy, Lee--every one of them was a fuck-up. Only Cassie was whole. No wonder she didn't want anything to do with him.

A bird fluttered close to his windshield and disappeared into the trees between MJ and the back of the old Republic Steel Youngstown works. Beyond some corrugated buildings and riveted storage tanks rose three metal towers, each with a tall smokestack--blast furnaces where iron ore and coke was turned, under extreme temperatures and hot air blasts, into molten iron. But the mill was closed and empty, the steel towers rusting, and the smokestacks poking impotently into the sky.

How could such a vast facility, the work of several generations, simply shutter up and go away, bleeding all of Youngstown's prosperity with it? No jobs, everyone on food stamps and welfare, drugs on every street corner. What the hell happened?

Maybe the commie Robert was right. The steel mill owners had raped the workers, stolen from them their youth and power, then left them lying face down in the dirt.

Or maybe it was more complicated. His father never thought he was raped. He thought he was lucky. But he also seemed to think that there would always be work for strong men like himself, that being steady and showing up was all that mattered, that the union, if not the company, would take care of him. At 48, he wasn't moving to any God-damned plant in Texas when he had a home and a family right here in Youngstown.

MJ's emotions finally quieted enough for him to drive again, but he felt empty and alone. Cassie was leaving tomorrow and he had to see her one more time. Maybe he could stop her from leaving, or maybe not. But he at least had to try, because he loved her and didn't know how he could go on without her now.

His pager sounded and he saw that it was Peggy's number. He wondered what she had found about Lee.

But first, Cassie.

***

It was mid-afternoon when he pulled up at the Wick Park house where Cassie lived, an imposing Victorian house with a colonnaded porch and a fairy-tale castle turret. Once grand, it now was weathered and shabby, with peeling paint and overgrown shrubbery that almost obscured the entrance. It had long since been broken into several apartments and was mostly occupied by student nurses from the school seeking cheap rent.

Cassie shared a room on the ground floor in the front, a former sitting room, now accessed by a makeshift foyer off the far end of the porch. The foyer door was locked and MJ rang Cassie's bell. He wasn't at all sure she would be home, but the apartment was closer than the school so he had decided to stop at the house first.

He rang the bell a second time, wondering whether it was working, when Jennifer Black, Cassie's roommate, came to the door. Jennifer knew him from when he had been dating Cassie over a year earlier.

"Oh, MJ, hello," she said, a frown on her face as she tried to process his unexpected appearance. "Are you going to Minneapolis too?"

"Minneapolis?"

"For the peace thing. The rally. Cassie's got protest signs all over her room."

"Is she in?"

"She's packing. I'll let her know you're here."

She started to close the door but MJ stopped her. "She's expecting me," he said.

Jennifer shrugged and led him across the makeshift foyer to an awkwardly placed wall which carved off their apartment. They passed through a flimsy door into a large, high-ceilinged room, with curtains over the windows to the porch.

Jennifer knocked at a closed bedroom door and called, "Cassie, your friend's here." Then she plopped into an oversized armchair in front of a droning TV, which she apparently had been watching. "Ever see *Another World*?" she called to MJ, motioning for him to have a seat. "It's really good."

But just then the door opened and Cassie was standing there, in faded blue jeans and a blousy pink top. To MJ she looked beautiful, even though it was obvious that her hair was tangled and her eyes puffy from crying.

"What do you want?" she said. He could tell from her tone that she was unhappy and upset.

"Cassie, can we talk a minute?"

"I told you we're through," she said sharply.

Jennifer looked up at them, surprised to see them arguing but interested in a soap-opera kind of way.

"I didn't come here for that."

"What then?" said Cassie, her voice rising. "To play your honcho businessman game again? Why can't you just leave me alone?"

"Cassie," he said, touching her forearm to calm her.

She gave him a shove. "Get out, get out, just get out of my life!" she screamed.

Jennifer popped up from the couch, looking alarmed now.

"It's okay," MJ said to her.

"Nothing's okay!" said Cassie. "Nothing's like you said it would be!" She turned and ran into her room.

But she left the door open. MJ took that as an invitation and followed her inside, closing it behind for privacy.

She sat on the edge of her bed, angrily wiping tears from her eyes. She had been packing for her trip and the suitcase lay splayed open on the bed. Against the wall were stacks of professionally-printed protest signs, "No U.S. Weapons in Space" and "Stop Reagan," with the president's face wrinkled and melting.

MJ moved some nursing books and sat in a chair at the desk. "Cassie, something bad happened."

She gave a bitter laugh. "Something bad always happens around you. Or haven't you noticed?"

He knew she was angry at him. Well, that was no surprise. She had every right to be angry. He pursed his lips and said nothing.

Her glare softened and she looked away. "What is it? Did you murder him?"

He flinched. "No, not that," keeping his voice level. "There was a girl that Danny was dating, a girl named Jane." He paused, not sure what to tell. "She got hit by a car this morning. Right in front of me."

Cassie put her hand over her mouth, then pulled it away. "I'm sorry to hear that. Is she okay?

"No," said MJ. "She's dead."

Concern flickered across Cassie's face before she re-composed it. "How did it happen?" she asked.

"She was flipped out on crack. I tried to help her but she ran and... she got hit. Really bad."

"Okay," said Cassie, her features softening. "I'm sorry you had to see that." She looked at him speculatively, as if wondering if he were possibly redeemable. "Is that why you came?"

He thought of the little grey baby and shuddered. "Well, that--and something else."

"What?" she said.

"That girl, she... she had something with her. Wrapped up in a handkerchief."

He looked up at her helplessly, not sure how to get out the words. He felt his eyes once more tearing up and he brushed them quickly with his hand.

Cassie saw the gesture and was looking at him closely now, with tenderness--and worry.

"What was it, Michael?" she prodded. "What did she have? Drugs?"

His cheeks were burning and he turned away, wiping his face with his sleeve and despising himself the way Cassie must despise him for his weakness.

"It, ah... it... it..." His eyes continued to water. He didn't know why the thought of the dead baby affected him so much. Something about it touched something in him. Maybe the waste, maybe the futility--maybe just the sadness of knowing that the baby's potential had been trampled and cut short.

Cassie, who had never seen MJ cry, had dropped her guardedness and was looking on him now without judgment--her eyes soft and loving, the way they used to look at him before he has messed everything up.

"What was it?" she said softly. "You can tell me."

"It was a baby, okay? My brother's baby that he had with Jane." He buried his face in his hands for a moment, then looked up. "And Cassie, it was so small! No bigger than my thumb. And it never had a chance."

He felt the tears coming and running down his face. He dropped his face into his hands again to hide the tears, and turned from Cassie. "The crack must of made her miscarry," he choked out.

He heard her rise and come toward him.

"Michael," she said, and she was there and her hand touched his shoulder to comfort him.

Chapter Twenty

Smoke Disappeared into Air

H e rose and hugged her to him, not sexually, but greedy for the love and understanding he hungered for. He found himself breathing in short little breaths, like a drowning man coming back to life.

"Oh, Cassie," he said. "I need you so much."

He clung to her tightly, his hands on her back, her body tight against his, his face in her soft, fragrant hair. He had to stop her from marrying Robert. He couldn't let her go. He couldn't live without her. There would never be another one like her.

And she wasn't stiff and resisting. She seemed soft, willing. He had to make her understand, now, while he still had her in his arms.

He kissed her neck, her ears.

"Cassie, I screwed up," he whispered. "You're the only good thing that ever happened to me. I'm so sorry for the way I hurt you. I never meant to. I only wanted to make you happy."

He drew her back so he could look her in the eyes. "Please forgive me, Cassie. Forgive me. I promise you I'll change. I'll never hurt you again, ever."

Her eyes stayed on his a long time. He wanted to kiss her so bad. But he had to have her forgiveness.

She looked away, then back at him. "What about Lee?" she said.

"He killed my brother," MJ said.

He could feel her stiffen. "You don't know that," she said. "And even if he did--will you leave him to the police?"

He could feel her, perfectly balanced, ready to pull away. He tried to kiss her but she put her hand between them. "Will you?"

She was so close. This was his last, his only, chance.

"Yes," he said.

"And the drugs? You'll stop all that?"

"If that's what you want," he conceded, all the fight out of him now. "But we'll be poor. I won't have any money."

"I don't care," said Cassie. "I'll have you."

She looked up at him, her eyes, a golden hazel, open wide. Her hand dropped from between their bodies and she hugged him tight. They kissed, a passionate, soft and loving kiss that seemed to melt the hard spike in MJ's chest.

"I love you, Michael," Cassie said. "You don't know how much I've longed and waited, hoping you would leave all that ugliness."

The bed was right there, a step away. Trembling with desire, he swept the suitcase aside and sat on the mattress, pulling her to him. They lay back on their sides and kissed again, MJ with his hand on her hip, no hurry now, everything would unfold, everything would work out, or so he hoped, it was hard to think with Cassie's lips on his, her tongue touching his, the soft skin of her neck, the heave of her breasts.

But bubbling up from beneath all that, like a worm burrowing through flesh, came the thought of Lee. The cops would never get Lee, no, he was too smart for them. He'd get away with it, just like Jimmy Verduci had gotten away with raping Kate Parknavy. The outrage on Danny's life would go unavenged, just like the outrage on Kate Parknavy--and where was the justice in that?

Even as Cassie moved nearer to him, brushing her fingers along the rim of his ear, new worries swirled in MJ's head. Maybe he had promised Cassie too much and too soon, he needed time to sort things out. But there wasn't any time, and there weren't any good choices. It was like that day when the brakes gave out on his '64 Impala. The memory was chillingly clear. He was rolling down Gypsy Lane when the brakes failed, with busy Federal Street coming up at the bottom. He had to decide whether to gun the car through against the light--risking a collision--or to try to thread the car through the school playground, steering around the little kids. Either way someone could get killed.

That time he had gunned through the intersection, and the crash that followed sent two people to the hospital though he himself was unscathed. Now he had to decide whether he could really keep his promise to Cassie. Getting out of the drug business would mean the end of easy cash, but he could learn to live with that if Cassie was by his side. But could he really trust that dingus Proferes to actually catch Lee?

He would have to decide, *really* decide, and fast.

His pager, under his right side, buzzed. He knew it had to be Peggy. He tried to ignore it and keep kissing Cassie, but it buzzed, and buzzed, and buzzed, until finally he reached down to shut it off.

Cassie looked at him. "Who is that?"

"My sister."

"Your sister, how do you know?"

He pulled the pager from his belt and showed her the little red display. "That's her number, see?"

"You're going to get rid of that thing now, right?" she said.

"I don't know," he said. "It's kinda handy."

"Really?" Cassie said.

She sat up, the mood ruined. "Well? Aren't you going to call her?"

"My sister? She can wait."

"I think you should call her," she said. She pointed to her nightstand, "The phone's right there."

MJ realized it was a test. She obviously thought Peggy was one of his drug contacts.

What the hell. He had to talk to Peggy anyway. He went to the phone, stood at the nightstand and dialed, with Cassie sitting up in bed watching.

"Hey, Sis," he said, when she answered.

"Where the hell have you been? I've been trying to call you. Didn't you get my page?"

"I've been busy," he said, with a reassuring smile at Cassie. She couldn't possibly hear what Peggy was saying but might have picked up on her angry tone. "What's up?"

"What's up is I found Lee is what's up," Peggy said. "But he's not at Mindi's house. He's at his aunt's."

Cassie had her arms folded now, watching him.

"His aunt? How do you know?" MJ asked, his voice serious now.

"My bartender friend talked to Mindi. Lee was with her but they had a fight and Mindi kicked him out. She said he went to his Aunt Jane's house in Steelton."

"You have an address?" he asked, turning away from Cassie to face the wall.

"1146 Waverly Avenue," Peggy said. "Across from the old Ohio Works."

There was a pen and pad on the nightstand and MJ wrote the address down, with a nervous look around to see if Cassie was still watching.

She was--intently.

He turned back to the phone. "Is he there now?" he asked.

"So far as I know. Mindi says he's laying low because word's out about Danny's murder."

"Okay, thanks."

"What are you going to do?" Peggy asked.

"What do you think?" he said, excited. He was too close now to let go of Lee, but Cassie would never accept that. The only way was, she didn't have to know.

"Be careful," Peggy said.

"Don't worry about me," MJ said, and hung up.

When he turned, a pillow whizzed past his head.

"*You fucking asshole,*" Cassie screamed. She was standing, angry as hell, at the end of the bed. "Your sister, huh?"

"Yeah, it was my sister."

"Right. 'Don't worry about me.' And now you're going over to some address to buy drugs."

"That's not what we talked about," MJ said.

"Bullshit!" Cassie screamed. "You are such a liar. I can't believe I fell for it again."

He took a step toward her to calm her but she stepped back and poked him in the chest. "Don't you know how much you hurt me, pretending to be a businessman just to get me in the sack? Telling me you loved me to suck me into your pathetic world of drugs and--and murder. I cried for weeks because of you."

He grabbed her wrist to keep her from poking him again. "Yes I lied. But I apologized for that. And I never meant to hurt you."

But she poked him with her other hand. "And then you come in here and butter me up and lie to me again. "'I need you, Cassie. I love you, Cassie.' Lies, all lies."

He grabbed her other hand and she tried to pull away. He pulled her to him and put his arms around her so she would listen.

"I do love you, Cassie. God only knows how I love you."

She wiggled from his embrace.

"Get out," she said. "Go to your stupid drug deal."

"Cassie, you've got it all wrong."

"Go to hell, you liar. I'll never believe another word you say. Now get out." She pulled open the door. "Get out!"

MJ suddenly realized the true depth of what had just happened. He had blown his last and final chance with her.

Defeated, he stepped out of the door, not even reacting when it slammed behind him.

So be it. He wasn't going to beg. Without a word, he brushed past a horrified Jennifer and left.

***

It was after five when he left Cassie's house. The sun was still shining, but with peculiar hazy light that seemed to drain everything of color, making the already-ugly grey buildings uglier and greyer. The address Peggy had given him was in Steelton, 10 miles north, and he turned onto Himrod and headed downtown. Somehow Youngstown had never looked more depressing--the brown trees, the weedy lawns, the boxy houses with falling-down porches and broken-down cars. When he reached Federal the homes gave way to dilapidated warehouses and closed businesses, after which came the parking lots and soot-covered brick buildings of downtown. The streets were empty and deserted, lifeless.

The way MJ felt.

All right, so he couldn't have Cassie. Fine. He didn't need Cassie or anybody. What an asshole he was for thinking she could ever understand. She puzzled him. Her mother was a whore and her daddy a runaway, so it wasn't like she grew up with a silver spoon in her mouth. She had told him some stories that made his hair curl, so she knew what it could be like on the streets. Yet she seemed to expect more of him than he or anyone could ever give.

The real problem, he knew, was those fucking nuns, who had filled her head with so much crap she couldn't escape, even though she had dropped the Catholic religion and was about to become--if that asshole Appel had his way--a full-fledged commie. Somehow she thought life was rainbows and unicorns when really it was Kate Parknavy, her skirt hiked up, a knife at her throat and Jimmy Verduci's dick shoved up her cunt.

And Kate's big eyes pleading with MJ for help. Instead of running he should have taken his chances and wrestled Verduci for the knife. If he didn't stab the bastard's guts out at least he would have gone down a man.

Kill or be killed, that was the law of the street, the only law that mattered now in Youngstown. Men were animals and the city was a cesspool and only the strong survived. The jungle law. That's the way it had been for thousands of years and that's the way it would always be. It didn't have to make sense.

Lee, that piece of shit, it would be a pleasure to put a bullet through his heart, or better yet blow off the back of his head the same way he killed Danny. Danny would get his justice.

Then MJ heard himself and laughed. Danny was dead and gone, smoke disappeared into the air. It wasn't about justice, that was just another rainbow story weak people told themselves. It was about strength, power, respect. MJ needed to kill Lee to prove to himself he was a man now, not the little-boy-ball-less coward who had run away and let Kate Parknavy get raped. And when he whacked Lee, word would get out, and nobody would ever fuck with him or his family again.

And if he didn't, if Lee killed him instead...

Then it wouldn't matter for shit what people said or didn't say. He would be smoke, too. Everything would be over and the pain would be gone.

So screw Cassie.

Screw it all.

The one thing he had left to do in life was to kill Lee Messina.

No more fucking around.

***

A quarter hour later MJ arrived in Steelton, famous as the former site of U.S. Steel's gargantuan Ohio Works, once the largest steel producer in the world. As he descended toward the address Peggy had given him, MJ could see the half-demolished remains of the mill spread out on the flats along the Mahoning River.

For decades the Ohio Works had seethed with activity, its blast furnaces relentlessly ladling out tons of liquid iron and pouring red smoke into the valley. Thousands were employed it its blooming, billeting and finishing mills, which literally stretched for miles up the river, and more thousands worked the ore loaders along the railway, tested the purity of the steel, and drove 18-wheelers loaded with coils, sheet bars and plates of steel from Youngstown to every part of the country. Steelton and nearby Girard were thriving towns, with restaurants, theaters, doctors, churches--everything to keep the worker and his family safe and secure, to make sure the river of steel never stopped flowing.

Now the mill, closed and demolished to make way for an "industrial park," looked like it had been bombed by the Nazis. The four huge blast furnaces had been famously razed some three years earlier and now were nothing more than a heap of girders and debris, the steel scrapped and sent to Japan for recycling. All of the towering smokestacks were gone too, but several conveyor structures and some immense production buildings remained, either fenced off or in the process of being torn down. Huge piles of rubble towered in every direction. While he watched, a lone yellow Caterpillar excavator poked about in the remnants of a bunker-like building by the tracks, reducing brick walls to rubble with its bucket.

As for the industrial park, a single new, pre-fab structure had been erected in the middle of a flattened plain of weeds and mud. It had a dozen garage doors and a sign that MJ was able to make out as he neared the bottom of the hill, "Youngstown Mini-Storage."

MJ shook his head in disbelief; a thousand storage warehouses wouldn't replace a tenth of the industry that had been knocked flat to the ground.

He turned left onto Waverly, a long street of two-story company houses facing across the tracks toward the remains of the mill. When he reached the 900 block, he pulled over beside a slant-roof structure along the tracks where his vehicle would be well-concealed.

His only weapon was the Browning 9 mm, but it should do the job if he surprised Lee like he intended. He inserted the clip, put a round in the chamber and de-cocked the piece. Then he dumped the spare ammo into his pockets and, with an air of finality, tossed the empty ammo carton on the passenger-side floor.

He was as ready as he was ever going to be. He took a deep breath and got out of the car.

The first step was to reconnoiter the place--to see if Lee was in the house and figure out how to take him. But he would have to proceed cautiously. MJ would be spotted for sure if he just walked up the street, and the houses were all on a hillside facing the mill, with no alley that would let him approach from behind.

His best bet were the tracks. Four parallel railroad tracks, rusted and disused, ran along the edge of the mill property, with a ditch and a line of scraggly trees between the rails and Waverly Avenue.

The ditch and trees provided good cover, and MJ began picking his way north toward his target, moving stealthily to avoid attracting attention. Not that there was much in the way of attention to attract. The row of closely-spaced identical houses--employee houses built by the company in the 30s--seemed strangely deserted, with empty windows and empty porches under sharply peaked roofs of asphalt shingles. The only signs of life were the starlings on the overhead wires and the incessant yapping of a dog in the distance. There weren't even many cars parked on the street. Maybe the workers had been demolished with the steel mills, MJ thought sourly.

Whatever had happened to his city? Did big-wig executives really destroy it all to live in new houses in Texas? Had the unions gotten so greedy the owners actually couldn't turn a buck? Or was it all just some cosmic joke, like Father Marchuk getting killed by the falling brick? Maybe God was poking a stick in man's proud creation the way MJ used to poke a stick in the ants' little anthill, to watch them panic and see what they would do.

Chapter Twenty-One

Fight is On

Ten minutes later, MJ was in place across from 1146, shielded from view by a copse of stunted sumac trees. A well-tended bed of daffodils and pansies lined the base of the house, with a yellow forsythia bush punctuating the steps. Old woman flowers, MJ thought--Lee's aunt's doings. A wind chime hung in the corner of the front porch, along with a wide wooden porch swing like the one his Mom used to like to sit on. He saw no movement, however, in the home's windows, and Lee's car was nowhere in sight, so he was out somewhere.

MJ considered what he'd do when Lee came back. If Lee parked his car in front of the aunt's porch, MJ would have a clear shot at him as he ascended the stairs to the front entrance. But the shot would be long, even if he braced the pistol on his elbows as he lay prone.

A better set-up suggested itself. The long narrow houses were only a dozen feet apart, and on the entrance side the neighbor's house appeared deserted. If MJ worked his way around it, he could conceal himself in the side yard and get an easy shot at Lee from twenty feet as he came up the steps. One shot and lights out; Lee would never know what hit him.

The only danger was being seen by a neighbor as he crossed the street--or even by Lee if he were somehow in the house. But the neighborhood seemed dead, and he could backtrack the way he came and cross far away from the aunt's house.

Decision made, he edged his way carefully out of his hiding place and began walking the ditch back in the direction he had come to get himself into position.

After walking back an entire block, MJ clambered up out of the ditch and started to cross the roadway--at a walking pace so as not to appear suspicious should anyone be watching.

He was almost to the opposite side when, far down the road to his left, a car turned the corner and started up Waverly toward him. MJ recognized it immediately as Lee's white Camaro. His mouth went dry and his hand reached toward his waist band for his gun, but the car was still a block away and he forced himself to relax and keep walking slowly--across the cracked asphalt, across the gravel margin of the road, across the ankle-deep lawn--until he reached the safety of the narrow space between two houses. There he lay on the ground behind the cover of a small lilac bush and waited for Lee's car to pass, his pistol drawn and cocked in case Lee had spotted him.

Lee drove by, however, without so much as a glance up the hill toward MJ's hiding place. His figure was shaded by the roof of the car, but there was no mistaking his outline, or the familiar white tee he liked to wear to show off his boxer shoulders. There was a passenger in the car with him, but obscured by Lee. The car bounced once on its springs as it hit a rough patch of road, then disappeared up the street, gone in a flash.

There was no way Lee could have spotted him.

Relieved, MJ stood and edged far enough toward the road so that he could see up the street, using the corner of a porch for cover.

Lee had pulled the Camaro up to the front of the house, the car parked parallel to the road but in the opposite direction of traffic. He emerged from the driver's seat, walked to the back of the vehicle and opened the trunk. Meanwhile, a skinny grey-haired woman in a flowery sun-dress climbed out of the passenger side and joined him. Lee handed her two bags of groceries before off-loading what looked like a 50 pound bag of potting soil.

The woman--Lee's aunt, presumably--started up the steps to the house. Lee closed the trunk and picked up the big bag of soil. Impossible as it seemed, Lee appeared unarmed. He liked to carry his Glock tucked into his waistband at the small of his back, but, as he bent for the soil, MJ could see no telltale bulge. Maybe the gun was inside the house? Or in the car?

In any case, Lee toted the bag up the steps, left it on the porch and followed his aunt indoors.

MJ's felt his initial plan going to pieces. He was too late to ambush Lee as he entered the house, and now Lee might not re-emerge for hours, maybe not until morning. And if he did come out and MJ wasn't in position, Lee could jump in his car and disappear for another day, week or month.

Long shadows were beginning to spread across the ruins of the mill and the sun would be setting soon. Having come this far, MJ couldn't risk Lee getting away.

A new plan gradually came into focus. MJ noted that all of the houses were identical and had two windows on the entrance side. The one toward the front was too high to look into because of the sloping ground, but the one at the rear was waist-level.

MJ crept up to the home in front of him and peered inside. The window looked across a small kitchen to a dining area opposite. So it would be possible to get a shot at Lee inside, while he was standing at the fridge or eating spaghetti at the table. The thin window glass would pose no obstacle, and MJ wouldn't have to wait around for hours for Lee to come out.

Decision made, MJ slowly picked his way through the back yards of the old homes, the sun dipping below the ridge of the hillside and the sky gradually darkening.

By the time MJ worked his way into position beside the kitchen window of Lee's aunt's house, darkness had descended and the air had grown chill. The kitchen was empty and dark, but wan light from the living room illuminated it clearly enough that MJ could see the layout, the same as the other house--counter and appliances along the near wall, dinette table in the far corner near the back door. When Lee entered the kitchen, MJ would have a clear shot.

He waited, gun in hand. He could hear the tv in the living room, tuned to what sounded like Tim Taylor on the Cleveland news, and voices periodically talking. From this angle, MJ could see only a sliver of the living room wall, but he pictured

Lee and his aunt on the couch in front of a big Zenith console, the aunt with her legs comfortably curled up, Lee sprawling and bored, his guard down.

Perfect.

He waited, the moon sailing overhead through scattered shreds of clouds.

It was cold and getting colder. He should have thrown on the sweatshirt from the back of the car. Instead he buttoned up his white church shirt and shifted his weight from side to side to ward off the cold creeping into his feet.

The news gave way to *The A-Team*, and then *Dallas*. Christ, how much tv could they stand? MJ considered breaking into the house through the back door, but through the kitchen window he could see it was double-locked with both a deadbolt and a chain.

He waited, the moon climbing higher.

Finally he saw a shadow stir in the living room as a figure rose from the couch. MJ's pistol was up and pointed at the window as he assumed a two-handed firing position. The kitchen light flicked on, almost blinding MJ, whose eyes had adjusted to the darkness.

It was the aunt.

The grey-haired woman sauntered to the stove, lit a burner with a match, and put a battered kettle on the flame. From a cabinet overhead, she took down a mug and a tea bag and waited in front of the stove for the water to boil.

MJ lowered his gun and moved back away from the window so as not to be spotted in the light now spilling out into the yard.

Just then, Lee entered. MJ raised the pistol but held his fire as Lee moved behind his aunt, giving her a peck on the neck as he stood behind her.

The two talked. MJ held the gun steady, waiting for Lee and the woman to separate. The aunt reached up into the cabinet for a second tea mug, dropped in a tea bag and filled it with boiling water.

When she turned to hand it to Lee, he finally took a slight step to the side.

MJ aimed at his chest and began to slowly squeeze the trigger. Simultaneously, inside, Lee bobbled the hand-off of the cup, spilling hot water down his shirt and jumping back.

Blam! The quiet night shattered like the glass in the window. Lee fell to the ground as the woman screamed and cowered.

MJ thought the shot had connected and lowered his gun, but suddenly Lee sprang to his feet and scrambled through the living room door unharmed.

MJ, incredibly, had missed.

A second later the front door slammed and then Lee's head poked around the corner of the house--sighting down the barrel of the 12 gauge Mossberg.

MJ, scrambling for cover around the corner of the neighbor's house, slipped on the wet grass just as the blast of the shotgun blew a hole in the siding where his head had been. He heard Lee pump another shell into the chamber and adrenaline propelled him up and around the corner just as Lee let loose with a second blast, this one taking out the molding from the corner of the house.

MJ kept going, scrambling desperately through the neighbor's yard until he had the whole house between himself and Lee. He ran toward the street front, hoping to surprise Lee from that angle. However, a glimpse through the porch railing showed that Lee was running furiously for his car, the shotgun gripped in his right hand.

Cursing, MJ steadied the Browning against the corner of the house, but his hands were shaking so violently that he couldn't hold a sight pattern. Lee had reached the driver side door and was fumbling with his keys. If he got in the car and took off, MJ knew it might take another month to find him. Lee had to be stopped--now.

MJ fought to steady his hands, but before he could get off a shot, Lee caught sight of him and swung the shotgun in MJ's direction. The shot went high and wide, blasting down a hanging plant as MJ dove for cover.

MJ crawled to the edge of the home's concrete block foundation and took a stupid, emotion-fueled shot at Lee, but the distance was too great and he missed.

Lee pumped the shotgun and pulled the trigger, but it clicked dully on an empty chamber. Cursing, he tossed the empty shotgun aside and dove over the Camaro's hood, trying to enter the car from the passenger side.

MJ scrambled over the block retaining wall and ran into the street, where he would be able to get a better shot at Lee.

But Lee, seeing MJ coming, abandoned his attempt to open the car and dashed across the road into the scrub, toward the ruined buildings of the mill.

Frustrated, MJ raised the gun and took three quick shots--all to no effect. Like it or not, Lee was out of range. The old steel plant was hundreds of acres of rubble and deserted buildings, and MJ knew that if he lost Lee in that mess, there would be no finding him.

MJ plunged into the brush, catching his belt loop on a branch, and after a moment of struggle to free himself scrambled up the drainage ditch to the line of parallel tracks. In the moonlight, he could see Lee a hundred feet ahead, too far off for a shot. But MJ was loathe to let Lee get away. Hoping for a miracle, he raised his gun, took aim and fired.

The gun's loud retort left MJ's ears ringing, but missed Lee completely. As he watched, Lee leaped a barricade and followed a rail spur across a small bridge onto the grounds of the mill. Up ahead on the left was some kind of overhead trestle roofed with a shed.

Only as Lee moved toward and under it did MJ realize the structure's huge scale. The elaborate steel truss work was as big as a small bridge, and the shed it carried large enough to drive a bus through.

Lee moved under the truss work and disappeared from sight.

MJ followed. With a start, MJ realized that the slanting structure had to house the conveyor system that fed raw materials to the blast furnace. As a kid, his fourth grade class, led by Father Wilson and Sister Mary Joseph, had toured the Republic Steel plant in Hazelton. One of the sights they had viewed was the conveyor, a wide belt carrying a river of ore, coke and limestone swiftly upward through the long slanted tunnel of the shed to the top of the blast furnace. MJ had been impressed by the conveyor's impossible length and the noise of its operation, and even got to handle some iron ore, which looked like black rock.

This structure before him, with its length and steep upward slant, had to be the same thing.

A path led into the shadows underneath and MJ followed it, straining to pick out Lee in the darkness. Then, in the moonlit shadows between the trusses, he saw Lee pull himself onto a steel ladder and disappear up into the conveyor structure.

MJ quickly followed, hoisting himself up the rusty ladder rung over rung some twenty feet into the air, until he finally reached a small platform with a door leading into the structure.

The door was ajar. Pistol in hand, MJ nudged it open and peered into the dark interior. Moonlight seeped inside, throwing sharp blue light into the blackness. As his eyes adjusted, he could make out machinery that indeed proved to be an ore conveyor like the one he had seen as a kid. A catwalk ran parallel, but Lee was nowhere to be seen.

MJ stepped inside.

Without warning, MJ found himself knocked flat, his gun slipping away as he threw out his hands for balance. Lee had dropped onto him from a truss in the ceiling, and now quickly wrapped a noose around MJ's neck, twisting it viciously and cutting off MJ's breath.

MJ flailed and gasped for air, even as the noose--Lee's belt, MJ realized--pulled tighter. Panicky, MJ strained to get his fingers under the leather, realizing that if he didn't break Lee's stranglehold, he would die right there.

"You want a fight, pussy boy?" Lee taunted, the way he used to taunt MJ when they fought in the ring. "I'll give you a fight."

In the dim moonlight filtering in, MJ saw his gun lying on the grate near his right hand. He reached for it, straining under Lee's weight to get the extra inches of extension he needed. With the noose, Lee twisted MJ's torso away from the weapon and gave the gun a kick, sending it skittering across the catwalk and over the side under the conveyor rollers.

MJ heard it slide and clatter for what seemed like forever, down into the bowels of the machinery--lost.

"No gun, pussy boy," Lee said, planting his knee in MJ's back for greater leverage as he pulled on the belt. "Just you and me."

Despair gripped MJ. Streaks of light like twirling sparklers danced in his eyes and he realized he was only moments away from blacking out.

He had to do something to break Lee's choke hold. *Now.*

Forcing himself to stop struggling with the belt, MJ braced his hands on the catwalk, then heaved himself up, grabbing the back of Lee's head and rolling him off his shoulders.

Lee smashed flat on his back onto the catwalk, grunting and momentarily losing purchase on the belt. Then he once more twisted the strands of leather in his hands, straining with the effort.

But now MJ was on his knees above his opponent. Even as the sparkles began to return, MJ tried to find some way to press his advantage. Desperately, he threw an arm and then a leg off over Lee's prone body, until finally he could get above and straddle him.

Lee spread his hands, trying to pull the ends of the belt tighter, but MJ stomped down on Lee's awkwardly-turned elbow. Lee gave a howl of pain and released the strap.

The chokehold broken, MJ tore the belt from his neck and gulped in a huge gasp of air, trying to fill his lungs with air. However, he had only managed that single breath when Lee brought his knee up into MJ's groin and squirmed out from under him, twisting as he stood to hook his left fist into MJ's head.

MJ shuddered and tried to regain his wits as Lee came at him again, this time with a right.

Reflexively, MJ raised a hand to block the punch. Like the time Jimmy Verduci had attacked him with the knife, MJ felt a jolt of overwhelming, primal fear. The fear shot through him like an electric jolt and, involuntarily, he sprang to his feet and stumbled back, away from Lee's attack. He had to catch his breath, put some distance between himself and Lee.

He turned and ran wildly up the sloping catwalk, his heart about to burst his chest, fear in full control now.

Lee followed behind, close enough at one point to grab at MJ's shirt. Adrenaline pushed MJ even faster and he sprinted ahead, only stopping when he finally realized he had out-distanced Lee. MJ turned and saw him hunched against the railing of the catwalk some 30 feet below, winded.

"You can't run, pussy boy," Lee said between breaths. "I'm coming for you."

More rational now, MJ grabbed the handrail and forced himself to continue upward, trying to make himself think. Lee was the better fighter but MJ had fought and beaten him before. So why was he so afraid now? Why was he so weak?

Shame burned through him. He had run from Jimmy Verduci, and what had that brought? Kate Parknavy raped and dead. Was he now going to run from Lee as well? In his innermost being, MJ knew he couldn't afford to be a coward this time. It was kill or be killed, the law of the jungle. He cursed himself for losing the Browning.

Fifty yards ahead, at the top of the catwalk, a crescent of moonlit clouds marked the end of the conveyor. MJ's lungs ached and he wanted desperately to sit, to get control of his breath, but Lee was coming on steadily, keeping up the pressure. MJ knew Lee's tactics and realized he wouldn't give him a chance to get his breath. Lee would keep pushing and pushing until they reached the top, and there he would press the fight.

So be it. MJ would make Lee pay for Danny's murder, or he would be killed himself.

Chapter Twenty-Two

Deserves to Die

MJ gulped down the fear he felt rising again and continued to climb up the catwalk toward the opening above. He needed a plan, but he had no idea what lay beyond the apex of the conveyor--whether there was another structure beyond, or a ladder to descend.

One thing was for certain: there was no longer any blast furnace. Everyone knew the huge furnaces at the Ohio Works had been blown apart with explosives several years earlier. MJ remembered seeing it on Walter Cronkite--the spectators, the explosions and the four huge multi-story blast furnaces crumbling slowly to the ground like dying giants, crumpling into clouds of dust.

So where did the conveyor lead, what was at the top now? The crescent of the opening above gradually grew bigger, the backdrop of clouds more distinct.

A plan, he needed a plan. But he couldn't form a plan until he knew what was waiting at the top. MJ could barely breathe, let alone think. The slope was as steep as the bleachers in high school where he used to train, and he concentrated on putting one foot in front of the other.

Now he was twenty yards away, then ten. He could see nothing but sky through the opening. Behind him, Lee.

Grimly, he forced himself forward, into the cold wind gusting in from the sky.

Then, finally, the enclosing shed came to an end and he was outside on a railed rectangular platform--suspended in mid-air.

It was a fifteen story drop to the black ground below, and MJ gripped the railing of the platform, fighting off vertigo.

On either side of him in the distance, MJ could see the lights of Steelton and Girard, but there was a yawning gap at the end of the platform where the stairway to a lower level had been ripped away. Once, apparently, the conveyor had dumped the steelmaking materials into a hopper a level below to feed the maw of the blast furnace--but now there was no blast furnace, no hopper, and only twisted remnants of the old second level, hanging and destroyed.

Lee was still climbing toward the platform, his face grim and determined.

There was no other way down, no stairwells or ladders. This was where MJ was going to have to fight Lee.

"Get ready for your maker, pussy boy," Lee hollered up.

MJ knew verbal intimidation was just another of Lee's fight tactics, but he felt unnerved just the same.

Desperately he looked around the platform for a weapon. He was standing on rectangle of screened grating, eight by twenty, with the conveyor on one side and a gaping hole on the far end, where the stairs had been shorn away.

But MJ saw nothing he could use as a weapon and he had no plan and suddenly Lee was on the platform with him, already hands-up in his boxing stance and closing in.

"Here it comes, pussy boy," he shouted, and then poked-out his quick left jab, a feeler punch for most boxers but one Lee had once used to knock MJ out cold.

MJ reacted instinctively with a down parry, already on the defensive, and countered with a jab of his own, all the while trying to think.

Lee parried his jab and countered with a jab and a cross.

MJ blocked those punches and stepped back out of Lee's range, keeping an eye on Lee's strong hand, his right. In Golden Gloves matches, MJ would hang back and try to let Lee exhaust himself, waiting for an opening. But this wasn't Golden Gloves. The narrow platform left little room to maneuver, and the hole in the railing led to death.

And the hole was where Lee--coming at him with a jab to MJ's body--was trying to force him. MJ attempted to cover himself and stay balanced so as to not give up ground, but his elbows were high and Lee's jab connected to his ribs in a sharp jolt of pain.

Lee followed-up with a right cross to MJ's face.

MJ parried and side-stepped, then skipped back several feet, trying to maneuver away from the gap in the rail and somehow get around to Lee's far side.

But Lee pressed his attack now, moving in close, faking a jab to MJ's face and landing a right cross to MJ's stomach that took MJ's breath away and backed him against the rail.

Lee came at him with a left hook.

This was it. MJ couldn't afford to play defense anymore.

MJ blocked Lee's hook, then threw a counter right, which connected squarely with Lee's chin.

Lee shook it off, but MJ saw the furrowed brow that Lee always got when he was rattled.

For the first time, MJ felt hope. He took a quick side step away from the rail, finally getting around the other side so that Lee had his back to the gap.

They traded jabs for a moment before MJ moved in with a right uppercut.

Lee blocked the uppercut and then threw a hard right cross, rotating his hips and upper body to put his entire weight into it.

It connected solidly, and a red jolt of pain exploded in MJ's head.

He felt himself stagger and go down.

***

The hard scrape of the catwalk against his shoulder blades brought MJ back to consciousness, and he realized he had momentarily blacked out. Lee was dragging him by his feet toward the opening in the railing.

The cloying fear rose up in him again, and for a moment it almost overcame him. He forced himself to think of Danny, of Cassie, to summon up some inner power that would squash the fear and finally make him a man, not the little boy who had run from Jimmy Verduci.

Lee was tired, gasping--but he kept jerking MJ closer and closer to the gaping hole in the platform.

MJ gave up trying to make sense of his feelings and kicked, hard.

Lee stumbled back, almost falling through the opening before recovering his balance and jumping onto MJ schoolboy style, trying to finish him off with a rain of punches.

MJ grabbed Lee's arms and wrapped his legs around Lee's waist, impeding the blows and trying to protect his face.

Lee tried to butt MJ's face with his head, then got a hand loose and smashed MJ in his left temple.

Once again MJ saw stars. He had to get Lee under control, fast. A wrestling move he had practiced a hundred times with Danny came back to him, and when Lee pulled his hand back to set up another blow, MJ quickly threw his legs up and around Lee's neck in a choke hold, locking his feet together and compressing Lee's neck.

Lee struggled to break the hold, trying to free himself from the steady pressure of MJ's thighs, then changed tactics and tried to pummel MJ in the temple to get him to release. MJ dodged the blows as best he could, feeling the power going out of Lee's fists as MJ's chock hold tightened and Lee began to lose blood flow to the brain.

MJ twisted Lee's body to the right for even more leverage, and now, finally, Lee began to black out. His arms became rubbery, then stopped working altogether. MJ kept up the pressure until Lee's whole body went limp.

MJ's heart, meanwhile, was pounding, and he could hardly catch his breath. In another minute Lee would be dead. All MJ had to do was keep applying the choke.

But there was one question he wanted answered yet, a question only Lee could answer, and now was the moment.

He kept his legs in place, but released the pressure on Lee's neck.

"Why?" he demanded. "Why did you kill Danny?"

He couldn't see Lee's face but he heard his gasping reply:

"I didn't."

"You lying sack of shit," MJ roared, tightening his legs once more.

"It was Peggy!" Lee screamed, panicking and trying to squirm out of MJ's hold. "Peggy did it. Peggy killed him."

Disgusted, MJ squeezed his thighs together with all of his might.

Lee's body began shuddering uncontrollably as he tried to pry MJ's legs apart. "Peggy killed him... the life insurance... Peggy..." Lee gasped, before finally passing out.

A cold chill swept over MJ, even as he kept up the pressure, choking the life out of Lee.

Lying. Lee had to be lying. What could Peggy possibly have to do with Danny's death?

Peggy.

His sister.

Impossible.

Not Peggy.

Lee was totally unconscious now, lifeless, his tongue lolling.

But Lee had said life insurance, and MJ thought back to the policies he had found in Lee's gym bag.

Could Peggy...?

He let off the pressure from his leg hold and slapped Lee hard on the face, trying to revive him, to bring him back from the brink of death.

Lee suddenly opened his eyes, wide with fear, all the fight out of him.

MJ should have felt triumphant but instead he said, "Answer my questions and I'll let you go. Do you understand?"

Lee brought his hands up to try to ease the pressure from MJ's legs, then croaked out a feeble, "Yes."

"Good," MJ said. "Now tell me, what did you mean about life insurance?"

"Peggy," Lee said hoarsely. "She took out policies on Danny, then killed him for the money."

"You bastard," shouted MJ. "My sister would never do that."

"She did it, I tell you. She was in the car with me, in the backseat. She shot him in the back of the head."

MJ felt sick. Angrily, he applied pressure to Lee's neck. "You fucking liar," he said, clamping down his legs until Lee was again on the point of passing out again.

"It was Peggy!" Lee yelled desperately, his face contorted. Reluctantly, MJ released the pressure. When Lee had found his breath again, he added, "She killed Danny for the money. Don't you see it? She had policies on his life."

The policies MJ had found in Lee's closet. "And so the two of you were going to kill him? After you bought up all those policies in your name?"

"Yes," Lee admitted.

"And you were going to split it? The policies I found in your gym bag?"

"What? No. I bought those after Peggy. They're chump change compared to Peggy's."

MJ was confused. "What do you mean?"

"She has her own policies, that she bought first. She showed them to me in her wood chest. That was how I finally knew she was serious. She was going to kill Danny with or without me. So that's when I got in on the deal."

"So you're saying it was Peggy's idea?"

"She came up with it out of her magazines."

MJ felt a numb chill. "And what about me? Whose idea was the car bomb?"

"Peggy's. She was afraid you'd keep digging, maybe turn us in to that cop."

"And Peggy was the one who shot Danny?"

"I swear to God, MJ! The plan was to just pass him a half-kilo of red rock--you know, crack with strychnine. Peggy figured he'd kill himself if he had enough of it.

"But then she goes and shoots him right there in the car. Shit, I didn't even know she had a gun."

Numbly, he tried to absorb what Lee was saying.

Peggy planned the insurance scam. Peggy was in the car with Lee. Peggy shot Danny, not Lee.

But...

He applied pressure to Lee's neck. "Why would Peggy kill Danny?"

"She said she was fed up," Lee gasped. "She said he was ruining her life. She said he was worth more dead than alive."

He had heard her voice those resentments many times in many different ways over the years, but never took her seriously, never realized she was reaching some sort of breaking point.

Sadly, MJ realized it was true.

His sister had killed their brother.

"Peggy shot him," Lee said. "The policies are in her chest, I swear to God, look for yourself."

If Peggy pulled the trigger, Peggy was the murderer. Peggy, not Lee, was the one who deserved to die.

His gut knotted like it was being squeezed. Lee by his own admission was planning Danny's death, but that was a different thing than putting a gun to his brother's head and pulling the trigger. His crazy fucking sister. How could she do such a thing? How could anyone.

Killing Lee would be satisfying but it wouldn't be right. Leave him to the cops, like Cassie would say.

"I'm going to let you up now," said MJ. "You're going to walk down that conveyor, back to your car and get out of Youngstown. If you're telling the truth, my beef isn't with you. Take your own chances with the police. But if you're lying I will track you down wherever you are and kill you on the spot. Get it?"

"Yeah," said Lee, still gasping in MJ's leg lock. "I get it."

Slowly, MJ unwrapped his legs.

Lee shook himself and got up, slowly. "I should never have listened to her," he said. "But, I swear, I never even thought the bitch was serious until she showed me those policies.

"I'm sorry, MJ. I really am sorry." He extended a hand to help MJ up.

MJ hesitated, then took the hand.

He had barely stood when, in one quick motion, Lee twisted MJ's arm behind his back and frog-marched him toward the gaping hole in the edge of the platform.

In horror, MJ spread his feet, trying to resist Lee's man-handling.

Lee cranked MJ's arm further up his back and shoved even harder.

To his right and left were the lights of the steel towns, and below him, nothing. The fear returned. In a second he would be over the side, and Lee, like Jimmy Verduci, would get away clean.

"No," screamed MJ. In visceral reflex, he twisted and swept Lee's feet out from under him in one fluid motion.

Lee went down and hit the ragged edge of the platform, wind milling his arms, trying to get his balance.

His eyes fixed on MJ, wide with disbelief.

And then he fell over the side, his hoarse cries following him down into the night, then silence.

MJ stepped back and gripped the rail, totally spent.

He put his head over the railing, gorge beginning to rise, then recoiled from the precipice and bent over the grate of the platform instead, heaving until his stomach was empty.

Finally he calmed and stood erect, still gripping the rail tightly.

First Danny, then Jane, and now Lee.

The world made no sense. No fucking sense at all.

And, if Lee was right, it was all because of his sister.

Grimly, he edged his way back off the platform onto the conveyor belt catwalk, dreading what he would have to do if he found the insurance papers in Peggy's cedar chest.

***

When MJ finally made it back to the car, his hands were shaking so badly he could barely jam a cigarette in his mouth and light it.

God knew that Lee deserved to die, but MJ couldn't erase from his mind the look of horror on Lee's face as he fell from the platform.

Lee. They had grown up together--and sure, they'd had some fun times--but somewhere along the line Lee had gone totally off the track. And why? MJ wondered. For money? Lee wasn't hurting for money. What made that shithead think he could murder Danny and get away with it?

But you murdered Lee, a small voice whispered.

No, MJ thought. He had tried to let Lee go, but Lee had forced his hand. MJ hadn't had any choice but to kill him. It was self-defense. Even Cassie would understand that, he felt sure. In fact, he realized with a start that in this instance she might even approve. She always seemed to know what was right and what was wrong.

He threw the shifter on the Nova and headed out of Steelton, toward Youngstown and his sister.

Lee's story had seemed believable in the life-and-death struggle atop the conveyor platform, but now MJ was wracked with doubt.

Peggy couldn't really have shot Danny--could she? She had put up with a lot of shit from him over the years, but deep down inside they all loved and helped one another. Like Mom said, family was all you got.

Lee said that the plan was to sell Danny some bad crack and hope he ODed on it. That would have been murder, too, and grizzly in its own way, but it wasn't as cold blooded as shooting a guy in the back of his head.

MJ thought back to the time Danny had actually ODed two years before. He had spent almost a week in the hospital detoxing and recovering. It was touch and go at first, and Peggy had been there day and night until they finally brought Danny out of his coma.

Peggy loved Danny.

(Unless, a little voice said, she had set him up to OD then, and failed.)

He tried to remember the dates on the insurance policies.

Lee said that Peggy had shot Danny from the back seat, using a gun he didn't know about.

That could be bullshit, but there was a gun at the house, a .38 snub nose police special that his Dad kept under the workbench in a Marsh Wheeling cigar box.

He turned up Andrews and started up the hill to Smokey Hollow.

And at the funeral home Peggy had shown him the one policy she had bought on Danny's life, $2,000. Surely she wouldn't kill him for that?

But according to Lee, there was a shitload of other policies in her cedar chest, adding up to many more thousands of dollars.

If the policies were there, Peggy had really, truly, actually killed their brother Danny.

And justice for Danny demanded that MJ kill Peggy.

He hoped to God he wouldn't have to do that.

He would know in a few minutes, when he looked into the cedar chest for himself.

Chapter Twenty-Three

Understanding the Situation

I t was after 11 when he pulled up outside the old family house. The upstairs bedroom windows were dark, and only the lights in the front room burned.

The entry door was locked. Peggy was probably in the living room watching tv but MJ wanted nothing to do with her right now. He gave the door a swift kick and sprang it open, the frame splintering and the door banging into the wall.

Peggy, alone on the couch in front of the tv, jumped in fear, and seemed to become even more fearful when she saw that it was MJ. She put a hand to her chest.

"Oh my God, MJ, you scared me coming in like that," she said. "What's wrong?"

He ignored her and tromped up the stairs, toward the bedrooms.

"MJ, what is it?" she said, following after him nervously. "Where's Lee? What the hell is going on?"

He pushed open Peggy's door. The cedar chest sat in the corner of the bedroom on the wall near the closet. It was a heavy, honey-stained piece of furniture that their mother had received as a wedding present and which Peggy had appropriated for herself. An embroidered doily sat atop it, and on the doily a fake fern in a basket and a porcelain Chinese dog.

MJ swept it all away and tugged on the lid. It was locked.

"Are you crazy?" Peggy demanded, coming up behind him.

"Where's the key?"

"I don't have no key," Peggy said. "Mom lost it. What the hell do you think you're doing?"

MJ stood back and began kicking at the lid, trying to break the inset lock.

"Stop, you're going to wake the kids. What did you do to Lee?"

MJ gave one last brutal kick, and lock popped. He pushed the lid back and knelt on the floor boards in front. The inside of the chest was also cedar, the boards set in a herringbone pattern for effect, and the interior smelled strongly of mothballs.

On the top of the chest were baby blankets and tiny knit garments--socks and hats--mementoes from the birth of Lee Jr. and Shannon. MJ tossed them aside.

Peggy came over and tried to close the lid. "Stop it, you're ruining my things, what's gotten into you?" she said.

"Get back," said MJ, pushing her away with such force that she tumbled onto the bed.

Next, under some tissue paper, he found Mom's old ermine hand warmer. He tossed that aside too.

"You pig," said Peggy, getting up off the bed and stooping to pick up the muff.

MJ ignored her and kept digging. Here were the family photo albums that Mom had kept over the years, containing carefully glued and labeled old pictures of birthday parties, family reunions, and vacations. Another album (bound in white leather and titled "Anne and Michael Shea, Sept 12, 1959") contained wedding photos. He lifted the albums out of the chest and dropped them to the floor as well.

"Stop it, MJ," said Peggy from behind. "Stop right now or I swear..."

Now MJ was down to the bottom of the chest, where he found several musty folders with legal papers, marriage licenses and death certificates.

One folder, newer and thicker than the others, had a string clasp.

He opened it and pulled out the contents.

Insurance policies, a dozen perhaps, neatly clipped and stacked and similar to the ones he had found in Lee's gym bag.

Except they listed "Margaret Beatrice Messina," not Lee, as the beneficiary.

He rocked back on his heels, tears stinging at his eyes, horrified.

So it was true after all. Peggy had killed Danny. MJ knew this beyond any doubt, for he was holding the evidence in his hands.

And now, to avenge Danny's murder, he had to kill Peggy.

Except he couldn't.

Except he had to.

He had seen Danny's mutilated face, the side of his scalp blown away and his brains leaking onto the pavement.

Peggy had killed their brother and it was up to MJ to make her pay.

Just then, MJ heard the unmistakable sound of a gun being cocked and, stiffening, turned.

Peggy was standing beside the dresser, a drawer open and Dad's pistol in her hand, pointing straight at him.

"Get away from my things, MJ," she said.

She had shot Danny so she was certainly capable of shooting MJ. But instead of moving he held out the insurance papers accusingly, demanding a rational explanation for Danny's murder.

"Is this why you killed Danny? For money? You fucking killed him for *money*?"

"Put the papers down and get away from my things. Step over by the bed."

Her hand was shaking so he put the papers down on the floor, slowly and carefully. But he didn't like the idea of standing by the bed, where she could shoot him down cold without getting blood all over her precious mementoes.

"If you needed money," he said, "you could have come to me."

"Ha," she said. "I did come to you. Many times. Like when the fridge broke and needed to be repaired. Or when the radiator plugged up on the Duster and ruined the engine. Or when they jacked up the property taxes and they were going to take the house away."

"What are you talking about?" said MJ. "I got the fridge fixed and got you a new car too. And I took care of the taxes myself. Didn't I help you out every time you asked?"

"You made me *beg*!" Peggy said, her voice quavering with emotion. "You never did anything until I nagged and nagged and nagged."

"Was that any reason to murder Danny?"

"Shut up," she snapped. "What do you know about Danny? Go stand by the bed."

"How could you kill him? Shooting him in the back of the head? What did Danny ever do to you?"

"What didn't he do to me?" Peggy said. "He took money from my purse and drained my savings passbook. He stoled my Valium and Vicodins so many times the doctor wouldn't give me any more prescriptions. He set the kitchen on fire making crack, and smoked it in front of the kids. He even took Mom's wedding ring and sold it."

"He was a crackhead."

"That's all you ever said, like that's some excuse? 'He's a crackhead, what do you expect?' As if it was some sort of justification for everything?"

"What was I supposed to do?"

"Get him into rehab, for one thing."

"I did get him into rehab, twice."

"Take him into your place, get him out of my hair! Why was everything my responsibility? 'Peggy do this,' 'Peggy do that.' I cooked and cleaned for you and Danny and Mom and Lee, and what thanks did I get? This old house, falling apart, with its bad plumbing and broken furnace, and not even a room air conditioner up here when it's sweltering and I've been asking for years."

"What does any of that have to do with Danny?" MJ asked sharply, trying to get her to make sense.

"Everything! It has everything to do with Danny!"

"Because things are tough, that's why you killed our brother?" MJ countered. "Things are tough for lots of people in Youngstown and they don't go killing over it."

"Don't you dare preach to me when you're the one that got Danny hooked."

"That's a fucking lie. I told him to stay away from that shit. Danny made his own choices."

"Yeah, well you really helped him with that, didn't you, leaving him for me to handle? How convenient for you. You have no idea what he was really like. I warned him over and over to stop stealing my stuff, to keep his crack friends out of the house, to get himself cleaned up or at least take the garbage out once in a while. But he never listened and you never helped because he had you wrapped around his little finger."

"That's not true, Peggy."

"You *want*ed me to babysit him so you could run around the country for that asshole Waylay, burning money in fancy bars and gambling with your sports buddies, while I sat at home cleaning up Queen Anne's shit."

"That's crazy. I came here plenty of times and took Danny with me, let him sleep at my place, tried to talk sense into him. But you can't talk sense to a crackhead."

"You don't understand the situation. You've never understood the situation. You never gave a flying fuck about me. You and Lee both. He wouldn't do anything about Danny either. You just put it all on me. So I had to do everything myself, just like I always have to."

MJ looked at her, really looked. Although her funeral hairdo was still rigidly in place, only half her lipstick was removed and there were bags under her eyes which her glasses, sliding down her nose, only seemed to magnify. There were shadows, too, under her cheeks and chin, as if her face were beginning to melt from stress she could no longer hide or control.

She was no longer the smart, funny, caring sister he had grown up with. Anger and resentment had taken over and were eating her from the inside. Maybe she was right that he didn't do enough with Danny, but that was no reason to kill him, for a fake butcher block countertop and some shit piece of money.

She had come unhinged, and MJ realized there wasn't going to be any rational explanation for Danny's murder.

She waved the pistol. "Now move away from my things. Go sit on the bed."

MJ hesitated. He had no doubt that when he sat on the bed she would shoot him.

She had done what she had done because that was what she wanted to do, and in the end Peggy always got her own way.

Except this time she wouldn't, couldn't.

He had to get the revolver away from her.

"Peggy," he said, holding out his hand. "Give me the gun."

"Shut up, you selfish pig," she said, the pistol not wavering. "Sit on the bed like I said."

Right hand still outstretched, he took a step closer.

"Stay back!" she said--then aimed and fired, the explosion of the gun ripping the night.

MJ felt a searing pain in his right forearm where the slug tore through.

He went down to his knees, screaming and holding his useless arm with his good one, trying not to black out.

"On the bed," Peggy said.

Just then Lee Jr., in an oversized tee shirt that passed for pajamas, appeared in the doorway.

Peggy's eyes flicked to the boy.

Before she could fire again MJ drove himself up and at his sister, knocking her against the wall and wrestling the gun from her grip with his good hand.

She squirmed and tried to twist away but he pinned her to the dresser with his shoulder.

Then he pressed the gun against her head and cocked it.

"No, MJ, don't!" she screamed, instantly going still.

"Mom!" Lee Jr. shouted, wide eyed and frightened.

"Get out!" MJ screamed at the kid. "Go back to your room!"

But the child seemed frozen.

"Lee," Peggy yelled. "Help Mommy. Uncle MJ's gone crazy. Call the police. Go!"

The child turned and disappeared, and MJ could hear him running down the stairs to the kitchen.

"The police aren't going to help you," MJ said, pressing Peggy's face harder against the wall.

"Don't shoot," she begged. "I didn't mean to kill Danny, I swear. It was an accident. I didn't mean for the gun to go off."

Her sickening lies disgusted him, and the adrenaline from the flesh wound made it hard to think.

He started to pressure the trigger, but stopped, the strawberry fragrance of Peggy's hair in his face.

Although awkward in his left hand, the gun was behind her ear and he could kill her right now exactly the way she killed Danny, a bullet in the back of the head.

"No, MJ, don't," she begged. "I'll make it up to you. We can split the insurance money. Lee's policies, too. Why are you being like this?"

Disgusted, horrified, he jammed the muzzle harder against her head.

She twisted and groaned, but still MJ held her pinned. A simple squeeze of the trigger and Danny's blood would be avenged, paid for by the blood of his murderer.

He steeled himself to pull the trigger, felt her heaving and sobbing under him as she now knew she was about to die.

A headache pain bloomed in his forehead, producing a hazy kind of light in his head that made him hesitate.

If he killed her Danny's blood would be avenged, but MJ would be the murderer of Peggy just as Peggy had been the murderer of Danny, and what would be the sense of that? The law of the jungle would prevail, but MJ would just be another animal in the jungle, mindlessly playing the role nature dealt, a falling brick like the one that struck down Father Marchuk.

Besides, he would go to jail for murder and never see Cassie again--never touch her, never hold her, never be held.

The hazy light in his head throbbed and finally MJ surrendered to it, realizing he was losing blood. He backed away from Peggy while holding the gun on her. "Lay down on the floor with your hands where I can see them," he said.

"MJ," she said as she complied, "think of what we could do with that money. I could fix up the house, finally have a decent place to raise the kids. And you could buy a new van, get rid of your old one. Or even buy a vacation place in that town you're always talking about. Where is it, New Jersey?"

"Shut up, Peggy," he said, wrapping a sweatshirt from her closet around his bleeding arm.

Lee Jr. was in the hallway, hanging back from the door, his fist in his mouth.

"Did you call the police?" he asked.

"Yes, Uncle MJ," he said. "They're coming." He looked at his mother on the floor, then at MJ's bleeding arm. "Did Mommy do that?" he asked.

"Yeah," said MJ. "She did it."

On the floor, Peggy sobbed. "You bastard," she said to MJ.

"Go back to your room and wait," MJ told Lee Jr.

Chapter Twenty-Four

Ocean Grove

A year later, MJ sat on the front porch of the little house on Atlantic Avenue, smoking a cigarette and waiting for Cassie to get back from her shift at Jersey Shore Medical Center. It was a little after four on a Sunday--MJ's day off, not because of any religious observance, but because Ocean Grove used to be a Methodist camp town, and nobody did business there on Sunday except ice cream vendors and bait salesmen.

The previous summer, after Cassie had graduated and gotten the job, they had rented in nearby Neptune, then the following February had found the Ocean Grove property and closed escrow. It was a decrepit bungalow, with two small bedrooms and a single bath with slanting floors and a leaky toilet.

But it was one block from the beach, had a charming dormer on the upstairs bedroom and a porch looking over a small lawn to the more substantial houses across the street. It had everything. But most of all, it had Cassie.

They had bought it without even fully inspecting it, all the while their poker faces trying to convince the seller that they were not really that interested. But they *were* interested--inescapable so. Cassie liked the dormer and MJ the price--a fiercely negotiated $23,950. MJ put $5,000 down--the last of his savings after getting his mother into All Saints Nursing Home and the kids settled in with cousins Rose and Gary.

Now MJ and Cassie were living on Cassie's nursing salary, supplemented a bit by MJ's roofing business, which he was slowly getting off the ground. He had completed two jobs in May, was currently finishing another, and had two more lined up for July, with possibly a third on the fence. In New Jersey, nobody worked as hard as they did in Youngstown, but MJ had managed to find a couple of men who were both competent and sober.

A car cruised down Atlantic Avenue toward the beach, a big white station wagon with a chrome luggage rack and fake wood sides. The driver was a man in a yellow short-sleeved shirt, with his wife and three children as passengers. MJ and Cassie weren't married yet and Cassie was on the pill for now, but they both wanted children. She said there was no hurry because they loved each other so much, but MJ had already picked out a ring and decided to propose on July 4th, before Peggy's trial in August.

He was a witness for the prosecution and would have to go back to Youngstown for that.

Lee Jr. and Shannon had spent eight months in the custody of the state before being fostered by Rose and Gary, who were in the process of adopting them.

Three seagulls flapped their grey wings overhead, then spiraled down and sat lined up side-by-side on his neighbor's fence posts. Despite their squawking noises he was learning to like seagulls, both for their beautiful white bodies and yellow beaks, and because they made a mess of people's roofs, giving him a second line of business installing seagull spikes--jagged steel wires positioned along roof lines, chimneys and gutters to discourage gulls from landing.

Ocean Grove was real different from Youngstown. The town was a little run down, but the people were friendly, and he and Cassie had already exchanged dinners with their neighbors and been out fishing on their postman's boat.

That night at Peggy's, the cops had come and taken away both his sister and himself. After an overnight in the hospital (where doctors had x-rayed and dressed his arm), MJ found himself facing a day of questioning at the homicide unit, mostly by Proferes, sometimes by his partners.

MJ told them, over and over again, how he had found out Lee was involved in the murder, what had happened in the fight on the conveyor platform, and how he had come to discover Peggy's real role in Danny's murder.

MJ was charged with involuntary manslaughter and held a night and day in a holding cell. Proferes found the insurance policies just where MJ said they were, and Lee's autopsy collaborated that he died from his fall, not from any wounds during the fight with MJ.

The D.A. declined to prosecute and the charges were dropped.

"You got a good thing going with your girlfriend there," Proferes had told him. "Stay away from Waylay and don't mess up again."

MJ had taken his advice, and a good thing he had because the Feds indicted Waylay a month later, just as Cassie was graduating and they were making plans to move to Ocean Grove.

Peggy was charged with over 20 felony and misdemeanor counts, including aggravated murder with death penalty specifications, attempted murder, conspiracy to commit aggravated murder, forgery, insurance fraud, telecommunications fraud, obstruction of justice and perjury.

And according to Proferes, Peggy wouldn't have gotten a dime from insurance in any case. There was a two-year contestability period in Ohio, and Peggy's misrepresentations would have made the policies worthless in any case.

The single attempted murder charge was the result of Peggy's attack on MJ in her bedroom.

Just then, Cassie's white Escort turned from Beach Avenue onto Atlantic and pulled up in front of the house. Cassie emerged from the car in her blue-checked hospital uniform, toting her canvas print bag. She smiled at MJ as she came up the walk.

MJ went to the top of the steps to greet her. "Hi, Nurse Cassie," he said, straightening her plastic name tag and kissing her.

"Oh my," she said. "The patient is frisky today."

"Frisky," he agreed. "But not too patient." He tugged on her blue fabric belt.

She laughed and escaped his grip. "You promised me the beach today, remember?"

"I remember," MJ said. He poked with his foot at the beach bag he had packed. "I've got the blanket right here. The wine, too. Even Danny's guitar, if I can play it." He had had the instrument repaired at a shop in Columbus.

"You've thought of everything."

"Everything."

"Then let's go up and change," she said, opening the screen door.

"I'm with you," MJ said.

Ocean Grove was real different from Youngstown. He didn't know life could be so sweet.

THE END

About the Author

James Dain writes fast-paced, character-driven mystery and suspense thrillers.

His work has won multiple awards, including "Best Novel" at the Los Angeles Neo-Noir Festival.

He enjoys an adventurous life in Palm Springs, California, where he teaches college, hikes with his dog and spends the winter snowboarding in the nearby mountains.

"Just wow! James Dain writes stories you can't put down!"
—Charles Anceney, author of *The Boy in the Boat*

SEE MORE OF JAMES DAIN'S WORK
AND SIGN UP FOR A FREE THRILLER. JUST CLICK

www.jamesdain.com

A Word from James Dain

If you enjoyed reading this book—there's a reason!

I strive to deliver a fun, fast-paced and enjoyable story, with interesting, real characters in difficult situations. Each novel is carefully crafted and generally takes one- to two-years to write.

My goal is to make every James Dain novel a reading experience you will not forget.

If I've succeeded, please leave a review on your favorite book sites, recommend me to your friends on social media, and pass along my books from hand-to-hand so that others may enjoy.

Word-of-mouth from you will enable me to keep creating the stories you like.

Thanks. And as a reward get a *free* thriller by me at my website:

www.jamesdain.com

www.ingramcontent.com/pod-product-compliance
Lightning Source LLC
Chambersburg PA
CBHW060324260626
47160CB00007B/2672